CW00865133

INSIDE THE GIANT ELECTRIC MACHINE

Volume four Steam Side

JOHN GUILIANO

Order this book online at www.trafford.com
or email orders@trafford.com

Most Trafford titles are also available at major online book retailers.

Print information available on the last page.

ISBN: 978-1-6987-0117-2 (sc)
ISBN: 978-1-6987-0119-6 (hc)
ISBN: 978-1-6987-0118-9 (e)

Library of Congress Control Number: 2020908825

Trafford rev. 05/18/2020

 www.trafford.com
North America & international
toll-free: 1 888 232 4444 (USA & Canada)
fax: 812 355 4082

WITH INSIDE THE GIANT ELECTRIC MACHINES UNIT ONE'S MAIN GENERATOR LESS THEN HALF WAY THROUGH THE FUEL CYCLE, IT CONTINUES TO PERFORM TO WORLD CLASS STANDARDS. THE CAPACITY FACTOR IS OFF THE CHARTS AND THERE ARE NO SIGNS OF A SLOW DOWN. THE GENERATION STATIONS GOAL OF A HIGH PERFORMING, HIGH PRODUCING RUN FROM BREAKER TO BREAKER APPEARS TO BE WITHIN REACH. THIS IS A TRUE REFLECTION OF THE CRAFTSMEN AND WOMEN, STATIONS OPPERATIONS DEPARTEMENT AND TEAM MANAGEMENT FROM THE ADMERIAL ON DOWN THE CHAIN OF COMMAND TO KIKEY THE FLOOR GUY, WHO KEEPS TURBINE HALL FLOORS SO CLEAN BRUCEY THE ELECTRICIAN, HAS BEEN SEEN EATING CRUMBS OFF IT.

SINCE THE TIME THE UNIT ONE GENERATOR, INSIDE THE GIANT ELECTRIC MACHINE, WAS BACK ON THE GRID PRODUCING ELECTRICITY FOR OUR HOMES AND BUSINESSES, THE TEAM HAS SHIFT GEARS IN PREPPERATION FOR THEIR NEXT CHALLENGE, A MAIN STEAM SIDE OUTAGE OF UNIT TWO'S HIGH PRESSURE TURBINE, THREE LOW PRESSURE TURBINES, ONE CONTROL VALVE, ONE STOP VALVE, ONE CROSS AROUND INTERMEDIATE VALVE, BYPASS VALVES AND LAST BUT NOT LEAST, A VERY IMPORTANT PART OF THE SAFETY OF THE PUBLIC, OF FELLOW TEAM MEMBERS AND EQUIPMENT, A MINOR INSPECTION OF THE HIGH-PRESSURE CORE INJECTION PUMP. (HPCI)

KISSY: We have all been so busy around here planning this outage, it's difficult to think straight sometimes.

PSUTOM:	How do you think I feel KISSY? At my age it's hard to keep this pace going into the outage making sure all the upfront paper work is in place.
GENO:	Being a planner has its challenges, especially when we're going from one major outage to the next with such high expectations.
KISSY:	That's why the ADMIRAL and JIMMY O always remind us to guard against complacency.
SCHAFFER CITY:	According to the paper work and the job screen on the computer the team is making progress on the set up of the MAIN TURBINE DECK in preparation for the full steam train overhaul.

SCHAFFER CITY BARELY COULD GET THE WORDS OUT OF HIS MOUTH AND THE DOOR TO THE LARGE GENERAL OFFICE AREA SWINGS OPENED IN WALKS THE JOB LEADERS CORONAL HOGAN ON VALVES, FATTY JOE AND GOON ON CENTERLINE, WOBY ON THE HPCI PUMP AND SCHAFER CITY (ALSO A PLANNER) IS AN ELECTRICIAN BY TRADE. OUR OLD FRIEND SQUAREHEAD IS NOT FAR BEHIND AND APPEARS READY TO GET THE SHOW ON THE ROAD.

PSUTOM:	Look what the cat drug in. Where have you guys been hiding?
SQUAREHEAD:	We have been hard at it trying to figure out who the best personnel for the individual tasks we have so we can align their skill sets accordingly.

GOON: Yea, I need some muscle on centerline especially when it's time to row the boat.

WOBY: One thing I know for sure is when the crew members get off the deck, there hungry.

COL HOGAN: We are going to be so busy during this Unit two outage the craft is going to have to eat on the fly.

KISSY: The ADMIRAL and JIMMY O agreed to allow JOR'GE THE SANDWICH MAKER to set up shop in the muster area.

SQUAREHEAD: That's great news JOR'GE THE SANDWICH MAKER always uses the best lunch meats and gets his bread from Conchocken or Norristown. I'm planning on bringing a couple coolers full of Fishtown kielbasa in to help feed the troops.

SCHAFFER CITY: BRUCEY also said he'll have the hot dog machine rolling.

FATTY JOE: Sounds good, we have a lot of work ahead of us but we have the experience and quality tradesmen and women to get the job done safely and right the first time.

SQUAREHEAD: We have to get up to the deck and see if the crew has any concerns.

THE JOB LEADERS ARE QUICK TO EXIT THE OFFICE AREA WITH THEIRE (PPE) HARD HATS, SAFETY GLASSES, GLOVES AND HEARING PROTECTION. FIRST STOP TURBINE HALL. THEY EXIT THE TURBINE BUILDING ELEVATOR AT ELEVATION 270' INSIDE THE GIANT ELECTRIC MACHINE THIS IS 270' ABOVE SEA LEVEL. FATTY JOE OPENS THE DOOR AND CAN TELL ALREADY THE CREW HAS BEEN VERY BUSY.

SQUAREHEAD:	Let's go take a look down the hatch and see what's next up to the deck.
COL HOGAN:	Looks like PLAIN BILL backed the trailer in with the SAND CRAB SHACK on it.

BIG JIM IS THE LEED FOR SAFE RIGGING PRACTICES AND MAKING SURE EVERYONE KNOWS OF THE OVERHEAD ACTIVITES TAKING PLACE USING THE SAFEST LOAD PATHS SO THE CREW CAN CONTINUE WORKING WITHOUT HAVING TO CONSTINTLY MOVE OUT FROM UNDER THE LOAD. EVERYONE KNOWS YOU NEVER WORK UNDER A SUSPENDED LOAD. RAYRAY CHONG IS OPPERATING THE UNIT ONE CRANE AND SMARKEY IS IN CONTROL OF THE UNIT TWO CRANE. PLAIN BILL HAS REMOVED THE LOAD BINDERS FROM THE I BEAMS AND THERE IS PLENTY OF ROOM TO SLIDE THE KEVLAR SLINGS UNDER THEM.

RAYRAY CHONG HAS THE UNIT TWO SMALL HOOK CENTERED RIGHT OVER THE TRAILER AND BEGINS TO LOWER THE HOOK. JUST THEN SUAVE RICO JUMPS UP ONTO THE TRAILER AND BLAZE HANDS UP THE RIGGING.

COL.HOGAN:	Hey! BIG JIM careful with those beams, the valve team is responsible for them.
FATTY JOE:	BIG JIM, where is the UNIT TWO crane?
BIG JIM:	UNIT TWO crane is dressed and waiting for the clearance to pull the floor plugs so we can get to the BYPASS VALVES STEAM CHEST, CONTROL VALVE number two and number one MAIN STOP VALVE.
SQUARE HEAD:	That should keep them to the front end of UNIT II for a while.

BIG JIM:	We're thinking we can build the CRAB SHACK while they are pulling the floor plugs.
COL. HOGAN:	That way we can stay out of each other's way.

RAYRAY CHONG HAS POSITIONED HIS UNIT TWO SMALL HOOK DIRECTLY CENTER ABOUT FIVE FEET FROM THE IBEAMS.

SUAVE RICO:	Thanks BLAZE, someone must have been thinking when they built the crab shack. In the old days they never had the lifting eyes for the rigging built in.
BLAZE:	Yea we could take a morning just to get it to the deck. We just have to hook it up and send it up the hatch. BIG JIM has PAPALUCHI and BIG O on the deck to disconnect the rigging and send the hook back down the hatch.
SUAVE RICO:	Beats running up and down. I got this BLAZE, a four-point pick using the four fifteen foot endless slings and four shackles or clevises.

SUAVE RICO DRESSES THE HOOK THEN CONNECTS THE SHACKLES TO THE LIFTING EYES WICH ARE STRATIGICALLY POSITIONED ON THE OUTSDE CORNERS OF THE LIFTING SKID OF THE SOON TO BE BUILT CRAB SHACK, AND ALLOWS FOR A LEVEL LOAD WHEN BEING HOISTED UP THE HATCH. SUAVE RICO AND BLAZE ARE WEARING A BRIGHT ORANGE VEST SO RAYRAY CHONG CAN SEE HIS FELLOW RIGGERS AND THE SIGNALS. SUAVE RICO LOOKS AT BLAZE AND GIVES A THUMBS UP, BLAZE IN TURN ESTABLISHES EYE CONTACT WITH RAYRAY CHONG AND GIVES THE SLOW UP, SLOW UP, SLOW UP TILL THE SLINGS GET TOTE. AGAIN, BLAZE GIVES A SLOW UP, SLOW UP AND SOON

ENOUGH ALL FOUR CORNERS OF THE SKID RISE UP OFF THE TRUCK BED.

SUAVE RICO INSPECTS THE HOOK TO MAKE SURE THE SLINGS ARE CENTER AND GIVES A NOD, THEN TAKES A FEW STEPS AWAY IN THE DIRECTION OF THE TRUCK CAB SO HE'S NOT UNDER THE LOAD WHILE IT'S MOVING UP THE HATCH. BLAZE THEN WINDES HIS HAND IN AN UP MOTION AND PARTS OF THE CRAB SHACK MOVE UP THE HATCH. BIG JIM AWAITS AND THEN SIGNALS RAYRAY CHONG TO DELIVER THE CRAB SHACK TO THE DESIGNATED AREA THE RIGHT SIDE OF THE" B" LOW PRESURE TURBINE.

PAPALUCHI: Here comes the crab shack BIG O. Just playing pitch and catch for now.

BIG O: You got it PAPALUCHI, disconnect the shackles and send the hook back down the hatch.

THAT QUICK BIG O DIRECTS THE CRANE TO PUT THE SKID OUT OF THE WAY FOR NOW, FREES THE LOAD AND SENDS THE HOOK ON IT'S WAY. RAYRAY CHONG CENTERS THE HOOK OVER THE TRAILER AND LOWERS IT BACK DOWN THE HATCH. THE HOOK STOPS ABOUT FIVE FEET FROM THE TRAILER.

BLAZE: Let's just take two beams at a time SUAVE RICO. Should be four verticals and three horizontals. The four verticals have the one-inch thick plate steel on the base so they are stable when they get stood upright.

SUAVE RICO:	They positioned the lifting eyes just perfect, one closer to the bottom plate and the other a few feet past center so when we make the pick they come up pretty close to level.
BLAZE:	You know what BIG JIM always says "any load over a five-degree pitch is not considered level.
SUAVE RICO:	He's always got something to say.

SUAVE RICO DOSE'NT WASTE ANY TIME, HOOKS UP THE SHACKLES AND GIVES BLAZE A NOD. BLAZE AGAIN, MAKES EYE CONTACT WITH RAYRAY CHONG AND GIVES A SLOW UP, SLOW UP, SLOW UP TILL THE SLINGS GET TOTE. SUAVE RICO LOOKS THINGS OVER AND MOVES AWAY FROM THE LOAD.

WITH HIS INDEX FINGER UP BLAZE WINDES HIS HAND AND NOTICES THE BEAMS COMING OF THE TRAILER AT THE SAME TIME AND SIGNALS THE CRANE TO PROCEED WITH THE LIFT. THE BEAMS ARE THIRTY FEET IN LENGTH AND HAVE PLENTY OF ROOM MOVING UP THE HATCH. BIG O AND PAPALUCHI ARE AWAITING AND GENTLY TURN THE BEAMS SO THEY ARE PARELLE TO THE "B" LP. AND GENTLY PUT THEM DOWN ON LAYDOWN METERIAL TO HELP PROTECT THE FLOOR. BIG O AND PAPALUCHI FREE THE LOAD AND RAYRAY CHONG RETURNS THE UNIT TWO CRANE BACK OVER THE HATCH THEN LOWERS THE HOOK STOPPING ABOUT FIVE FEET FROM THE TRAILER. BLAZE THEN HANDS SIX MORE SLINGS TO SUAVE RICO.

SUAVE RICO:	Let me hook up the big beams first then I can hook up the eight-inch web beams and deliver all five with one pick.

BLAZE: Good thinking SUAVE, as long as the slings
                    are centered on the hook. Let me get six more
                    shackles.

BLAZE HANDS SIX MORE THREE QUARTER INCH SHACKELS TO
SUAVE RICO WHO IN TURN FINISHES UP PREPARING THE LOAD.
SUAVE RICO LET'S BLAZE KNOW EVERYTHING IS PROPERLY
POSISIONED AND THE SHACKLES ARE HAND TOTE (BUT NOT
TO TOTE) AND GETS OUT FROM THE MIDDLE OF THE FIVE
REMAINING BEAMS AND GETS OFF THE TRAILER. BLAZE THEN
SIGNALS THE CRANE A SLOW UP, SLOW UP, SLOW UP THEN
THE BEAMS BEGIN TO SLIDE TOGETHER AND MAKE A CLANKING
SOUND AS THEY COME TOGETHER AND SLOWLY RISE UP OFF
THE DECK OF THE TRAILER. BLAZE GIVES A QUICK STOP

AND CLOSELY CHECKS EVERYTHING OUT.

SUAVE RICO: How does it look BLAZE?
BLAZE: All good Suave.
PLAIN BILL: As soon as security opens up the door I can
                    dump this trailer and bring the last two roller
                    assemblies in.
BLAZE: Thanks, PLAIN BILL we are happy to have such
                    a reliable truck driver who understands what
                    we need to get done in support of THE GIANT
                    ELECTRIC MACHINE.

BLAZE WITH HIS INDEX FINGER POINTING UP, WINES HIS HAND
IN AN UPWARD MOTION AND RAYRAY CHONG UNDERSTANDS
THE LOAD LOOKS GOOD AND PROCEEDS TO THE LAYDOWN
AREA IN PREPERATION TO BUILD THE CRAB SHACK. BIG O

AND PAPALUCHI GENTLY SITCHUATE THE BEAMS SO THEY ARE PARELLE TO THE B LP. PAPALUCHI SIGNALS THE CRANE FOR A SLOW DOWN, SLOW DOWN, SLOW DOWN AND THE FIVE BEAMS COME TO REST ASIDE THE OTHER TWO. BIG O FREE'S THE LOAD AND THE CREW IS NOW READY TO BUILD THE SAND CRAB SHACK WHERE A LOT OF THE PARTS WILL BE SAND BLASTED AND CLEANED PRIOR TO INSPECTION FOR CRACKS AND WASHOUTS.

JUST THEN POOPDECK PAPPY AND CHARDY SHOW UP IN THEIR FALL PROTECTION, ON A SCISSORS LIFT ALONG WITH A SECOND SCISSORS LIFT WITH JAKE AND DELCO JOE ON BOARD DAWNED IN THEIR FALL PROTECTION. AFTER ROPEY AND PEACHES CAREFULLY MARK OUT THE EXACT LOCATION OF THE CRAB SHACK, TWISTED STEELE, GEGGY AND GOOGLY TAKE FOUR BY EIGHT FOOT SHEETS OF ONE QUARTER INCH THICK PLASTIC AND PUT IT ON THE FLOOR THEN TAPE THE SEEMS. THE CRAB SHACK IS THERTY FEET BYE TEN FEET.

BIG O: DELCO JOE, JAKE you guys ready? We can start with the two laterals' in the front then tie them together with a ten-footer. Then we can do the same with the back end, slide the right side, left side the center beam then racks it all together.

JAKE: CHARDY, POOPDECK PAPPY did you guys hear the plan?

CHARDY: Yea JAKE, we got the right side and you guys can have the left. Remember we have to use new hardware.

DELCO JOE:	We set each lift up with the hardware, pinch bars, opened end wrenches, ratchets and the proper sockets.
POOPDECK:	Ok, let the show begin.
BIG O:	I got this PAPALUCHI two six-foot slings each choked on the top end about two feet from the top of the beam, opposite sides of each other.
PAPALUCHI:	Set them tote BIG O.

RAYRAY CHONG IS UP IN THE BOX READY TO CONTINUE OPPERATING THE UNIT TWO CRANE INSIDE THE GIANT ELECTRIC MACHINE.HE'S EXPERIENCED WITH WHAT IS GOING ON THE FLOOR AND HAS AN IDEA OF WHAT IS NEXT SO HE SENDS THE SMALL HOOK DOWN TO ALMOST FLOOR LEVEL, CENTER OF THE TOP OF THE BEAM THAT IS GOING TO BE STOOD UP. BIG O THEN TAKES THE TWO OPENED ENDS OF THE SLINGS AND SLIDES THEM ONTO THE HOOK MAKING SURE THE MOUSE IS IN ORDER. PAPALUCHI ESTABLISHES EYE CONTACT WITH RAYRAY CHONG AND GIVES A SLOW UP, SLOW UP, SLOW UP TILL THE CHOKES GET TOTE AROUND THE TOP OF THE BEAM. BIG O TAKES HIS HANDS AND MAKES SURE THE CHOKES ARE POSITIONED PERFECTLY BEFORE CONTINUING THE LIFT THEN NODS TO PAPALUCHI.

PAPALUCHI AGAIN GIVES THE SLOW UP, SLOW UP THE CHOKES GET TOTE AND APPEARS TO BE CENTER. PAPALUCHI AGAIN SLOW UP, SLOW UP, SLOW UP AND NOW THE TOP END OF THE BEAM IS ABOUT FOUR FEET OFF THE GROUND AND THE BASE SLIDES EVER SO SLIGHTLY. PAPALUCHI SIGNALS BRIDGE FORWARD, BRIDGE FORWARD, BRIDGE FORWARD THEN STOP, SLOW UP,

SLOW UP AND SLOW UP TILL THE BEAM IS STANDING STRAIGHT UP AND THE BASE IS JUST A FEW INCHES OFF THE GROUND.

BIG O THEN GUIDES THE BEAM OVER TO THE CORNER OF THE AREA WITH PAPALUCHI CLOSELY WORKING TOGETHER WITH THE CRANE SLOW DOWN, SLOW DOWN AND PERFECT RIGHT ON THE MARK.CHARDY AND POOPDECK PAPPY POSITION THE SCISSORS LIFT AND GO UP TO REMOVE THE SLINGS AND LET THEM FALL TO THE FLOOR. NUMBER ONE VERTICLE IBEAM WAS NOW IN PLACE AND USING THE SAME TECHNIQUE SOON ENOUGH THE LEFT SIDE WAS IN PLACE. JAKE AND DELCO JOE POSITIONED THE LIFT AND REMOVED THE RIGGING. NEXT WAS A TEN FOOT IBEAM THAT TIED THE TWO TOGETHER ACROSS. PAPALUCHI AND BIG O HAD THE IBEAM ALREADY TO BE INSTALLED. THE IBEAM WAS SUSPENDED FROM THE HOOK AND STRAIGHT OVER ITS TARGET FIT.

PAPALUCHI MAKES SURE THE CREW IS READY AND REMINDS THEM TO WATCHA YOUR FINGERS. PAPALUCHI THEN REESTABLISHES EYE CONTACT WITH THE CRANE OPPERATOR AND GIVES THE SLOW DOWN, SLOW DOWN THEN A STOP. WITH DELCO JOE AND JAKE ON ONE SIDE AND POOPDECK PAPPY AND CHARDY ON THE OTHER THE CREW SHOULD BE ABLE TO GUIDE THE IBEAM RIGHT INTO THE SLOTTED FIT. PAPALUCHI RUBS HIS HANDS TOGETHER THEN TOUCHES HIS CHIN TO LET RAYRAY KNOW ONE INCH AT A TIME NOW.

A QUICK POINT DOWN, A QUICK POINT DOWN, A QUICK POINT DOWN ANOTHER QUICK POINT DOWN AND THE CREW WAS ABLE TO GUIDE THE BEAM RIGHT INTO THE FIT. EACH SIDE STRUGGLED WITH THE PINCH BARS FOR A LITTLE, BUT WAS ABLE

TO GET THE BOLTS STARTED AND SNUG BUT NOT TOTE YET.
NOW THE THREE IBEAM STRUCTURE IS STANDING ALONE IT'S
IMPORTANT THE CREW KEEPS MOVING ONTO THE BACK END AS
THEY SUCCESSFULLY COMPLETE THAT PART OF THE STRUCTURE
USING THE SAME TECHNIQUE.

BIG O: Next, we have to attach the three thirty footers
            right side, left side and the one that spans the
            middle so the SAND CRABS have something to
            hang the trolley and chain block from.

PAPALUCHI: Hey BIG O, you want to talk about busy?
            The SAND CRABS have got all four turbines,
            diaphragms, flow guides and valve parts to
            blast.

THE SCISSORS LIFTS HAVE BEEN REPOSITIONED AND RAYRAY
CHONG IS READY FOR BIG O TO ATTACH THE RIGGING. BIG
O IS USING TWO FIFTEEN FOOTERS AND SHACKLES BECAUSE
THE IBEAM NEEDS TO FLOAT A LITTLE TO GET IT IN THE FITS. BIG
O LOOKS AT PAPALUCHI AND GIVES THE OK. SLOW UP, SLOW
UP, SLOW UP TILL THE IBEAM IS ABOUT SHOULDER HIGH. BIG
O POSITIONES THE IBEAM SO IT'S THE LENGTH OF THE CRAB
SHACK THEN PAPALUCHI SENDS IT ON IT'S WAY DIRECTLY OVER
THE TARGET.

JAKE AND DELCO JOE ON ONE END AND POOPDECK PAPPY AND
CHARDY ON THE OTHER ALLIGN THE IBEAM UP WITH THE FIT.
PAPALUCHI THEN ESTABLISHES EYE CONTACT WITH RAYRAY AND
LOOKS UP TO THE CREW THEN GIVES A SLOW DOWN, SLOW
DOWN AND STOP, RUBS HIS HANDS TOGETHER SCRATCHES HIS
CHIN LETTING RAYRAY CHONG KNOW INCH AT A TIME. THEN

WITH A QUICK INDEX FINGER DOWN, QUICK INDEX FINGER DOWN AND A THIRD QUICK INDEX FINGER DOWN THE CREW GUIDES THE IBEAM RIGHT INTO THE FIT. LEAVING THE RIGGING HOOKED UP, THEY STRUGGLE FOR A FEW MINUTES BUT EVENTUALLY GET THE BOLTS IN AND SNUG UP ON THE NUTS. PAPALUCHI SIGNALS SLOW DOWN AND LOSENS UP THE SLINGS SO THEY CAN BE REMOVED AND USED FOR THE RIGHT SIDE. THE CREW DON'T TAKE LONG TO FINISH THE NEXT TWO IBEAMS SAFELY, TORQUE EVERY THING UP NICE AND TOTE, CLIMB DOWN FROM THE SCISSORS LIFT AND REMOVE THE FALL PROTECTION.

COL. HOGAN: Nice job, the outside walls and hanging the lights is up to the SAND CRABS all I have to do is let HIGH VOLT know so he can provide a temporary lighting circuit. CHARDY?
We need to find your genius curtain rack to cover the tops.

CHARDY: We found it on unit one side already, HOGE. We can get it when we need it.

SQUARE HEAD, FATTY JOE, GOON, COL. HOGAN, WOBY AND SCHAFFER CITY ARE ABOUT ONE HUNDRED FEET AWAY FROM WHERE THE UNIT I CRANE APPEARS TO BE ON THE MOVE AND FROM WHERE THE CRAB SHACK HAS BEEN BUILT, ON THE RIGHT SIDE OF UNIT II "A" LP. TURBINE. THE JOB LEADERS MAKE THEIR WAY TO THE FRONT OF UNIT II AND ARE STANDING NEXT TO THE FRONT STANDARD. SMARKEY IS IN THE BOX (OPPERATOR UNIT I CRANE) WITH EEFFY AND SKIN WEARING THE FLYER ORANGE VESTS.

STANDING BYE IN SUPPORT OF THE RIGGERS K, MOE, GEGGY, TWISTED STEEL AND GOOGLY ARE PREPARRED TO FENCE OUT THE HOLES IN THE FLOOR THAT ARE LEFT WHEN THE FLOOR PLUGS ARE REMOVED. IT'S VERY IMPORTANT TO HANDLE THIS TASK IMMEDIATELY DUE TO THE POSSIBILTY OF SOMEONE NOT FAMILIAR WITH OR PAYING ATTENTION TO THE JOB CONDITIONS CHANGING.

BUTCH, A JOB PLANNER FOR THE VALVE TEAM LETS EEFFY KNOW WE HAVE THE CLEARENCE TO REMOVE THE NECESSARY FLOOR PLUGS. BYE REMOVING THE FLOOR PLUGS THE VALVE TEAM WILL BE ABLE TO HAVE ACCESS TO THE EQUIPMENT TO BE WORKED ON AND THE USE OF THE CRANE IS VITAL.

EEFFY: Ok, SKIN we have the clearance to pull the floor plugs.

SKIN: How are we going to get SMARKEY's attention? He looks pretty comfortable up there.

EEFFY: Oh, there he goes, he moved, he just gave us the thumbs up. We're ready to go.

SKIN: We cleaned out the lifting rings in the corners of the floor plugs and are going to use a four-legged bridal, each leg is eight-foot-long, one-inch stranded wire rope with a moussed hook on the end. It looks brand new.

SKIN ESTABLISHES EYE CONTACT WITH SMARKEY (UNIT I CRANE OPPERATOR) AND POINTS ALMOST DIRECTLY UNDER THE BOX. SMARKEY IS FAMILIAR WITH THE TASK AT HAND AND HAS AN UNDERSTANDING THAT THE FIRST PICK WILL BE THE BYPASS VALVE FLOOR PLUG. SMARKEY POSITIONS THE SMALL HOOK DIRECTLY

CENTER OVER THE PLUG AND LOWERS THE SMALL HOOK, WITCH IS RATED TO FIFTY TON.

THE HOOK STOPS AT ABOUT WAIST HEIGHT AND SKIN IS QUICK TO PUSH THE BRIDAL THROUGH THE MOUSE AND ON TO THE HOOK. SKIN THEN TAKES EACH LEG OF THE BRIDAL AND ATTACHES IT TO THE LIFTING RINGS BUILT INTO THE FLOOR PLUGS MAKING SURE, EACH LEG WAS STRAIGHT AND THE TIPS OF THE HOOKS WERE POINTING OUT.

THE BYPASS VALVE FLOOR PLUG IS SHAPED LIKE A RECTANGLE RUNNING THE LENGTH OF THE STEAM CHEST. FOUR-FOOT-WIDE, TWELVE-FOOT-LONG AND THREE FEET THICK OF HIGH TENESIAL, REINFORCED CONCRETE. SKIN GIVES EEFY A NOD AND IS READY TO PROCEED WITH THE PICK. EEFFY LOOKS UP TO THE BOX AND CAN TELL SMARKEY IS SET TO GO. EEFFY SIGNALS SLOW UP, SLOW UP, SLOW UP TILL THE SLACK IN THE LEGS OF THE BRIDAL TOTEN UP. EEFFY SIGNALS A STOP TO ALLOW SKIN TO TAKE A CLOSE LOOK AT THE HOOKS AND POSITION OF THE BRIDAL. SKIN GIVES THE NOD TO PROCEED WITH THE LIFT.

EEFFY WITH HIS RIGHT ARM UP AT A NINTEY DEGREE ANGLE AND A CLINCHED FIST LOOKS UP AT SMARKEY AND OPENS HIS FIST THEN CLOSES HIS FIST, OPENS HIS FIST THEN CLOSES HIS FIST, OPENS HIS FIST AND CLOSES HIS FIST AND WITH EVERY OPENEND FIST THE CRANE LIFTS THE FLOOR PLUG FROM IT'S RESTING PLACE. SKIN HAS A CLOSE EYE ON THE CLEARENCE OF THE FLOOR PLUG SO NOT TO LIFT IT HIGHER THEN NECESSARY, THEN NODS TO EEFFY LETTING HIM KNOW THE PLUG WAS SAFLEY CLEAR AND CAN BE MOVED TO THE RIGHT SIDE OF THE HOLE. SKIN THEN GUIDES THE FLOOR PLUG, AS EEFFY DIRECTS

THE CRANE TO TROLLY JUST A COUPLE FEET TO THE RIGHT OF THE HOLE IN THE FLOOR. EEFFY MAKES SURE SKIN IS CLEAR AND THE PLUG IS POSITIONED AT THE PROPPER LOCATION THEN GIVES THE SLOW DOWN SIGNAL AS THE PLUG FINDS REST ON THE DECK. EEFFY SIGNALS ANOTHER SLOW DOWN TO CREAT SLACK IN THE LEGS OF THE BRIDAL SO SKIN CAN DISCONNECT THE RIGGING AND PREPARE FOR THE NEXT FLOOR PLUG TO BE REMOVED. K, MOE, GEGGY, TWISTED STEELE AND GOOGLY ARE READY TO SPRING INTO ACTION.

MOE: I'm glad we were thinking outside the box when we reviewed the work package. We had a really good idea to build the safety barriers prior to the job.

K: Yea, that way we can carry the safety barriers over to the hole, slide them in so they rest on the lip where the floor plugs rest and then hang our signage on them.

THEN AS SOON AS THE HOOK GETS OUT OF THE WAY K, MOE, GEGGY, TWISTED STEELE AND GOOGLY TAKE A SPOT AND USING EEFFY AND SKIN AS THEIR SPOTTERS SLOWLY WALK THE SAFETY BARRIERS OVER THE HOLE AND SLID IT DOWN INTO PLACE.

EEFY: Ok SKIN that's one down. What's next?

SKIN: SMARKEY is in the know and he has the hook directly over the number two control valve.

EEFFY: Let's do it. I'm getting hungry for my fried bananas and plantains.

SKIN DRAGGS THE SAME BRIDAL OVER TO THE NEXT FLOOR PLUG AS SMARKEY BRINGS THE HOOK TO A STOP, ABOUT WAIST HIGH. SKIN CLIPS THE BRIDAL ONTO THE HOOK THEN IN THE SAME MANNOR MAKES SURE THE LEGS ARE STRAIGHT AND THE HOOKS ARE ATTACHED TO THE LIFTING RINGS WITH THE TIPS OF THE HOOKS POINTING OUT. SKIN NODS TO EEFFY THEN EEFFY ESTABLISHES EYE CONTACT WITH THE CRANE OPPERATOR. EEFFY, WITH HIS ARM OUT AND CLOSED FIST AT A NINETY DEGREE ANGLE OPENS HIS FIST, CLOSES HIS FIST, OPENS HIS FIST CLOSES HIS FIST AND THE SLACK IN THE FOUR LEGS OF THE BRIDAL IS QUICK TO DISAPEER. SKIN, THEN TAKES A CLOSE LOOK TO MAKE SURE EVERYTHING IS ORIENTED CORECTLY THEN KICKS ONE OF THE HOOKS TO STRAIGHTEN IT OUT AND GIVES EEFFY THE NOD. EEFFY LOOKS UP TO SMARKEY AND OPEN FIST, CLOSE FIST, OPEN FIST, CLOSE FIST, OPEN FIST, CLOSE FIST THEN SKIN IS QUICK WITH A TWO HAND WAVE LETTING EEFFY KNOW THE PLUG IS CLEAR. EEFFY SIGNALS TO BRIDGE THE CRANE TOWARDS THE FRONT OF THE HOLE A COUPLE FEET AWAY AND SKIN, WITH HIS FEET OUT OF THE WAY GENTLY GUIDES THE NUMBER II CONTROL VALVE FLOOR PLUG TO REST. EEFFY THEN SIGNALS A SLOW DOWN, SLOW DOWN TILL THE SLACK IN THE LEGS OF THE BRIDAL ALLOW SKIN TO DISCONNECT THE HOOKS.

THIS TIME SKIN LEFT THE BRIDAL ON THE HOOK AND SMARKEY WAS QUICK TO LOCATE THE NEXT FLOOR PLUG, NUMBER ONE STOP VALVE, TO BE LIFTED OUT. WITH K, MOE, GEGGY, TWISTED STEELE, GOOGLY STANDING BYE WITH THE PRE-MADE SAFETY BARRIERS. THE HOLE ALLOWS CRANE ACCESS TO THE NUMBER II CONTROL VALVE AND IS SAFELY MARKED AND IDENTIFIED SO NO ONE CAN ACCIDENTLY FALL.

EEFFY:	Ok SKIN, that's two plugs down just the number one stop valve to go.
SKIN:	They are the same size EEFFY six-foot bye six-foot bye three foot of high tensile reinforced concrete. SMARKEY must be hungry too because he has the hook ready to go

USING THE SAME TECHNIQUES, THE TEAM SAFELY PULLS THE FLOOR PLUG FOR THE NUMBER ONE STOP VALVE AND PUTS IT TO REST A COUPLE FEET IN FROT OF THE HOLE. K, MOE, GEGGY, TWISTED STEELE AND GOOGLY SECURE THE HOLE IN THE FLOOR WITH THE SAFETY BARRIERS AND DOUBLE CHECK TO MAKE SURE EVERYTHING IS NEAT AND WELL MARKED TO PREVENT ANY CONFUSSION WHEN THE UNIT TWO STEAM SIDE OUTAGE BEGINS INSIDE THE GIANT ELECTRIC MACHINE.

SQUARE HEAD, WOBY, FATTY JOE, COL. HOGAN AND SCHAFFER CITY (JOB LEADERS), AFTER WATCHING THE EVELOUTION OF THE FLOOR PLUG REMOVAL, WALK AROUND TO THE LEFT SIDE OF THE FRONT STANDARD WHERE THEY BUMP INTO KULPPIRNICUS, AMMO, LAZALOON AND COOL EARL. THE CABNET DOORS OF THE DRY POCKET ON THE RIGHT AND LEFT SIDES OF THE FRONT STANDARD ARE OPENED AND THE CREW LOOKS TO BE CLOSLY EXAMINING EACH SIDE LOOKING FOR ANY LEAKS THAT WILL NEED TO BE ADDRESSED DURING THE OUTAGE. KULPPIRINCUS SLIDES OUT TILL HIS FEET HIT THE GROUND ARMED WITH A FLASHLIGHT.

SQUARE HEAD:	Don't forget KULPPRINCUS, the unit is still at full power.

KULPPRINICUS: Hard to forget that fact. We can barely hear ourselves think working on the deck.

FATTY JOE: Makes sense, when you have both units operating, remember each unit weighs about four hundred ton, rotating at eighteen hundred revolutions per minute, supported bye babbitt faced bearings on a four to eight thousand of an inch oil wedge it's going to be loud and hot.

KULPPRINICUS: Cheese FATTY JOE, you been at this for too long. We're being very careful to identify any small leakers, we need to fix and make sure we have the correct O-rings, ferrell's and fittings on hand to make repairs.

LAZALOON: Talk about a confined space!

SQUARE HEAD: How's it look in there?

KULPPRINICUS: We have some repairs plus what the procedure requests. MITTS and JOHNNYOBOTT are performing a visual inspection of the electro hydraulic pump as well, so we're ready to go.

THE JOB LEADERS ARE MOVING ALONG THE LEFT SIDE OF THE UNIT AND KNOW WHAT THEY ARE LOOKING FOR.

SCHAFFER CITY: I can see the electricians have been hard at work, the high-pressure turbine rollers are set and have temporary power. Also, the temporary bolt induction heater circuits are in place but I have to check with HIGH VOLT to make sure their tied into the disconnect.

AS THE JOB LEADERS CONTINUE TO WALK THE LEFT SIDE OF UNIT II SCHAFFER CITY NOTICES THAT "B" LP., AND "C" LP. TURBINE ROLLERS ARE ALSO READY TO GO. TO THE RIGHT SIDE OF THE JOB LEADERS IS THE NUMBER THREE CROSS AROUND INTERMEDIATE VALVE.

COL. HOGAN: The valve crew has a minor inspection on the number three cross around intermediate valve. We have to take an actuator rod measurement and inspect the spring tension rod assembly. I hope we don't have to get into that this time around, were going to be busy enough.

THE JOB LEADERS MAKE THEIRE WAY ALONG THE LEFT SIDE OF THE UNIT II MAIN GENERATOR THEN PAST "E" COUPLING TO THE DOG HOUSE CAPPY AND DOC (ELECTRICIANS) ARE INSIDE THE DOG HOUSE INSPECTING THE BRUSH RIGGING AND SEE HOW DIRTY THEY GET DURING THE LIFE OF A BREAKER TO BREAKER RUN. THEY WILL ALSO BE IN CHARGE OF MAKING SURE THERE IS NO POTENTIAL FOR ANY GROUNDING OF THE GENERATOR DURING THE RUN OF THE NEXT CYCLE. THE JOB LEADERS MAKE THEIR WAY PAST THE HATCH. ALONG THE RIGHT SIDE OF THE OPPERATING UNIT AND ON THE LEFT IS THE MOBILE RIGGING ROOM WITH IT'S DOORS FACEING THE HATCH, BACK TO BACK WITH MOBILE TOOL CAGE (LOPEZ LAND) WITH IT'S DOORS FACEING TOWARDS THE FRONT STANDARD.

SQUARE HEAD: LOPEZ how's things going? You opened for business yet?

LOPEZ: Not quite SQUARE HEAD we still have to make sure our calibrated tools are up to date and put away, but were getting there. If I could only get MIC to stop practicing the light tree, drag racing thing. But he is very dependable and knows the tools required for the job.

AIRY SUE: I'm also taking inventory of the cleaning chemicals and making sure they are on the approved list. We have a lot of parts to clean.

LOPEZ: Soon we are going to receive more work gloves, safety glasses and hearing protection that we'll have to store away as well.

BLAZE AND SUAVE RICO SENT THE LAST SET OF ROLLERS AND THEIRE BASES TO BIG O AND PAPALUCHI, WHO SET THEM UP PERFECTLY ON THERE MARKS IN FRONT OF THE CRAB SHACK. IT'S VERY IMPORTANT ROPEY AND PEACHES PRECISELY MARK WHERE THE ROLLERS GO BECAUSE WHEN THEY ARE HOISTED OUT OF THE GIANT ELECTRIC MACHINE FOR CLEANING AND TESTING THEY ARE SET TO REST ON THE JOURNALS OF THE SPINDLES. AS THE JOB LEADERS HAVE THERE BACK TO THE TOOL ROOM THEY PROCEED ON THE RIGHT SIDE OF THE GIANT ELECTRIC MACHINE AND SEE OTTO, BOOGER, GONESKI, LAURY AND CARLEY FINISHING UP BUILDING THE TEMPORARY WELD SHACK. ABOUT TEN FEET IN FRONT OF THE CRAB SHACK.

THE WELD SHACK IS THERTY FEET LONG AND TWENTY-FIVE FEET WIDE. THE WELDERS USE A FLAME RETARDENT FABRIC TO PROTECT THE FLOOR AND IS BUILT OUT OF A LIGHT WEIGHT CORROGATED ALLUMINUM WITH EACH PANNEL ATTACHED TO THE OTHER AND ONE INCH ANGLE TO TIE IN THE CORNERS. THE

ROOF IS LEFT OPENED SO THE CRANE CAN FLY FLOW GUIDES
AND DIAPHRAMS, THAT NEED REPAIR DUE TO STEAM WASH, IN
AND OUT. BOOGER SEES THE JOB LEADERS AND HEADS OVER TO
FILL THEM IN ON THE PROGRESS.

BOOGER: The MIG, TIG machines along with the bottle farm rack is on its way. Looks like we'll have just enough room to land two full diaphragm racks in here as well. Plus, only one fire watch is required.

GOON: Hey listen BOOGER, we have a lot of centerline work, we're critical path to start up. We need high quality work in a timely manner your well-staffed with a great crew.

BOOGER: I understand GOON, don't worry we are going to MAKE IT HAPPEN!

SCHAFFER CITY LEADS THE JOB LEADERS FURTHER ALONG THE
RIGHT SIDE OF THE GIANT ELECTRIC MACHINE AND FINIALLY
HAS A CHANCE TO CATCH UP WITH HIGH VOLT, BRUCEY, SISTER
T AND CUPCAKE WHO HAVE JUST FINISHED UP HANGING A
TEMPORARY, FOUR CONDUCTORS, NUMBER EIGHT WIRE ABOUT
SIXTY FEET LONG FROM A DISCONNECT SWITCH TO THE FORTH
SET OF ROLLERS.

BRUCEY: I'm starving.

SISTER T: Your forever hungry BRUCEY, I can't believe your out of food.

BRUCEY: I hope JOR'GE the sandwich maker is ready to feed the hungry.

SQUARE HEAD: JOR'GE is not fully set up yet. The ADMIRAL and JIMMY O ordered out for all of us.

WOBY: The generating station is going to feed us during the pre-job brief then JOR'GE Is going to take over from there.

SCHAFFER CITY: The electricians make me proud. Obviously, you all have been hard at it.

CUPCAKE: You're not kidding, this is heavy wire with the rockspestos insulation.

HIGH VOLT: Teamwork is key, SISTER T is ready to tie into the disconnect, then before the steam side outage starts we'll have to energize our temporary circuits. (close disconnects)

CUPCAKE: Everything from the induction bolt heaters, power rollers, temporary lighting and weld machines should be ready to go.

SCHAFFER CITY: That's a great start let's keep our fingers crossed.

FATTY JOE LOOKS TOWARDS THE NUMBER THREE BEARING AND IS RELIEVED TO SEE ROPEY, PEACHES, YUM YUM, COOL DADDY, SUNNY AND JOWEE STAGEING THE THRUST PLATES AND TOOLING UP FOR ONE OF THE FIRST MAJOR EVELUTIONS OF THE OUTAGE. A FULL TRAIN THRUST MEASUREMENT IN ORDER TO ESTABLISH FULL AS FOUND AXIAL MOVEMENT.

WOBY: I must go to the basement to make sure the HIGH-PRESSURE CORE INJECTION PUMP crew is good to go. Sometimes it's difficult to get our tooling down there.

WOBY MAKES HIS WAY DOWN THE ELEVATOR AND GETS OUT AT ELEVATION MINUS FORTY-EIGHT FEET. WALKS THROUGH THE DOOR OF THE TOTE CONFINES AND THE CREW IS PREPARING FOR THE HIPCI MINOR INSPECTION. ON THE JOB IS DUDDLEY, NOSEALEO AND SOME TEAM SPECIALISTS JOSEPH STRANGLEHOLD AND RAPPING RODNEY.

WOBY:	So much quieter down here, you can hear a pin drop. How's things going?
DUDDLEY:	Pretty good WOBY, RAPPING RODNEY finished the crane inspection and we have our tool box down here
NOSEALEO:	I have the tools to replace the cooling water filters, oil filters and packing where required.
STRANGLEHOLD:	Also, we are tooled up for alignment check and overspeed testing.
WOBY:	Ok sounds good, once you feel like your set up head to the muster area for the pre-job and a bite to eat.

WOBY IS CONFIDENT THE CREW HAS A VERY GOOD UNDERSTANDING OF THE TASK AT HAND, BEING A MINOR INSPECTION, IF ALL GOES WELL, THE MEN SHOULD BE ON CENTERLINE BEFORE LONG. ON HIS WAY OUT OF THE TURBINE BUILDING, HE MAKES SURE TO LET EVERYONE KNOW ON THE TEAM TO FINISH UP, GET TO THE MUSTER AREA FOR THE PRE-JOB BRIEF/ SAFETY MEETING WITH JIMMY O AND POSSIBLY THE ADMIRAL TO ATTEND.

SQUARE HEAD, COL.HOGAN, FATTY JOE, GOON AND SCHAFFER CITY ARE STANDING NEAR THE RIGGING CAGE LOOKING

DOWN THE HATCH AT SUAVE RICO AND BLAZE WHO ARE HOOKING UP THE LAST OF THE BOLT BINS AND DIAPHRAM RACKS THAT ARE PLACED ALONG BOTH SIDES OF THE TURBINES USED FOR ORDERLY PARTS STORAGE AND CLEANING DURING THE DISASEMBLY, CLEANING, INSPECTION AND REASSEMBLY OF THE MAIN STEAM TURBINES INSIDE THE GIANT ELECTRIC MACHINE. THE BINS ARE IN THE AIR AND THE TRAILER IS EMPTY. PLAIN BILL JUMPS UP INTO HIS TRACTOR, GIVES A WAVE UP THE HATCH, SECURITY OPENS UP THE BIG ROLL UP DOOR AND PLAIN BILL DRIVES THE TRACTOR TRAILER OUT THE TURBINE BUILDING THEN IMMEDIATELY SECURITY CLOSES THE DOOR AND STANDS BYE. RAYRAY CHONG (UNIT II CRANE OPPERATOR), PAPALUCHI, BLAZE, EEFFY, BIG O, SUAVE RICO AND SMARKEY (UNIT I CRANE OPPERATOR) FINISH SETTING THE LAST BOLT BINS ALONG BOTH SIDES OF THE "C" LP. (LOW PRESSURE TURBINE) AND MEET UP WITH BIG JIM WHO IS STANDING BYE THE HATCH, WAITING FOR RAYRAY CHONG TO CLIMB DOWN FROM THE BOX OF THE UNIT TWO CRANE. ONCE HE JOINS THE REST OF THE CREW, THE TEAM OF FIRST CLASS, HEAVY LOADS RIGGERS MAKES THEIR WAY TO THE ELEVATOR TO JOIN THE REST OF THE MAIN STEAM/ TURBINE GANG, IN THE MUSTER AREA INSIDE THE GIANT ELECTRIC MACHINE.

WITH THE CREW FULLY ASSEMBELED IT GETS VERY LOUD, SOME HAVENT SEEN EACH OTHER IN A FEW MONTHS DUE TO WORKING AT DIFFERENT STATIONS THEN GETTING BACK TOGETHER FOR THE BIG JOBS. SQUARE HEAD WALKS IN THE DOUBLE PERSONEL DOORS AND DOES HIS BEST TO KEEP THEM OPENED AS FIVE, FOUR WHEEL CARTS COME PLOWING INTO THE MUSTER AREA.

EACH CART WAS STACKED TO ALMOST THE TOP OF THE DOOR JAMB AND JUST BARLEY ABLE TO BE PULLED IN. A WHOLE LOT OF FOOD FOR A WHOLE LOT OF HUNGRY FOLKS. BRUCEY, JOR'GE THE SANDWICH MAKER, GOOGLY, K, HIGH VOLT WERE ALL AVAILIABLE TO SPREAD THE FOOD AROUND THE COUNTER TOPS ON THE PERIMITER OF THE LARGE MUSTER AREA WITHOUT GETTING TO CLOSE TO THE HOTDOG ROLLER OR JOR'GE THE SANDWICH MAKER'S AREA. ON THE MENUE OF COURSE, PHILLY FAVORITES CHEESE STEAKS FROM PLAIN TO SAUCE AND ONIONS, MUSHROOM CHEESE, HOAGIE STYLE WIT OR WIT OUT. ALSO, PIZZA STACKED HIGH AND STILL HOT EVERYTHING FROM HAWIAN STYLE, BUFFALO CHICKEN, VEGGIE, PLAIN, PEPPERONI ALMOST EVERY KIND OF PIZZA YOU COULD THINK OF. THAT'S NOT ALL INDIVIGUAL HALF CHICKENS FRIED AND BARBACUED ALONG WITH SIDES OF POTATO WEDGES, SWEET POTATO WEDGES WITH LITTLE CUPS OF HONEY, COLE SLAW, BROCOLI RAB, COLD COLIFLOWER SALAD REGULAR SALAD WITH DRESSING OPTIONS AND JUST ABOUT EVERY NON ALCHOL BEVERAGE AVAILIABLE FROM POP TO FLAVORED WATER.

THE ADMERIAL WENT ALL OUT IN FEEDING THE TROOPS AND HE IS WELL AWARE OF THE TEAMS CHALLENGES AHEAD. EVERYONE IS VERY ORDERLY IN THE BUFFET STYLE ARRANGEMENT BUT IT DID'NT GET ANY QUIETER. THE CREW IS IN CHOW MODE, AND DESERVINGLY SO A LOT OF WORK GOES INTO A SOUND PRE-JOB SET UP. THERE IS ALWAYS ONE TABLE LOUDER THEN EVERYONE ELSE BIG O, CUPCAKE RAYRAY CHONG, COOL EARL TWISTED STEELE, EEFFY AND SOMETIMES EVEN FATTY JOE WILL SIT IN TO PLAY A CARD GAME THEY ARE VERY PASSIONATE ABOUT. AN HOUR OR SO LATER EVERYONE IS FULLY FED AND

LOUIE, SQUARE HEAD AND KISSY MAKE THEIRE WAY TO THE FRONT OF THE ROOM.

KISSY RINGS A SMALL BELL TO BRING THE MUSTER AREA TO A VERY SLOW ATTENTION, AS THE CARD PLAYING TABLE ERRUPTS IN A LOUD ROAR AND LAUGHTER. KISSEY RINGS THE BELL AGAIN AND THE ROOM GRADUALLY COMES TO A SLOW ATTENTION.

LOUIE: Great crew we have here, good to see everyone. Just to let you know the ADMERIAL and JIMMY O are on their way for a pre-job brief.

TEAM MEMBERS ARE QUICK TO CLEAN UP THE MUSTER AREA, CLEAN UP AND TAKE OUT THE TRASH, NEATLY ARRANGE ANY LEFTOVERS AND WIPE OFF THE TABLES. THE PERSONEL DOOR SWINGS OPENED AND IN WALKS EAGLE ED, JIMMY O, KRINE DOG, BOW TIE AND THE ADMERIAL. THE CRAFTSMEN AND WOMEN GET IT, THEY KNOW WHY THERE THEIR AND ARE THANKFUL FOR THE HOSPITATILITY OF THE ADMERIAL INSIDE THE GIANT ELECTRIC MACHINE. KISSY RINGS THE BELL AGAIN AND THE ADMERIAL STEPS UP.

ADMERIAL: For me personally, it's good to see so many familiar faces. Having a group with a great track record helps give me the confidence I like to have when preparing for such a challenging STEAM SIDE outage. I want to thank all of you on behalf of the station for your commitment to excellence, your safe work practices, your questioning attitude, your housekeeping and your past results in keeping THE GIANT ELECTRIC MACHINE a world class facility with the highest capacity factors in the industry. I also want to challenge you to not get complacent always work safe, watch out for each other, ask questions and follow the procedures associated with the task. Again thank you and I'll see you on the deck.

THE ADMERIAL IS VERY BUSY, AND MAKES A QUICK EXIT NOT ONLY CONCERNED FOR THE UNIT II STEAM SIDE OUTAGE INSIDE THE GIANT ELECTRIC MACHINE, BUT THE UNIT ONE OPPERATING UNIT AND ITS WORLD CLASS RUN, FROM BREAKER TO BREAKER PROVIDING ELECTRICITY FOR OUR HOMES AND BUSINESSES.

JIMMY O: I don't want to take much time, but I want to second everything the ADRERIAL had to say, and like to welcome our engineers KRINE DOG, BOW TIE the SAND CRABS who play a very important role in blasting our rotors and valve parts for thorough inspections and balancing and our instrument and control techs DANDAMAN and SJUNG who will be working in the control room and making sure the indicators and vibration probe monitors are working to one hundred percent satisfaction. Also, I want to assure you we are critical path and only people who have work on the deck are welcome, the ADMERIAL made that perfectly clear he expects no distractions. Let's be safe out there, plan the work, work the plan, stay out from underneath a suspended load always. KRINE DOG has something to say then the job leaders will make the rounds and get us pointed in the right direction as the countdown to the UNIT II main steam outage INSIDE THE GIANT ELECTRIC MACHINE continues.

KRINE DOG: I was asked to remind everyone to make sure you have the proper and most up to date prints and procedures in front of you ANTHILL and the ANTHILL MOB are here to provide us with the infield hard copies when needed.

LOUIE STEPS FORWARD AND HANDS THE FLOOR TO THE JOB LEADERS. LOUIE, KRINE DOG, BOW TIE, EAGLE ED, DANDAMAN, SJONG, JIMMY O, PSUTOM, GENO AND KISSY HEAD OUT TO A CONFRENCE ROOM TO GO OVER ANY LOOSE ENDS PRIOR TO THE START OF THE OUTAGE. SQUARE HEADS FIRST STOP WILL BE A VISIT WITH BIG JIM AND THE RIGGERS.

SQUARE HEAD: Here we go again, you guys have a lot of work ahead of you, I'm glad we had time up front for crane inspections. So far so good? Looks like the rigging cage is set up and there shouldn't be anyone around who's not supposed to be.

BIG JIM: Right off the top were all familiar with the task at hand, heavy loads trained and have worked together before.

SUAVE RICO: We set up the rigging cage with all our specialty slings, wire ropes, softeners, shackles, eyebolts, chain blocks and BIG JIM promised he's going to keep it orderly and have our gear ready for us when we must redress the hook according to the task.

BIG O: BLAZE, SKIN, PAPALUCHI and I also had the time to set the cribbing on the unit I side so when we have a hood or inner shell in the air we have a place to go with it.

EEFFY: We are well set up but were going to have a lot of heavy picks. Like the high-pressure head one hundred and twenty tons and the three low pressure rotors at sixty tons each.

PAPALUCHI: Bye the time this steam side outage is over were all going to be rolling in Eagles green.

BIG JIM: SMARKEY is going to be operating the unit I crane with BLAZE, BIG O and Suave RICO floating around in support. Then in the unit II crane RAYRAY CHONG is operator with EEFFY, PAPALUCHI and SKIN available on the ground. What's nice this time is RAPPING RODNEY is going to be handling the rigging on the HPCI job, so we won't have to run back and forth.

SKIN: Don't forget when we send parts to the SAND CRABS for blasting they must be hanging from wire rope or chain because Kevlar and nylon, no matter what grade will tare from the blasting and load and could really injure someone.

SQUARE HEAD: Very important heads up SKIN that's another reason FATTY JOE likes you so much. Don't forget the FLYERS orange vests, make sure you stick to the proper load path, set the pace and watch out for each other. Oh, yea be careful of the floors don't want to tick off KIKEY or his helper FUZZY.

SQUARE HEADS NEXT STOP IS THE ELECTRO HYDRAULIC CONTROL TEAM BECAUSE ITS IMPORTANT THEY GET TO THE DECK AND OPEN UP THE FRONT STANDARD PRIOR TO THE COUNTDOWN AND THE UNIT II MANUALTRIP. KULPPIRNICUS, AMMO, GONESKI, JOHNNYOBOTT, JOEWEE, COOL DADDY AND MITTS WHO WILL BE WATCHING AND PERFORMING AN EHC PUMP INSPECTION, ARE WAITING FOR SQUARE HEAD TO SEND THEM ON THEIR WAY.

KULPPRINICUS: Waiting on you SQUARE, GONESKI's got to visit the store room and pick up a few more o rings from CHICKEN SALAD KEITH and meet us on the deck.

MITTS: I've got to stand by the EHC pump and monitor discharge pressure, check for leaks, then when we get the clearance, check pump alignment and look for soft foot.

AMMO: We also need to replace the in-line filters.

SQUARE HEAD: Very important system, no FME zone. Foreign materials exclusion.

SQUARE HEAD KNOWS HOW IMPORTANT THE TOOL ROOM IS AND WANTS TO MAKE SURE LOPEZ LAND IS IN ORDER.

SQUARE HEAD:	LOPEZ is everything ready in LOPEZ LAND?
LOPEZ:	Our calibrated tools are all up to date and put away. We should be opened for business. GOON and FATTY JOE have kept us informed as to what to expect. All the airlines and tools are in place and staged for the thrust work and outer hood removal.
AIRYSUE:	We also have the torque machines, coupling bolt removal tools and plenty of gloves for the razor sharp, bronze packing replacement work.
SQUARE HEAD:	We can't have anyone get cut from that stuff, but it tightens up the steam path. Also, the ADMERIAL made it perfectly clear no one is to raid our tool room unless you have work on the deck.

THE WORDS SOUND LIKE MUSIC TO MICS EARS, HE EVEN PICKED HIS EYES UP OF THE RED LIGHT, YELLOW LIGHT, GREEN LIGHT DRAG STRIP RACING TREE GAME FOR A SPLIT SECOND. NEXT STOP FOR SQUARE HEAD IS THE VALVE TEAM HEADED UP BYE CORNAL HOGAN. CORNAL HOGAN IS STANDING WITH FATTY JOE AND GOON THE THREE OF THE JOB LEADERS ARE OLD SCHOOL AND HAVE ACQUIRED A LIFETIME OF EXPERIENCE. THEY WORKED THEIR WAY UP FROM HELPER AND KNOW WHEN ITS TIME TO LAUGH AND WHEN ITS TIME TO WORK.

SQUARE HEAD:	CORNAL HOGAN how's the valve team looking?

CORNAL HOGAN: We have all the floor plugs up and can access the valves. I just hope we don't have to get deep into the number three cross around intermediate valve. It's scheduled for a minor inspection, packing replacement, measure the actuator arm and check push rod spring tension. If it passes inspection, we won't have to get into it!

SQUARE HEAD: CORNAL HOGAN cheese no need to yell. I'm standing right here, in the muster area. You blow out my ear drum.

JAKE: SQUARE HEAD, he can't hear that well anymore all those years working in the loud environment he can't tell how loud he speaks.

TWISTED STEELE: It don't matter where he is he is a very loud talker.

JAKE: A lot of times you think he's yelling at you but he's harmless.

SQUARE HEAD: I'm standing right next to you don't yell.

GEGGY: Yea, turn it down CORNAL HOGAN.

CORNAL HOGAN: I can't help it, you know that SQUARE HEAD!

SQUARE HEAD: You all set up?

CORNAL HOGAN: We have a lot of experience JAKE, POOPDECK PAPPY and DELCO JOE are going to be working on the Main Control Valve number two. BUTCH, CHARDY and GOOGLY are going to be on the number one Main Stop Valve and TWISTED STEELE and GEGGY are going to handle the bypass valves.

SQUARE HEAD:	Remember all hands-on centerline until we get disassembled then we can break off into our valve work. Remember as soon as we open the valves up, we create an FME zone. Work safe and I'll see you on the deck. GOON, FATTY JOE you guys ready?
FATTY JOE:	Looks like the gang is ready as we'll ever be.
GOON:	We have a good plan going in and our team is loaded with experience. The fitters and welders are going to help on centerline until we get the machine apart and they know what to expect.
FATTY JOE:	MOE, K, JOEWEE, JOHNNYOBOTT, OTTO, BOOGER, LAZALOON are going to be working on the high-pressure turbine. Also, CHARDY and SKIN know where the spring cans are to gag before we work on the main steam flanges.
GOON:	On the low-pressure turbines ROPEY, PEACHES, COOL DADDY, YUMYUM, SUNNY, KOCHY and CUBBY the two old steam heat guys. Good hard-working men.
SQUARE HEAD:	I think were as ready as we can be. We all know what needs to get done.

GOON IS STANDING BYE ROCKING BACK AND FORTH ON HIS FEET WITH HIS HANDS BEHIND HIS HIPS, LICKING HIS LIPS IN ANTICIPATION OF THE CHALLENGES AHEAD.

GOON: BOOGER, I expect the welders and fitters to be ready to go. I want a quality response to the work and expect high quality repairs on any washed-out diaphragms or flow guides. When it comes to the packing replacements everyone needs to have the heavy gloves on, we all know how sharp that brass is. Another thing before you guys get to the deck, If we need to crack any inner shell cylinder nuts to remove the upper halves don't try to get cute with the torch, if you hit the hardened US STEELE fine threads I'm going to be seeing PHILLIES red.

BOOGER: Alright GOON we've all been over this before. Only so far with the torch then split the nut with a hammer and chisel and chase and clean the threads. Then double check to make sure the nut threads on the stud.

SQUARE HEAD: It's important to remember before we unstack the lower half they want us to install air bags in the steam lines to prevent foreign material from entering the system. Ok see you on the deck.

GOON: I want everyone to know we have the paper work to remove the bolts to the outer low-pressure hoods and have them jacked up ready to be picked as soon as were done with the thrust check. We also have the clearance to remove every other bolt on the oil side coupling covers, but not the dowels. So, let's get busy.

THE MUSTER AREA IS EMPTYING OUT AS THE CRAFTSMEN AND WOMEN ARE GRADUALLY FINDING THEIRE WAY BACK TO THE DECK. NAVY MIKE AND MR. URRIGHT LET SQUARE HEAD KNOW THEY ARE STILL IN SET UP MODE IN THE PRECISION MACHINING SHOP. WOBY AND THE HPCI TEAM IS NEXT FOR SQUARE HEAD TO TUCH BASE WITH LEAVING THE ELECTRICIANS AND SCHAFFER CITY.

WOBY: DUDDLEY and the HPCI pump specialist JOSEPH STRANGLEHOLD are going to handle the minor inspection.

DUDDLEY: We are ready to go SQUARE HEAD; our tools are staged down there, and we reviewed the procedures. EAGLE ED and ICEMAN are ready to support us when the clearance comes down and they know the importance of the task also to make sure we get our work done within the window provided.

WOBY: We know the auxiliary steam valve needs to be blocked and tagged and the importance of the system. Until then DUDDLEY is going to help on the high-pressure flanges. NOSEALEO is working on the lube oil system and making sure he has the "Q" parts at hand if required. RAPPING RODNEY is on the rigging team, but he needs to be prepared for anything in the HIPCI room and requires all "Q" rated rigging equipment and procedures.

R A P P I N G   No worry SQUARE all good down there.
RODNEY: A hundred feet below the deck what more
                 to expect. We wait on the clearance no
                 interference, that turbine kick on, the pump
                 goanna hum, move more water than ever
                 before, push that water right to the core. Don't
                 worry SQUARE I been there before.

STRANGLEHOLD RUBS HIS CHIN, SHAKES HIS HEAD AND
CHUCKLES AS SQUARE HEAD TRACKS DOWN SCHAFFER CITY.

SCHAFFER CITY: I had to bring in SEESAU as an extra pair of
                 hands and in case we need parts. Plus, he is a
                 great planner. Also, our work load is huge, so
                 RJ is also going to help, first class electrician.
SQUARE HEAD: Great to have you guys back. We know you do
                 quality work and are familiar with our procedures.
SCHAFFER CITY: CUPCAKE and SISTER T are going to stand by
                 and support the thrust bearing work. Once we
                 get the thrust measurement and the clearance
                 they will tie in with HIGH VOLT and BRUCEY on
                 clam shell and links removal. DOC, CAPPY and
                 RJ are going to have their hands full in support
                 of the front standard work, brush removal, dog
                 house cleaning and inspections. ESKIN, ELANE
                 are going to handle the vibration probes and
                 thermocouples stationed at each bearing,
                 working closely with DANDAMAN and SJONG
                 who will be in the control room making sure the
                 annunciator lights are true. Outside of that, I
                 think we're ready.

SQUARE HEAD: Thanks electricians for a proficient set up I know running the temporary circuits using the heavy rockspestos wire is no easy chore. Work safe and always test before you touch. Oh yea, quick BRUCEY, COOL EARL, LAURY and CARLEY are going to put together a grill for us, CORNAL HOGAN has some extra angle iron and a clean drum that way we won't need the hotdog roller for the kielbasa.

BRUCEY NODS HIS HEAD BUT HIS NOSE IS STUCK IN THE LEFTOVERS HE CONTINUES TO PICK AND FILLS POCKETTS WITH ENOUGH FOOD TO GET HIM THROUGH TILL HE GETS A CHANCE TO GET OFF THE DECK AND VISIT JOR'GE THE SANDWICH MAKER, WHO ALSO HAS BEEN HARD AT WORK READY TO KEEP THE TROOPS FED DURING THE MAIN STEAM OUTAGE INSIDE THE GIANT ELECTRIC MACHINE. WITH THE FUEL RUNNING DOWN AND UNIT TWO HOVERING AT ABOUT SIXTY PERCENT, IT WON'T BE LONG TILL THE ADMERIAL REACHES THE FINIAL COUNTDOWN. SQUARE HEAD SPENDS A LITTLE TIME WITH KISSY, PSU TOM AND GENO AND MAKES SURE THEY ARE READY TO GO, THEN MAKES HIS WAY TO THE DECK.

JUST A QUICK EXPLANATION OF THE MAIN STEAM PATH INSIDE THE GIANT ELECTRIC MACHINE. THE SUPER HEATED, DRY, HIGH PRESSURE STEAM COMES ROLLING OUT OF THE HOT WATER BOILER OR REACTOR AND THROUGH THE MAIN STEAM CONTROL VALVES. THE CONTROL VALVES ACT AS A GOVONER AND HAVE THE ABILITY TO THROTLE THE STEAM MOST EFFICIENTLY. THE MAIN STEAM MOVES THROUGH THE MAIN STOP VALVES THEN COMES UP OVER HEAD THROUGH FOUR, THREE FOOT INSIDE DIAMETER,

INLET FLANGES AND BLASTS THE HIGH-PRESSURE TURBINE. INSIDE THE HIGH PRESURE TURBINE AND LOW-PRESSURE TURBINES IS FLOW GUIDES AND DIAPHRAMS. THE FLOW GUIDES DIRECT THE STEAM TO HIT THE BLADES OF THE TURBINES AT THE PERFECT ANGLE WHILE THE DIAPHRAMS HELP THE CYLINDERS TO MAINTAIN A MAX PRESSURE BETWEEN EACH STAGE. AS THE MAIN STEAM MAKES ITS WAY THROUGH THE HIGH-PRESSURE TURBINE AND IS DIRECTED TO THE BOTTOM SIDE OF THE CYLINDER THEN PULLED UNDER THE FLOOR INTO A REHEAT, HEAT EXCHANGER.

TOP VIEW INSIDE THE GIANT ELECTRIC MACHINE NORMANCLATURE

COLLECTOR END
ALTEREX/
DOG HOUSE

UNIT II
G
E
N
E
R
A
T
O
R

C
LOW
FIVE PRESSURE SIX
CIV TURBINE CIV

B
LOW
THREE PRESSURE FOUR
CIV TURBINE CIV

```
                    A
                   LOW
     ONE        PRESSUR        TWO
     CIV        TURBINE        CIV


                  HIGH
                PRESSURE
                TURBINE
                                       B
            FRONT                      Y
            STANDARD                   P
            GOVONOR END                A
ONE         TWO            THREE       S
MAIN        MAIN           MAIN        S
STOP VLV    STOP VLV       STOP VLV    V
                                       L
                                       V
ONE         TWO            THREE       S
CONTROL     CONTROL        CONTROL
VLV         VLV            VLV
```

THE HEAT EXCHANGER REHEATS THE STEAM, DRYS IT OUT THEN SENDS IT SUPER HEATED, UP THROUGH THE BOTTOM SIDE OF THE CROSS AROUND INTERMIDIATE VALVES WHERE IT IS STRAINED AND CAN BE THROTLED FOR MAX EFFICENCY. THEN ROLLS UP THROUGH THE BOTTOM OF THE "A" LP TURBINE WHERE IT'S DIRECTED BY THE FLOW GUIDES AND MAINTAINS PRESSURE WITHIN THE STAGES OF THE TURBINE, BY THE DIAPHRAMS FOR MAXIMUM PERFORMNCE. PULLED BYE VACUME THE STEAM MOVES THROUGH ANOTHER HEAT EXCHANGER BECOMES SUPER HEATED AND DRY, THROUGH ANOTHER SET OF CROSS AROUND

INTERMEDIATE VALVES WHERE IT IS STRAINED AND CONTROLLED AND BLASTED INTO THE BOTTOM HALF OF THE "B" LP TURBINE. THE MAIN STEAM IS PULLED THROUGH THE "B" LP TURBINE DIRECTED BYE THE FLOW GUIDES SO ITS DELIVERED TO THE BLADES OF THE TURBINE AT THE PERFECT ANGLE THE DIAPHRAMS HELP MAINTAIN THE PRESSURE BETWEEN THE STAGES OF THE TURBINE. THEN FOR THE LAST TIME THE MAIN STEAM IS PULLED THROUGH, UNDER THE FLOOR TO ANOTHER HEAT EXCHANGER AND COMES OUT ROLLING, SUPER HEATED AND DRY.

THROUGH ANOTHER SET OF CROSS AROUND INTERMEDIATE VALVES, WHERE ITS STRAINED AND CONTROLLED THEN BLASTS THE CENTER STAGE OF THE "C" LP TURBINE THEN DIRECTED ACCORDING TO THE FLOW GUIDES AND IS ABLE TO MAINTAIN THE PROPER PRESSURE DUE TO THE DIAPHRAMS. ONCE THE STEAM BLASTS THE FINAL STAGE OF THE "C" LP TURBINE, UNDER THE FLOOR IS THE HUGE CONDENSER, WHERE THE MAIN STEAM HITS THE COOLING WATER, INSIDE THE CONDENSER PIPEING, AND RETURNS TO WATER TO BE PUMPED BACK TO THE BOILER OR REACTOR. THE BYPASS VALVES ARE AVAILIABLE TO RELIEVE ANY PRESSURE DURING A SHUT DOWN OR SCRAM LEFT BETWEEN THE MAIN CONTROL VALVES AND THE MAIN STOP VALVES. THE EXCESS PRESURE OPENS UP THE VALVES INSIDE A STEAM CHEST AND DIRECTS INTO THE CONDENSER. NOW WE CAN JOIN THE REST OF THE CREW ON THE DECK AS WE AWAIT THE ADMERIAL AND EAGLE ED TO PULL THE MANUAL TRIP LEVER AND BEGIN THE MASSIVE STEAM SIDE OUTAGE INSIDE THE GIANT ELECTRIC MACHINE.

THE ADMERIAL, EAGLE ED, ICEMAN, KRINE DOG AND TIE BOW ARE IN THE CONTROL ROOM PATIENTLY WAITING FOR THE RIGHT TIME TO REMOVE UNIT II'S GENERATOR FROM THE POWER GRID.

EAGLE ED: ICEMAN before you make your way to the two hundred kv yard, we need to make sure of a seamless, event free unit II manual trip. As soon as the ADMERIAL gives us the go ahead I'm going to use the manual trip lever located on the governor end. Once the the unit is in coast down mode you are to open the main disconnect, lock and tag it. Make sure you tie in with SATCH the substation guy and let him know the unit II steam side outage is underway.

ICEMAN: On my way EAGLE ED. I have my face shield, hard hat, safety glasses, flame retardant coveralls and insulated rubber gloves. Oh, and my radio.

JIMMY O, LOUIE, SQUARE HEAD, JOHNNYOBOTT, COOL DADDY, JOEWEE ARE STANDING BYE THE GOVERNOR END DOOR WITH FLASHLIGHTS PEEPING THROUGH INSPECTION HOLES, STUDYING THE MANUAL TRIP MECHANISM AND OVERSPEED TRIP MECHANISIMS TO THE UNIT. KULPPERNICUS, AMMO AND GONESKI HAVE THE RIGHT SIDE AND LEFT SIDE CABNET DOORS OPENED TO THE FRONT STANDARD, WITH FLASHLIGHTS IN HAND, CLOSELY LOOKING IN THE DRY POCKETS FOR ANY UNIDENTIFIED LEAKERS IN THE ELECTRO HYDRAULIC SYSTEM.

ALL ALONG CENTERLINE THE CREW IS WELL UNDER WAY REMOVING THE BOLTS TO THE OUTSIDE HOODS OF THE LOW

PRESURE TURBINES. EACH OUTSIDE HOOD HAS OVER THREE HUNDRED ONE INCH IN DIAMETER X FOUR INCHES LONG HOLD DOWN BOLTS THAT KEEP THE OUTSIDE HOODS SECURLEY FASTENED. WITH THE THREE-QUARTER INCH AIR GUNS, THE CREW MAKES REMOVAL LOOK TRIVIAL. THE CREW MAKES SURE TO GATHER UP THE BOLTS AND STORE THEM IN THE BOLT BINS STATIONED ALONG EACH SIDE OF THE MACHINE. THE NEXT STEP FOR THE CREW IS TO PREPARE THE HOODS FOR REMOVAL, USING JACK BOLTS AND OPENING UP THE HOODS OF THE HORIZONTAL JOINT SO THE RIGGERS CAN LINE UP AND GET THEM OUT OF THE WAY.

EAGLE ED GETS THE OK FROM THE ADMERIAL AND MAKES HIS TO THE MANUAL TRIP LEVER.

EAGLE ED:	ICEMAN, ICEMAN do you copy? ICEMAN do you copy?
ICEMAN:	Yes, I copy EAGLE ED, Yes, I copy.

LOUIE LEANS OVER AND SAYS TO JMMY O, SQUAREHEAD AND EAGLE ED.

LOUIE:	I can remember we used to wear greens, grays, and blues. These days it's hard to tell who's who with everyone wearing Seventy Sixers blue.
EAGLE ED:	Me to LOUIE. Ok, yes ADMERIAL I copy. Yes, ADMERIAL I copy. Alright were in countdown mode.

EAGLE ED PUTS ONE HAND ON THE MANUAL TRIP LEVER AND IS LISTENING TO THE ADMERIAL 3, 2, 1 AT THAT PRECISE MOMENT

EAGLE ED PULLS DOWN ON THE MANUAL TRIP LEVER AND THE START OF THE MAIN STEAM OUTAGE UNIT II INSIDE THE GIANT ELECTRIC MACHINE BEGINS. JOHNNYOBOTT HAS THE BEST SEAT IN THE STATION?

JOHNNYOBOTT: As soon as EAGLE ED pulled down on the trip lever, the spring released tension on the dog, and because of the centrifugal force, the dog swung opened, came around made contact with the hydraulic control switch. The control switch opened then dumped all the hydraulic systems fluid and pressure into the systems reservoir.

KULPPRINICUS: With the loss of pressure in the hydraulic system all the main steam supply valves closed, and the main steam turbine /generator moves into coast down mode.

AMMO: Don't forget the bypass valves which opened and relieved any leftover steam pressure into the condenser.

EAGLE ED: ICEMAN, ICEMAN you can open the main breaker. I repeat, open the main breaker.

ICEMAN: Yes, EAGLE ED the main breaker is opened and SATCH is here to double verify lock and tag the main breaker to the two hundred kv yard.

EAGLE ED: Great job ICEMAN, now get back to the control room. We must block the oil side of the thrust bearing so the crew can measure the full axial thrust of the GIANT ELECTRIC MACHINE. Remember ICE were critical path and unit two is full STOP.

BIG JIM, RICO SUAVE AND THE RIGGERS ARE SET UP AND READY TO REMOVE THE OUTER HOODS OF THE THREE LOW PRESSURE TURBINES. RAYRAY CHONG OPPERATING THE UNIT TWO CRANE IS DIRECTLY CENTERED OVER THE "B" LP HOOD. EEFFY, PAPALUCHI AND SKIN DRESSED THE BIG HOOK WITH FOUR ENDLESS KEVLAR SLINGS, THERTY FOOT LONG. EACH HOOD WEIGHS IN AT FIFTY TONS.

SMARKEY IS OPPERATING THE UNIT ONE CRANE WITH BLAZE, BIG O, AND RAPPING RODNEY AS THE GROUND HANDS. RICO SUAVE HAS THE UNIT ONE CRANE SET PERFECTLY CENTERED OVER THE "C" LP HOOD. THE RIGGERS ON EACH TEAM MAKE SURE THEIRE IS NO TWISTS IN THE SLINGS AND HOOK ONE END AROUND THE CENTER OF THE HOOK, ALMOST PERFECTLY ON TOP OF EACH OTHER. THE RIGGERS TAKE THE OTHER END OF THE SLINGS AND PUT THEM AROUND THE OUTSIDE CORNERS, FIXED LIFTING HORNS. BOTH TEAMS WORKING TOGETHER, GIVE BIG JIM THE THUMBS UP. BIG JIM IS GOING TO SIGNAL TO BOTH CRANE OPPERATORS AT THE SAME TIME. SLOW UP, SLOW UP, SLOW UP AND STOP AS THE SLINGS GET TOTE. SKIN AND RICO SUAVE CHECK THE SLINGS AROUND THE HOOK AS THE REST OF THE RIGGERS MAKE SURE THE SLINGS ARE TOTE ON THE HORNS. BIG JIM DOUBLE CHECKS TO MAKE SURE EACH CRANE IS PERFECTLY CENTER, THEN PROCEEDS. SLOW UP, SLOW UP AND BEING ALREADY UP OFF THE JOINT DUE TO THE JACK BOLTS THE HOODS ARE FLOATING AND OUT OF THE FIT. THE RIGGERS ARE WATCHING VERY CLOSELY AS BIG JIM SIGNALS SLOW UP, SLOW UP, SLOW UP THEN UP.

THE HOODS ARE CLEAR OF THE INNER SHELLS AND BIG JIM SIGNALS TO THE CRANE OPPERATORS BRIDGE THE HOODS TO

THE DESIGNATED LAY DOWN AREA. USNG THE SAFE LOAD PATH, OVER THE UNIT TWO GENERATOR, THEN OPEN FLOOR SPACE TO OVER TOP OF UNIT ONE GENERATOR AND THE "C" AND "B" LP'S WHERE THE CRANES COME TO A STOP, ALWAYS ALLOWING A SAFE DISTANCE BETWEEN THE TWO. PAPALUCHI SIGNALS TO RAYRAY CHONG AS BLAZE SIGNALS TO SMARKEY TO TROLLY THE HOODS TO THE RIGHT SIDE OF THE "C" AND "B" LP HOODS OF THE OPPERATING UNIT I AND CENTER THEM TO COME DOWN ON THE CRIBBING. WHEN THE HOODS ARE DIRECTLY OVER THE CRIBBING PAPALUCHI AND BLAZE SIGNAL SLOW DOWN, SLOW DOWN, SLOW DOWN AS THE RIGGERS GENTLY GUIDE THE OUTTER HOODS RIGHT ONTO THE CRIBBING. THE HOODS COME TO REST AND THE HOOKS CONTINUE TO COME DOWN, SO THE RIGGERS CAN REMOVE THE SLIGS FROM AROUND THE LIFTING HORNS AND SEND THE CRANES ON THEIR WAY.

UNDER BIG JIM'S DIRECTION RAYRAY CHONG TAKES HIS UNIT TWO CRANE TO THE "A" LP HOOD WHERE HIS TEAM IS WAITING EEFFY, SKIN AND PAPALUCHI. WITH HELP FROM SUAVE RICO, SMARKEY IN THE UNIT I CRANE STOPS AT THE RIGGING CHAGE TO HAVE HIS HOOK RE DRESSED. BLAZE AND BIG O REMOVE THE THERTY FOOT KEVLAR SLINGS FROM THE BIG HOOK AND DRESS THE SMALL HOOK WITH TWO, TWO INCH WIRE ROPE, EYE AND EYE SLINGS IN PREPERATION TO REMOVE THE THRUST BEARING COUPLING COVER. ICEMAN HAS THE OIL SIDE CLEARENCE AND WAS ABLE TO ISOLATE THE LUBE OIL LIFT PUMP FOR THE THRUST BEARING COUPLING COVER. (B COUPLING). PEACHES, ROPEY AND POOPDECK PAPPY AS SOON AS THE LIFT OIL PUMP WAS LOCKED OUT AND TAGGED WERE ABLE TO REMOVE THE DOWELS AND THE INCH AND A HALF X FOUR INCH BOLTS HOLDING THE COUPLING COVER DOWN.

USING THE THREADED JACK BOLT HOLES IN THE CORNERS OF THE COUPLING COVER THE CREW USED THE AIR GUNS AND SLOWELY OPENED UP THE JOINT EVENLY. SMARKEY DOES HIS BEST TO CENTER THE UNIT ONE CRANE DIRECTLY OVER THE COUPLING COVER WHILE BLAZE GIVES THE SLOW DOWN SIGNAL, SLOW DOWN, SLOW DOWN, SLOW DOWN THEN A STOP. BIG O HAS TWO ONE INCH SHACKLES IN HIS HANDS AND ATTACHES THEM TO THE CAST IN LIFTING EYES OF THE COVER. POOPDECK PAPPY AND PEACHES ARE STANDING BY READY TO WIPE DOWN THE INSIDE OF THE COUPLING COVER OF ANY OIL THAT IS LEFT ON IT TO PREVENT ANY TYPE OF SLIPPERY FLOOR HAZARD. BIG O TAKES A STEP BACK AS BLAZE SIGNALS SLOW UP, SLOW UP, SLOW UP UNTIL THE COVER IS UP AND CLEARED OF THE COUPLING, POOPDECK AND PEACHES WIPE DOWN THE COVER OF ANY RISIDUAL OIL AND BLAZE SIGNALS SMARKEY TO TROLLY THE COUPLING COVER OUT OF THE WAY TO THE RIGHT SIDE. BIG O GUIDES THE COUPLING COVER GENTLY TO THE COVERED FLOOR AND DISCONNECTS THE SHACKLES.

WITH THE "B" COUPLING COVER OFF THE MACHINE IT ALLOWS ACCESS FOR THE TEAM TO SET UP FOR THE FULL THRUST MEASUREMENT. BIG JIM GIVES SMARKEY A BIG WAVE TO BRIDGE ALL THE WAY TO THE FRONT OF UNIT ONE AS RAYRAY CHONG AND THE UNIT TWO RIGGING CREW HAVE THE "A" LP HOOD ON THE MOVE TO THE LAYDOWN AREA RIGHT ASIDE THE "A" HOOD OF THE OPPERATING UNIT. EEFFY, PAPALUCHI AND SKIN ARE WAITNG THE ARRIVAL AS SUAVE RICO SIGNALS TO TROLLY THE HOOD TO THE PROPER LOCATION AND LOWER IT DOWN. THE HOOD COMES DOWN UNDER CONTROLL AT ALL TIMES, AS THE TEAM GENTLY GUIDES IT RIGHT ON TOP OF THE CRIBBING THAT WAS SET THERE DURING THE JOB SETUP. THE RIGGERS

REMOVE THE SLINGS FROM AROUND THE OUTSIDE CORNERS OF THE LIFTING HORNS, AND RAYRAY CHONG DRUMS UP ON THE BIG HOOK AND HEADS FOR THE RIGGING CAGE TO REMOVE THE THERTY FOOTERS AND DRESS THE SMALL HOOK WITH THE EYE AND EYE WIRE ROPES TO HELP IN THE COUPLING COVER REMOVALS WHEN READY. SQUARE HEAD IS FAMILIAR WITH THE NEXT EVELOUTION OF THE PROCESS AND HEADS FOR THE THRUST BEARING. EAGLE ED, ICEMAN, PEACHES, ROPEY, POOPDEK PAPPY, CUPCAKE AND SISTER T ARE STANDING BYE.

ICEMAN: Substation SATCH and his crew have a lot of work in the two hundred kv yard. His team is responsible for installing the new capacitor bank. The capacitor bank removes excess flux from the sign wave and aligns IT in a more concentrated wave which allows IT to travel along the high volt lines more efficiently on ITS way to our homes and businesses.

EAGLE ED: That plant mod is going to increase our capacity factors substantially. ICEMAN take CUPCAKE over to the disconnect switch to the turning gear motor and wait on SISTER T to give you the close or energize signal. YUMYUM is greasing the gear and will be checking the mesh when ready.

FATTY JOE: I just checked in with SUNNY at the collector end "E" coupling and he has his dial indicator set, JOHNNYOBOTT is set on the governor end. Both understand we are thrusting the unit hard to the collector end first.

EAGLE ED:	All the lube oil pumps are still on except for the thrust bearing pedestal.
ROPEY:	I have plenty of oil to dump in the bearing when required. We don't want to wipe out the Babbitt face bearing.
PEACHES:	The joint has been cleaned and we bolted the thrust plates to each side of the coupling face.

THE THRUST PLATE IS FABRICATED WITH THE EXACT SAME BOLT PATTERN AS THE COUPLING COVER. IT IS MADE OF TWO-INCH-THICK USA STEELE. THE PLATES WRAP AROUND THE OUTSIDE FACES OF THE COUPLINGS. THEY HAVE A HORIZONTAL, RAISED, THREADED CONNECTOR WITH LONG JACK BOLTS AND A BRASS ROLLER ON EACH BOLT, FOUR TOTALS. ROPEY DOUBLE CHECKS TO MAKE SURE SUNNY AND JOHNNYOBOTT HAVE THE INDICATORS SET TO ZERO. ROPEY ALSO HAS AN DIAL INDICATOR SET UP ON THE INBOARD SIDE OF THE THRUST PLATE TO LET FATTY JOE KNOW WHEN THE UNIT GETS PUSHED.

| FATTY JOE: | Let's get this done. SISTER T ready? |

PEACHES AND POOPDECK PAPPY ARE KNELLING TOTE TO THE THRUST PLATES WITH LARGE OPEN END WRENCHES IN THEIR HANDS, THEY NEED AS MUCH LEVERAGE AS THEY CAN GET TO PUSH THE MACHINE.

SISTER T:	Were ready FATTY JOE, YUMYUM is watching the greased bull gear and the gear on the putt putt motor to make sure of engagement of the two.
FATTY JOE:	Everyone here ready?
POOPDECK:	Come on already.

FATTY JOE SIGNALS TO SISTER T, SISTER T SENDS CUPCAKE A THUMBS UP, CUPCAKE CLOSES THE DISCONECT TO THE TURNING GEAR AND YUMYUM MAKES SURE OF FULL ENGAGEMENT OF THE GEARS. YUMYUM WATCHES AS THE SMALLER GEAR GETS PUSHED UP INTO THE BULL GEAR VIA COMPRESSED AIR. THE TURNING GEAR IS FULLY ENGAGED AND STRUGLES TO GET THE UNIT TO TURN. PUTT, PUTT, PUTT AND WITH ALL THE LUBE OIL PUMPS ON EXCEPT FOR THE THRUST BEARING PEDESTOL, ROPEY DUMPS LUBE OIL DOWN INTO THE BABBIT FACED BEARING. PEACHES AND POOPDECK PAPPY HAVE THE WELL GREASED, THRUST PLATE ROLLERS ORIENTED TO PUSH TOWARDS THE COLLECTOR END. THE JACK BOLT ROLLERS ARE HARD ON THE FACE OF THE COUPLING AND GETTING TIGHTER AND TIGHTER, WITH THE UNIT UP ON OIL AND ROPEY WATCHING THE INDICATOR THE UNIT SLIDES TOWARDS THE COLLECTOR END. ROPEY WATCHING THE INDICATOR WAVES HIS HANDS, THEN SISTER T WAVES HER HANDS THEN CUPCAKE OPENS THE DISCONECT, THE UNIT COMES TO A QUICK STOP.

FATTY JOE: What's it look like ROPEY? .006 FATTY.

SUNNY AND JOHNNYOBOTT REPORT TO THE THRUST BEARING AND AGREE .006. THEN RETURN TO THEIR STATIONS UNDERSTANDING THE NEXT MOVE WILL BE HARD TO THE GOVONOR END. ROPEY ASKED THEM TO RE ZERO THE INDICATORS FOR THE INITIALL FULL THRUST MEASUREMENT. PEACHES AND POOPDECK PAPPY ADJUST THE ROLLERS TO PUSH THE OTHER DIRECTION.

FATTY JOE: This time were going hard to the governor end.

ROPEY MAKES SURE EVERYONE IS READY AND HAS ANOTHER LARGE CONTAINER OF LUBE OIL. FATTY JOE SIGNALS SISTER T WHO GIVES CUPCAKE THE GO AHEAD. CUPCAKE, WITH FACE SHIELD INTO THE BULL GEAR. YUMYUM IS MAKING SURE OF FULL ENGAGEMENT AS THE PUTT PUTT STRUGLES TO MOVE THE MACHINE. ROPET DUMBS A LOT OF LUBE OIL ON TOP OF THE THRUST BEARING AS PEACHES AND POOPDECK PAPPY STRUGGLE TO GET ENOUGH STRENGTH TO TIGHTEN THE JACK BOLT ROLLERS AGAINST THE OTHER SIDE OF THE COUPLING. IT LOOKS LIKE THE HARDENED JACK BOLTS ARE READY TO SNAP IN HALF WHEN ALL THE SUDDEN THE ENTIRE INNERS OF THE MACHINE GETS PUSHED HARD TO THE GOVERNOR END. ROPEY WATCHING THE DIAL INDICATOR GIVES FATTY JOE A QUICK HAND WAVE, THEN FATTY WAVES HIS ARMS TO SIGNAL SISTER T WHO SIGNALS CUPCAKE WHO OPENS THE DISCONECT. THE UNIT AGAIN COMES TO A QUICK STOP.

FATTY JOE:	What's it look like ROPEY.
ROPEY:	Sixteen thousand of an inch FATTY JOE. Easy to remember is Bobby Clarkes number.
PEACHES:	Wow ROPEY that was a great couple parades, broad street bullies.
SUNNY:	I see .016.
JOHNNYOBOTT:	The indicator measurement shows .016, hard to the governor end.
ROPEY:	One more time. This time hard to the collector end and then we leave it there.
FATTY JOE:	Re zero the indicators so we have no questions. KRINE DOG and BOW TIE are interested in the measurement.

EVERYONE RETURNS TO THEIR WORK AREA AND ROPEY MAKES SURE HE HAS PLENTY OF LUBE OIL. FATTY JOE MAKES SURE PEACHES AND POOPDECK PAPPY ARE ORIENTED TO PUSH THE MACHINE HARD TO THE COLLECTOR END AND SIGNALS SISTER T. SISTER T THUMBS UP CUPCAKE WHO ENERGIZES THE PUTT PUTT AND IMMEDIATELY THE GEAR GETS PUSHED UP INTO THE BULL GEAR.

YUMYUM IS WATCHING FOR FULL MESH OF THE GEARS AS ROPEY POURS MORE LUBE OIL INTO THE THRUST BEARING. PEACHES AND POOPDECK HAVE A GOOD SWEAT ON AS THEY TIGHTEN UP ON THE WELL GREASED ROLLERS SET UP TO PUSH THE MACHINE INNERS HARD TO THE COLLECTOR END. THE MACHINE IS UP ON OIL PREVENTING ANY WIPEING OF THE BEARING FACES AND THE JACK BOLTS ARE IN FULL STRESS MODE.

FATTY JOE: Come on put some back into it!

POOPDECK PAPPY LOOKS POOPED, PEACHES GIVES EVERYTHING HE HAS AND WITH KRINE DOG AND BOW TIE STANDING WATCHING THE INDICATOR THE UNIT THRUSTS HARD TO THE COLLECTOR END. ROPEY WAVES HIS HAND THEN FATTY JOE SIGNALS SISTER T WHO HAS CUPCAKE OPEN THE DISCONECT AND THE UNIT IS QUICK TO COME TO REST.

ROPEY: .016 FATTY JOE
SUNNY: .016 collector end FATTY.
JOHNNYOBOTT: Minus sixteen from the face of the governor end FATTY JOE.

| KRINE DOG: | Great .016-inch full thrust collector end. As found ill put that number in the package of paper work. |

WITH THE CREW FINISHING UP THE FULL THRUST MEASUREMENT, ICEMAN PROCEEDS WITH THE LUBE OIL SIDE BLOCKS AND TAGS ON THE LUBE PUMPS AND VALVES. AS SOON AS HE IS FINISHED WITH EACH BEARING PEDESTOL THE MACHINISTS, MILLWRIGHTS, FITTERS AND RIGGERS WORK TO REMOVE THE DOWELS, BOLTS AND COUPLING COVERS MAKING SURE THE DOWELS ARE LABELED AND THE BOLTS ARE STORED IN THE BOLT BINS. THEY USE THE JACK BOLTS TO OPEN UP THE JOINT AND MAKE ABSOLUTLY SURE, TO WIPE DOWN THE COUPLING COVERS OF ALL EXCESS LUBE OIL TO PREVENT ANY SLIPPING HAZARDS. THE RIGGERS SET THE CRANES UP DIRECTLY OVER THE COUPLING COVERS, HOIST THEM OUT OF THE WAY AND PUT THEM ON THE PROTECTED FLOOR TO THE RIGHT. LEAVING THE LUBE OIL OFF AND EXPOSEING THE COUPLINGS SO THE CREW CAN REMOVE THE COUPLING BOLTS AND SPACER. WITH UNIT II INSIDE THE GIANT ELECTRIC MACHINE IN COLD SHUT DOWN, SQUARE HEAD TRACKS DOWN SCHAFFER CITY STANDING AND TALKING WITH SOME ELECTRICIANS NEAR THE RIGHT SIDE OF THE DOG HOUSE.

| SCHAFFER CITY: | Now that were off the gear HIGH VOLT, CUPCAKE, SISTER T and BRUCEY (with three chicken legs wrapped up in hanky) head down under the main generator and start removing the clam shells and links. |
| HIGH VOLT: | Yep we got that SQUARE HEAD. |

CUPCAKE: GOON also want's us to be available to work the turning gear when needed for the coupling bolt removal team.

SCHAFFER CITY: CAPPY, RJ and DOC are going to handle the brush removal and cleaning. Also, ESKIN and ELANE are getting started with the vibration probes and thermocouple removal and identification process. The thermocouples and vibration probes are stationed on the top of each bearing and signal to the control room bearing status and temperature. DANDAMAN and SJONG are handling the control room work and are making sure the correct annunciators are matched up to the correct bearing.

SEESAU is also with us incase we need any last second planning or parts.

SQUARE HEAD: You have your hands full like the rest of us
BRUCEY: Plus, we have valve work and HPCI work. SQUARE HEAD we'll never get a chance to visit JOR"GE THE SANDWICH MAKER or cook the dogs and the old school kielbasa.

THE HIGH- PRESSURE TURBINE PLUS THE THREE LOW PRESSURE TURBINES ARE COUPLED TOGETHER AND DRIVE THE MAIN GENERATOR EIGHTEEN HUNDRED ROTATIONS PER MINUTE. EACH TURBINE AND THE MAIN GENERATOR ARE SUPPORTED BY ONE BABBITT FACED BEARING, ON EACH END THE TURBINES AND GENERATOR TURN INSIDE THE BABBIT FACED BEARINGS.

THE BEARINGS HAVE A CONSTANT SUPPLY OF LUBE OIL BEING PUMPED UP AND AROUND THE BEARINGS. AS THE LUBE OIL PASSES THROUGH THE BEARINGS THE JOURNALS OF THE TURBINES AND GENERATOR ARE LUBRICATED WITHIN THE BEARINGS ABOUT FOUR TO EIGHT THOUSAND OF AN INCH OIL WEDGE IS CREATED. THE OIL IS COLLECTED IN THE BASE OF THE COUPLING COVER HOUSING AND DRAINS TO THE LUBE OIL COOLERS TO COME BACK AROUND AGAIN. THE TOTAL WEIGHT OF THE ROTATING EQUIPMENT, WITHIN ITS HOUSING IS ABOUT FOUR HUNDRED TON. THE MAIN GENERATOR(DRIVEN) ARMATURE WEIGHTS IN AT ONE HUNDRED AND NINETY-EIGHT TONS. THE ARMATURE IS MAGNETIZED AND ROTATES INSIDE THE STATOR WHICH IS STATIONARY INSIDE THE GENERATOR HOUSING.

AS THE MAGNETIZED ARMATURE ROTATES INSIDE THE STATOR ELECTRICITY IS CREATED AND COLLECTED ON THREE SEPARATE CONDUCTORS. THE CONDUCTORS ARE CONNECTED TO SOMETHING THAT LOOKS LIKE A GIANT SPARKPLUG THAT ACTS LIKE AN INSULATOR AS IT PASSES THROUGH THE BOTTOM OF THE GENERATOR HOUSING. THAT'S WHERE YOU FIND THE CLAM SHELLS AND LINKS. THE CLAM SHELLS ATTACH TO THE BOTTOM OF THE SPARKPLUGS, THEN THE LINKS CONNECT TO TO OTHER CLAM SHELLS WHICH ARE ATTACHED TO THE THREE CONDUCTORS THAT CARRY THE ELECTRICITY TO THE SUBSTATION. EACH CLAM SHELL IS HOUSED IN ITS OWN INSULATED BOX.

THE THREE COMING OUT OF THE GENERATOR AND THREE GOING TO THE SUBSTATION. THE LINKS ARE CONDUCTORS THAT PROVIDE THE ELECTRICITY TO MOVE FROM ONE LOCATION TO ANOTHER. HIGH VOLT, SISTER T, CUPCAKE AND BRUCEY HAVE THE JOB TO SAFELY REMOVE THE CLAM SHELLS AND LINKS, CLEAN,

INSPECT AND REPLACE PARTS IF NEEDED. THE CLAM SHELLS EACH WEIGHT AROUND ONE HUNDRED POUNDS EACH. SOLID COPPER. GIANT "U" BOLTS HOLD THEM IN PLACE AND WHEN YOU LOOSEN THEM UP THE CLAM SHELLS STICK THERE UNTIL YOU BANG ON THEM WITH A SOFT BLOW HAMMER OR MAYBE USE A WOODEN PRY DEVICE BUT YOU BETTER BE READY WHEN THEY DECIDE TO COME FREE. THE LINKS ARE LIKE A COPPER BELT WITH HOLES IN THE END, SO THEY THREAD TO THE FACES OF THE CLAM SHELLS. EVERYTHING UNDER THE GENERATOR IS TOURQUED ACCORDING TO THE PROCEDURE. NOW WITH LOUIE IN TOW SQUARE HEAD MAKES HIS WAY TO THE "D" COUPLING AND COUPLING BOLT REMOVAL. STANDING BESIDE THE "D" COUPLING IS GOON AND FATTY JOE AS THEY WATCH THE MACHINISTS REMOVE THE COUPLING BOLTS.

LOUIE: I can't spend much time in the field anymore, with all the meetings.

FATTY JOE: Better you LOUIE then me.

GOON: You used to be a good machinist LOUIE. You trained a lot of the crew.

FATTY JOE: I wouldn't go that far GOON.

LOUIE: OK men that's enough. I got to get to the next critical path meeting.

SQUARE HEAD: That's funny, what a great way to get him off the deck. How's things going?

GOON: It usually takes a little while to figure out the vague procedure but once we figure it out the crew can get on a roll.

WORKING ON THE "D" COUPLING BOLT REMOVAL SUNNY, JAKE AND YUMYUM. THEY HAVE EIGHT INCH ROUND SCREEN

COVERED MESH OVER TOP OF THE LUBE OIL RETURN LINES TO HELP PREVENT FOREIGN METERIAL FROM ENTERING THAT VERY IMPORTANT SYSTEM. JAKE IS STANDING IN THE BOTTOM OF THE COUPLING COVERS OIL PAN AND ITS PRETTY TITE BECAUSE OF THE BULL GEAR.

JAKE REMOVES THE ELEVEN O'CLOCK POSITION NUT AND SLIDES A SLEEVE OVER THE TAPERED BOLT TILL THE SLEEVE COMES IN CONTACT WITH THE PERMENENT SLEEVE SPANNIG THE TWO COUPLING FACES AND IN THIS CASE A SPACER. THEN JAKE TAKES A SMALL HYDRAULIC JACK WITH A HOLE IN IT UNTIL ITS TITE ON THE TEMPORARY JACK SLEEVE THEN THREADS THE NUT BACK ON THE TAPERDED BOLT TILL IT GETS TOTE. JAKE SIGNALS TO SUNNY TO TURN ON THE PUMP.THE PUMP KICKS ON, SUNNY KEEPS A CLOSE EYE ON THE PRESSURE GUAGE WHILE JACK IS LISTENING CLOSELY FOR A POP SOUND.

THE HYDRAULIC PRESSURE IN THE JACK HEAD PUSHES THE REMOVAL SLEEVE AGAINST THE PERMENENT SLEEVE ALONG THE TAPERED FIT. SUNNY AGAIN HAS A CLOSE EYE ON THE PUMPS PRESSURE, IT GETS INTO THE PROPPER RANGE AND THEN ALL THE SUDDEN POP. JAKE WAVES A HAND AND SUNNY TURNS OFF THE PUMP AND THEN WITH A HALF A TURN OF A THUMB VALVE RELEASES THE PRESSURE ON THE JACK.

JAKE LOOSENS THE NUT, REMOVES THE JACK HEAD, AND REMOVAL SLEEVE THEN YUMYUM PULLS THE ELEVEN O'CLOCK COUPLING BOLT OUT FROM THE OTHER SIDE OF THE COUPLING AND PUTS IT IN PROPPER POSITION ON THE COUPLING BOLT RACK. EACH COUPLING BOLT WEIGHTS ABOUT EIGHTY POUNDS AND IS MADE SPECIFICALLY FOR THAT POSITION IN THAT

COUPLING USING THAT SAME SLEEVE. EVERYTHING IS STAMPED OR ETCHED TO TRY TO LIMIT CONFUSSION. JAKE REMOVES THE NUT ON THE TWO OCLOCK POSITIONED BOLT NEXT, TAKES THE REMOVAL SLEEVE SLIDES IT OVER THE TAPPERED BOLT THEN PUTS THE JACK HEAD ONTO THE BOLT, THREADS THE NUT BACK ON TILL EVERYTHING IS SNUG. LOOKS AT SUNNY, SUNNY TURNS ON THE SMALL HYDRAULIC PUMP AND WATCHES THE PRESSURE GUAGE. THE HYDRAULIC PRESSURE IN THE JACK TOTENS EVERYTHING UP, SUNNY WITH A CLOSE EYE ON THE GUAGE REALIZES THE PRESSURE IS IN THE POP AREA AND THEN POP THERE IT GOES THE REMOVAL SLEEVE PUSHED THE PERMENENT SLEEVE ALONG THE BOLT TILL THE SLEEVE CAME OFF THE TAPER AND BECAME LOOSE IN THE HOLE. JAKE LOOSENS UP THE NUT REMOVES THE JACK AND THE REMOVAL SLEEVE THEN SLIDES THE BOLT THROUGH THE COUPLING WHERE YUMYUM GRABS IT AND SETS IT IN THE PROPPER POSITION ON THE RACK.

SQUARE HEAD: You guys seem to be moving in the right direction

SUNNY: Remember we used to use a sledge hammer and a three-inch punch? Sometimes one would get stuck for a shift or two.

SQUARE HEAD: Let's go see what 's up on "C" coupling.

COOL DADDY, GEGGY AND GOOGLY ARE HARD AT IT, ALSO IN THE PROCESS OF REMOVING COUPLING BOLTS. COOL DADDY IS STANDING IN THE COUPLING COVERS OIL PAN AND THEY ALSO HAVE TAKEN THE PROPPER FOREIGN METERIALS EXCLUSION PREVENTION MEASURES. GEGGY IS MANNING THE HYDRAULIC PUMP AND GOOGLY IS IN CHARGE OF THE BOLT REMOVAL AND STORING THEM IN THE PROPPER LOCATION IN THE RACK.

COOL DADDY SLID THE REMOVAL SLEEVE ONTO THE COUPLING BOLT, THE JACK THEN SNUGGED IT UP WITH THE NUT. GEGGY MAKES SURE COOL DADDY IS READY AND TURNS ON THE PUMP, THE JACK TOTENS UP ON THE REMOVAL SLEEVE AND PUSHES, PUSHES, PUSHES AND THEN POP GOES THE SLEEVE RIGHT OFF THE TAPER. GEGGY TURNS OFF THE PUMP AND RELIEVES THE PRESSURE ON THE JACK WITH THE THUMB SCREW. COOL DADDY LOOSENS THE NUT AND SLIDES THE JACK HEAD OFF THE BOLT, REMOVES THE JACK AND SLEEVE THEN PUSHES THE COUPLING BOLT THROUGH THE COUPLING WHERE GOOGLY IS THERE TO TAKE IT AND STORE IT FOR INSPECTION AND CLEANING.

GOON:	GEGGY why are you on the pump? Aren't you strong enough to carry a bolt?
GEGGY:	Just keep moving GOON! You know my specialty is the bypass valves.
GOON:	Don't forget to leave the three o'clock and the nine o'clock bolts loose in the sleeves because we must use the turning gear to get the coupling bolts on the bottom.
COOL DADDY:	We got it GOON. Were almost ready.
SQUARE HEAD:	Let's see how the "B" coupling is coming along.

FATTY JOE MOVES AHEAD TO THE "A "COUPLING. WHILE SQUARE HEAD AND GOON WANT TO SEE HOW THINGS ARE GOING ON THE "B" COUPLING. PEACHES IS STANDING IN THE OIL PAN, ROPEY IS REMOVING THE BOLTS AND STOREING THEM, POOPDECK PAPPY IS ON THE HYDRAULIC PUMP

PEACHES:	Ok POOPDECK let it fly.

POOPDECK PAPPY TURNS ON THE PUMP, PEACHES WATCHES EVERYTHING GET NICE AND TOTE.

ROPEY: POOPDECK you awake over there? You look half asleep.

OUT OF ONE EYE POOPDECK PAPPY IS WATCHING THE GUAGE THE PRESSURE IS A LITTLE HIGHER THEN NORMAL AND THEN ALL THE SUDDEN POP GOES THE COUPLING BOLT SLEEVE. IT GETS PUSHED RIGHT OFF THE TAPER. POOPDECK PAPPY TURNS OFF THE PUMP, YAWNS AND THEN RELIEVES THE PRESSURE ON THE JACK HEAD.

ROPEY: Ok GOON we left to in at the joint loose and were ready for the roll.
GOON: Let me see how everyone else is doing first.
SQUARE HEAD: Looks like they removed the stub shaft.

"A" COUPLING HAS DELCO JOE, DUDDLEY AND K AND ARE READY FOR THE ROLL. K WAS IN THE HOLE WITH DELCO JOE ON THE PUMP AND DUDDLEY STOREING THE COUPLING BOLTS. WITH THE HELP OF RAYRAY CHONG WHO IS OPPERATING THE UNIT TWO CRANE, EEFFY, PAPALUCHI AND RAPPING RODNEY HAVE THE SMALL HOOK CENTERED DIRECTLY OVER THE TOP OF THE STUB SHAFT. THE STUB SHAFT CONNECTS THE HIGH-PRESSURE TURBINE TO THE GOVERNOR END WHICH IS CONSIDERED THE FRONT OF THE UNIT WHERE THE MANUAL TRIP LEVER IS. THE STUB SHAFT IS FOUR FEET LONG, IS HOLLOW BUT MADE OF A VERY STRONG, HEAT TREATED CARBON FIRED STEELE THE COUPLING FACES ARE TWO FEET IN DIAMETER. JOHNNYOBOTT, JOEWEE, AND MOE WERE ABLE TO WORK THEIRE WAY AROUND THE COUPLING FACES RELIEVING TENSION IN A STAR PATTERN. THE

COUPLING BOLTS ARE TWO INCHES IN DIAMETER AND HAVE NUTS ON BOTH ENDS. ONCE ALL THE NUTS WERE LOOSE EEFFY, PAPALUCHI AND RAPPING RODNEY USED TWO CHAIN BLOCKS, TWO NYLON SLINGS, SIX FEET LONG AND PUT A CHOKE ON THE STUB SHAFT AT EACH END, CENTERED THE CHOKES ON THE TOP RADIAL AND ATTACHED THEM TO THE SMALL HOOK. PAPALUCHI GIVES A SLOW UP, SLOW UP AND THE SLACK QUICKLY DISAPEARS. THE SLINGS ARE JUST TOTE ENOUGH, BUT NOT TO TOTE. JOHNNYOBOTT, JOEWEE, AND MOE WORK THEIR WAY AROUND BOTH COUPLING FACES AND REMOVE MOST OF THE BOLTS LEAVING FOUR IN BOTH ENDS. PAPALUCHI GENTLY PULLS UP ON THE CHAIN BLOCKS LOOKING FOR HE SWEET SPOT AS THE MACHINISTS WORK THE COUPLING BOLTS OUT. MOE WAVES HER HAND AND SIGNALS PAPALUCHI A LITTLE DOWN ON THE COLLECTOR END AND WITH JUST TWO CLICKS OF THE CHAIN THE MACHINISTS WERE ABLE TO REMOVE THE FINIALE EIGHT COUPLING BOLTS.

PAPALUCHI THEN CONTINUES TO PULL UP ON THE CHAIN BLOCK TILL THE STUB SHAFT CLEARS THE THE HIGH-PRESSURE COUPLING FACE AS EEFFY DIRECTS RAYRAY CHONG TO GENTLY PUT THE STUB SHAFT DOWN CLOSE BYE ON THE LEFT SIDE. RAPPING RODNEY REMOVES THE SLINGS FROM THE CHAIN BLOCK AND RAYRAY CHONG GETS READY FOR THE NEXT LIFT. FATTY JOE AND SQUARE HEAD ASUME THE POSITIONS AND ARE READY FOR THE TURBINE BUMP. THE MACHINISTS AND MILLWRIGHTS ARE ALL SUPPLIED WITH LUBE OIL TO DUMP INTO THERE ASSIGNED BEARINGS. SISTER T AND CUPCAKE ARE READY TO ENERGIZE THE TURNING GEAR AND AWAITING FATTY JOE'S SIGNAL. SQUARE HEAD HIS ROUNDS TO MAKE SURE EVERYONE WAS READY ESPICIALLY WITH THE LUBE OIL. FATTY JOE GIVES THE

SIGNAL, SISTER T WAVES TO CUPCAKE, CUPCAKE ENERGIZES THE TURNING GEAR, YUMYUM MAKES SURE OF THE GEAR MESH AND THE MOTOR STRUGLES TO MOVE THE UNIT AS EVERYONE IS DUMPING OIL INTO THERE ASSIGNED BEARINGS THEN ALL THE SUDDEN THE UNIT CREEPS AROUND GETS UP ON OIL THEN FATTY JOE WAVES. SISTER T SIGNALS CUPCAKE WHO OPENS THE DISCONECT AND THE UNIT SLIDES AROUND JUSTA LITTLE MORE AND COMES TO A REST.

FATTY JOE: HOW' that?
ROPEY: We can work with that FATTY JOE.

THE BOTTOM COUPLING BOLTS ARE NOW TOP SIDE AND IT DOSENT TAKE LONG FOR THE CREW TO REMOVE THE REMAINING BOLTS. EXCEPT FOR "D" COUPLING WHERE SUNNY, JAKE AND YUMYUM ARE GOING TO REMOVE THE SPACER BETWEEN THE TWO COUPLING FACES. SMARKEY, IN THE UNIT ONE CRANE SETTLES IN DIRECTLY OVER TOP OF THE" D" COUPLING. SUNNY LEAVES TWO COUPLING BOLTS UN SLEEVED IN PLACE AT THE THREE AND NINE O'CLOCK POSITION OR PRETTY CLOSE.

THE SMALL HOOK IS DRESSED IN A TWO AND A HALFTON CHAIN BLOCK AND A FOUR FOOT EYE AND EYE, ONE INCH IN DIAMETER WIRE ROPE. BIG O THREADS A LIFTING EYE INTO THE ALMOST TOP OF THE SPACER THEN CONNECTS THE WIRE ROPE AND LIFTNG EYE WITH A ONE INCH SHACKEL. BLAZE SIGNALS SLOW UP, SLOW UP TILL THE SLACK IS OUT OF THE ROPE. WITH FATTY JOE, GOON AND CORNAL HOGAN WATCHING YUMYUM AND JAKE THREAD JACK BOLTS THROUGHT THE 'C'LP COUPLING FACE UNTIL THEY CAN'T TURN ANY MORE THEN YUMYUM AND JAKE

TAKE AN AIR GUN AND RUN THE JACK BOLTS IN TOWARDS THE GENERATOR. SLOWELY THE COUPLING FACE OPENS UP, JUST A LITTLE MORE THEN FATTY JOE WAVES HIS HANDS TO STOP. YUMYUM AND JAKE BACK OUT THE JACK BOLTS BLAZE STAYS TOTE ON THE CHAIN BLOCK AND SLOWLY PULLS UP ON THE BLOCK TILL THE SPACER IS CLEAR OF THE COUPLING FACES. NAVY MIKE AND MR. URRIGHT ARE STANDING BYE WITH A CART TO TAKE THE SPACER TO THE MACHINE SHOP FOR CLEANING AND POLISHING AND INSPECTION.

GOON IS EXPECTING TO GET THE "L' MEASUREMENT IMMEDIATELY SO USING AN INSIDE MICROMETER SUNNY FINDS THE STAMPED "L" JUST BELOW THE HORIZONTAL JOINT OF THE PEDESTOL ON THE RIGHT SIDE AND YUMYUM LOCATES THE "L" ON THE LEFT. EACH MACHINIST MEASURES WITH A UP TO DATE CALIBRATED MICROMETER FROM THE "L" TO THE COUPLING FACE OF THE GENERATOR THEN THEY MEASURE THE INSIDE MICROMETER WITH A CALIBRATED OUTSIDE MICROMETER AND SWITCH SIDES. THEY BOTH GO THROUGH THE SAME MEASUREMENT PROCEDURE AND HAND THE PAPER WORK TO KRINE DOG. GOON FEELS LEFT OUT. KRINE DOG EXAMINES THE MEASUREMENTS AND HANDS THEM TO BOW TIE.

KRINE DOG: That works 18.088 we just charted the generator and now know exactly where it has to be when its time for the rebuild.

WITH ALL THE COUPLINGS APART MOST OF THE CREW IS GOING TO SEE JOR'GE THE SANDWICH MAKER. SQUARE HEAD, GOON AND FATTY JOE ARE HEADING TO THE HIGH-PRESSURE TURBINE.

CHARDY, LAZALOON, OTTO, BOOGER CLIMB UP THE STAIR WELL FROM BELOW THE HIGH-PRESSURE TURBINE.

BOOGER:	CHARDY showed us the spring cans.
CHARDY:	Yep, we found all four on the first time.
OTTO:	SKIN helped to. Its like he came out of the rafters, like a stray cat or something.
CHARDY	Like the great Wallenda with fall protection.
LAZALOON;	SKIN dropped out of the rafters walked the pipe right to the spring cans then slid the five-inch x five- inch blocks of steel under the springs and on top of the bottom of the housing.
BOOGER:	We must gag the spring cans so when we detention the four main steam flanges the steam supply flange face remains at the same height.
OTTO:	Then when we finish with removing the flange nuts, bolts and metaltalic gaskets, the riggers using come alongs and slings pull the flanges away from the high pressure head, a few inches, so they can pick the one hundred twenty-ton, space ship looking top half of the head off the diaphragms and flow guides to get to the turbine rotor.
SQUARE HEAD:	Maybe SKIN is more like Peter Pan.

THE CREW OF CARPENTERS JUST FINISHED BUILDING THE SCAFFOLD AROUND THE MAIN STEAM INLET FLANGES THAT CONNECT THE MAIN STEAM PIPES TO THE TOP HEAD OF THE HIGH-PRESSURE TURBINE. TWENTY-TWO, ONE-INCH X SIX-INCH

HIGH GRADE ALL THREAD WITH TWO AND A QUARTER INCH NUTS ON EACH END SECUREING THE FLANGE FACES TOGETHER WITH THE METALTALIC GASKET INBETWEEN. OTTO AND BOOGER ARE GOING TO WORK ON THE RIGHT SIDE WITH CHARDY AND LAZALOON WORKING THE LEFT. NO REASON FOR THE TOURQUE MACINE UP THERE EACH SIDE HAS A HOLD BACK WRENCH AND A SLUGGING WRENCH. USING THE STAR PATTERN TO EQUALY DETENSION THE FLANGES, ONE FITTER HAS A HOLD BACK WRENCH TO HOLD THE NUT IN PLACE, WHILE ANOTHER HAS THE SLUGGING WRENCH. ONE CREW MEMBER BANGS ON THE SLUGGING WRENCH HANDLE USING A FIVE POUND SLEDGE HAMMER, TO THE LEFT TO LOSSEN THE NUT, WHILE THE OTHER IS HOLDING BACK THE OTHER NUT KEEPING IT FROM TURNING. ON THE FIRST PASS THEY JUST LOOSEN THE NUTS AROUND THE ENTIRE FLANGE FACE USING THE STAR PATTERN. ON THE SECOND PASS THEY AGAIN HAVE TO LOOSEN THE NUTS USING THE STAR PATTERN AS THE FLANGES BEGIN TO RELAX. ON THE THIIRD PASS AGAIN, USING THE STAR PATTERN, THE NUTS ARE STILL NOT LOOSE ENOUGH TO REMOVE THEM BY HAND.

AFTER THE FORTH TIME AROUND THE FLANGES BEGIN TO OPEN UP THE ALLTHREAD AND NUTS ARE NOW ABLE TO BE REMOVED BYE HAND WITHOUT DESTROYING THE THREADS. EACH SIDE OF THE HIGH PRESSURE TURBINE MAIN STEAM SUPPLY PIPES ARE NOW FREE FROM THE HIGH PRESSURE TURBINE HEAD. THE FITTERS PASS DOWN THE HARDWARE AND TOOLS FROM THE SCAFFOLD AND THEY ARE ABLE TO SLIDE A LARGE NYLON BAG OVER THE INLET FLANGES TO ELEMINIATE ANY POSSIBILTY OF FOREIGN METERIAL FROM ENTERING THE SYSTEM. NEXT THE RIGGNG CREW CLIMB UP THE SCAFFOLD SO, THEY CAN RIG EACH SUPPLY LINE FLANGE TO PULL THEM AWAY FROM THE HIGH-PRESSURE

HEAD FLANGE TO CREATE A FEW INCHES OF CLEARANCE WHEN IT COMES TIME TO REMOVE THE HIGH PRESSURE HEAD. EEFFY, SKIN, PAPALUCHI AND SUAVE RICO ARE ON THE JOB. SUAVE RICO CLIMBES UP THE SCAFFOLD WITH TWO, EIGHT-FOOT-LONG EYE AND EYE WIRE ROPE SLINGS AND REACHES UP TO CHOKE THE FIRST MAIN STEAM INLET PIPE. PAPALUCHI ON A LADDER BEING FOOT BY EEFFY, HANGS THE FIXED END HOOK OF THE COMEALONG ON A PERMENENT RIGGING EYE THAT WAS BUILT INTO THE FILLED BLOCK WALL ADJACENT TO THE INLET PIPE. SKIN WALKS THE OTHER HOOK ATTACHED BYE QUARTER INCH WIRE TO THE COMEALONG OVER TO RICO SUAVE. RICO SUAVE HOOKS IT TO THE CHOKED AROUND THE PIPE WIRE ROPE THEN PAPALUCHI CRANKS THE WRATCHTING COMEALONG TILL ITS LIKE A GUITAR STRING. SUAVE RICO IS LOOKING VERY CLOSE AT THE SUPPLY LINE PIPE UNTIL HE SEES IT MOVE A COUPLE INCHES THEN WAVES HIS HANDS TO STOP PAPALUCHI.

THE RIGGING TEAM MOVES POSITION TO THE NEXT INLET FLANGE ON THE RIGHT SIDE. SUAVE RICO AGAIN, REACHES UP AND USING AN EIGHT FOOT EYE AND EYE ROPE PUTS A CHOKE ON THE MAIN STEAM INLET PIPE. PAPALUCHI IS UP THE LADDER WITH EEFY ON THE FOOT. SKIN WALKS THE WIRED HOOK OVER AND UP TO SUAVE RICO THEN PAPALUCHI WRATCHETS DOWN ON THE COMEALONG TILL IT GETS LIKE A GUITAR STRING. SUAVE RICO LOOKING VERY CLOSE FOR THE MAIN STEAM SUPPLY LINE TO MOVE AND SLOWELY AS PAPALUCHI CRANKS IT TOTER AND TOTER THE PIPE PULLS AWAY A COUPLE INCHES FROM THE FLANGE FACE OF THE HIGH-PRESSURE HEAD. SUAVE RICO WAVES A HAND NOT A SECOND TO SOON BECAUSE PAPALUCHI WAS RUNNING OUT OF STRENGTH AS THE SECOND HIGH PRESSURE SUPPLY FLANGE WAS NOW OUT OF THE WAY. THE CREW

MOVED OVER TO THE LEFT SIDE MAIN STEAM SUPPLY PIPES AND USED THE SAME TECHNIQUE EXCEPT ON THE LEFT SIDE EEFY WAS UP THE LADDER AND PAPALUCHI WAS STILL CATCHING HIS BREATH FOOTING THE LADDER. BEFORE LONG ALL FOUR MAIN STEAM SUPPLY LINE FLANGES WERE OUT OF THE WAY FOR WHEN ITS TIME TO LIFT THE HEAD.

A LOT OF THE CREW RETURN BACK TO THE DECK AFTER ENJOYING A QUALITY SANDWICH JOR'GE THE SANDWICH MAKER PUT TOGETHER FOR THEM. EVERY SANDWICH IS CUSTOME MADE BY JOR'GE. HE CUTS ALL THE MEAT AND CHEESE AS HE NEEDS IT FOR EACH SANDWICH AND ONLY WILL USE PHILLYS FINEST CUTS OF LUNCHMEAT AND CHEESE. LOPEZ, AIRYSUE AND MIC WERE BUSY SETTING UP THE TORQUE MACHINES AT EACH LOW PRESSURE TURBINE. AFTER GETTING BACK TO THE DECK SQUARE HEAD, GOON AND FATTY JOE WANTED TO TOUCH BASE WITH SENIOR MANURE (LOPEZ NICKNAME)

GOON: How are the tools holding up LOPEZ?

LOPEZ: So far so good, we just spent time staging the torque machines.

AIRYSUE: We have four torque machines, so we set up two on CLP turbine.

LOPEZ: One on each side, with the right sized castle sockets to remove the nuts.

GOON: We need to start with CLP turbine, so it will be first cleaned, inspected, balanced and ready for reassembly.

LOPEZ: Also, two torque machines on BLP turbine so the crew can start working on relieving the tension on the six-inch diameter studs and removing the nuts for cleaning and inspection.

FATTY JOE: How about the high-pressure turbine, LOPEZ?

LOPEZ: MIC worked with HIGH VOLT, CAPPY and DOC to make sure the induction heater circuits are holding, so the team can also start relieving the tension on the ten-inch diameter studs and removing the nuts for cleaning and inspection. The castle nuts to the HP turbine weigh one hundred pounds each and are the size of a basketball.

SQUARE HEAD: When MIC is not on the red, yellow, green light drag strip game he's effective and very helpful.

AIRYSUE: He says it helps him focus. I wonder if it helps him on race day?

SUNNY, JAKE AND YUMYUM WERE READY TO GET STARTED ON THE RIGHT SIDE. COOL DADDY, GEGGY AND GOOGLY WERE GETTING STARTED ON THE LEFT SIDE. THE SIX MACHINISTS WERE WORKING ON RELIEVING THE TENSION ON THE STUDS OF "C" LP TURBINE BY USING THE TORQUE MACHINE TO LOOSEN THE NUTS. KRINE DOG AND TIE BOW USED A WHITE PAINT MARKER TO NUMBER EVERY NUT AND ALSO NUMBERED THE OUTSIDE OF THE "C" LP SHELL TO MAKE SURE EACH NUT STAYS AT THE SAME LOCATION AND WITH THE SAME STUD COME TIME FOR REASSEMBLE. KRINE DOG AND BOW TIE ARE RESPONSIBLE FOR MARKING ALL THREE LP. TURBINES AND THE HP. TURBINE. THE ENGINEERS REALIZE THAT AS THE STUD IS BEING STREATCHED THE

NUT KEEPS IT TOTE AND THE THREADS OF THE STUD AND THE NUT STREATCH TOGETHER AT THE SAME RATE. IT'S ALSO IMPORTANT TO START RELIEVING THE STUDS IN THE MIDDLE THEN WORKING YOUR WAY ALONG THE SIDES TILL YOU MAKE IT AROUND THE CORNER TO THE JOURNALS OF THE ROTOR. THAT METHOD HELPS KEEP THE JOINT FLAT. THE SHELLS TO THE LP. TURBINES IS SIX INCHES THICK US STEEL AND EACH UPPER HALF WEIGHS ONE HUNDRED TONS.

YUMYUM: Were ready to get started, we must make sure we loosen the nuts in the proper sequence starting from the center and working our way around the joint.

SUNNY: The torque machine is set to maximum pressure.

JAKE: LOPEZ and the crew set us up for success. The castle nut socket is the right size we just need to make sure we set the reaction arm so when it gets tote it reacts against the bottom of the horizontal joint of the "C" LP turbine upper half shell.

YUMYUM: Yea JAKE, and make sure your fingers aren't between the reaction arm and the shell.

JAKE TAKES THE TORQUE MACHINE WITH THE RIGHT CASTLE SOCKET AND PUTS IT ON TOP OF THE NUMBER ONE NUT THEN GIVES SUNNY THE THUMB UP. SUNNY USING A THUMB SWITCH, HITS THE ON BUTTON. JAKE HOLDS THE TOP OF THE TORQUE MACHINE ON TOP OF THE NUT AND THE REACTION ARM SWINGS AROUND AND TOTENS UP ON THE NUT. THE REACTION ARM IS USED FOR THE TORQUE MACHINE TO GET LEVERAGE ON THE NUT. SUNNY IS WATCHING THE GUAGE OF THE TORQUE

MACHINE AND IT'S ALMOST MAXXED OUT. JAKE IS CLOSELY
WATCHING THE TORQUE MACHINE AS EVERYTHING, TORQUE
MACHINE ON THE NUT, REACTION ARM TOTE ON THE BOTTOM
HALF OF THE SHELL LOOKS LIKE IT'S READY TO GIVE. EVEN THE
HYDRAULIC LINES ON THE BASE OF THE TORQUE MACHINE IS
TOTE.

JAKE: Ok the socket is starting to move. Keep it going
     SUNNY.

THEN CLICK THE TORQUE MACHINE GETS ONE RATCHETING
CLICK ON THE NUT THEN RRESETES ITSELF. EVERYONE IS KEEPING
A VERY CLOSE EYE ON THE PROCESS AS THE TORQUE MACHINE
EVER SO SLOWLY MOVES TOWARDS ANOTHER CLICK. JAKE
KEEPS HIS EYE ON THE TOP OF THE CASTLE SOCKET AND CLICK
THE TORQUE MACHINE PICKS UP ANOTHER CLICK. THE TORQUE
MACHINE PICKS UP ANOTHER RATCHETING CLICK THEN RESETS
ITSELF. YUMYUM IS NOT FAR AWAY READY TO PICK UP THE
TORQUE MACHINE AND SET IT ONTOP OF THE NUMBER TWO
NUT WHEN READY. WHEN THE TORQUE MACHINE RESETS ITSELF
EVERYTHING RELAXES FOR A SHORT TIME THEN GETS BACK TO
RELIEVING THE TENSION ON THE NUT.

EVERYTHING GETS SUPER TOTE AGAIN WITH JAKE MAKING SURE
HIS FINGERS ARE NOT GOING TO GET BETWEEN THE REACTION
ARM AND THE "C" LP SHELL. SUNNY KEEPS HIS THUMB ON THE
SWITCH AS JAKE HAS HIS EYES ON THE TOP OF THE SOCKET.
THIS TIME THE TOP OF THE SOCKET TURNS TO THE LEFT JUST
A LITTLE QUICKER, AS THE STUD BEGINS RELAX. AT THIS POINT
JAKE HOLDS THE TORQUE MACHINE STEADY ON TOP OF THE
NUT AS IT RESETS. SUNNY KEEPS HIS THUMB ON THE SWITCH AS

THE TORQUE MACHINE IS QUICKER TO PICK UP THE RATCHETING CLICKS TURNING THE SIX INCH DIAMETER NUT TO THE LEFT RELIEVING THE TENSION ON THE STUD. SUNNY AND JAKE CONTINUE TO RUN THE TORQUE MACHINE UNTIL THE NUT IS ABOUT A HALF INCH OF THE JOINT.

JAKE SIGNALS TO SUNNY TO CUT IT AND YUMYUM MOVES IN QUICKLY TO REMOVE THE TORQUE MACHINE FROM THE NUMBER ONE NUT AND PUT IT ON THE TOP OF THE NUMBER TWO NUT. JAKE USING HIS HANDS CONTINUES TO TURN THE SIXTY POUND NUT TO THE LEFT TILL HE CAN REMOVE THE NUT AND PUT IT IN A BIN FOR CLEANING AND INSPECTION. YUMYUM SIGNALS TO SUNNY AND BEGINS THE PROCESS AGAIN ON THE NUMBER TWO NUT. THE CREW TAKES TURNS REMOVING THE NUTS STARTING FROM THE CENTER AND EACH WORKING AROUND THE CORNERS TO THE "C" LP ROTOR. ON THE LEFT SIDE OF THE "C" LP TURBINE COOL DADDY, GEGGY AND GOOGLY ARE WORKING TOGETHER USING THERE OWN TORQUE MACHINE AND MAKING PROGRESS.

THE MACHINISTS AND MILLWRIGHTS ARE ALSO TEAMED UP ON THE" B" LP TURBINE RELIEVING THE TENSION ON THE STUDS USING THE SAME TORQUE MACHINES AND PROCEDURES. PEACHES, ROPEY AND POOPDECK PAPPY ARE TEAMED UP ON THE RIGHT SIDE WITH DELCO JOE, DUDDLEY AND K ON THE LEFT. GOON IS WATCHING CLOSELY AS THE TEAMS CONTINUE TO RELIEVE THE STREATCH OF THE STUDS BY USING TORQUE MACHINES TO TURN THE SIX-INCH CASTLE STYLE NUTS TO THE LEFT. HOWEVER THE TORQUE MACHINE CAN NOT BE USED ON THE HIGH-PRESSURE TURBINE BECAUSE THE NUTS ARE TO BIG AND TO TOTE. FATTY JOE HAS A CLOSE EYE ON THE MACHINISTS, MILLWRIGHTS AND ELECTRICIANS AS THEY MAKE

PROGRESS USING THE INDUCTION HEATERS. THE CREW OF THE HIGH-PRESSURE TURBINE MUST ALSO START FROM THE MIDDLE, ALTERNATE BACK AND FORTH RELIEVING TENSION FROM THE STUDS BY TURNING THE TEN INCH IN DIAMETER NUTS TO THE LEFT. THE ELECTRICIAN DOC WILL BE CONTROLLING THE ON / OFF SWITCH TO THE INDUCTION HEATER ON THE RIGHT WHILE JOHNNY OBOTT AND MOE WILL BE RELIEVING THE TENSION ON THE STUDS. ON THE LEFT SIDE CAPPY IS THE ELECTRICIAN WITH JOWEE AND NOSEOLEO RELIEVING THE TENSION ON THE STUDS. FATTY JOE AND SQUARE HEAD ARE WATCHING THE TEAMS PROGRESS.

FATTY JOE: Were moving right along, the induction heaters are holding up and so far, just a couple nuts got jammed but MOE banged them free with a dead blow hammer while JOHNNYOBOTT was turning the nut two the left. They aren't cross threaded but the Threads must have gotten some dirt in them.

MOE: Okay, DOC I put the induction heater rod into the top of the next nut, you can power up

DOC: Got it MOE.

DOC TURNS THE POWER ON TO THE INDUCTION HEATER AS MOE STANDS BY FOR A FEW MINUTES TO ALLOW THE INDUCTION HEATER TO HEAT UP THE NUT. AS THE INDUCTION HEATER HEATS UP THE NUT MOE USING A TWO-FOOT-LONG BREAKING BAR SETS THE BAR IN THE OPENED CASTLE SQUARE AND TRYS TO PUSH THE NUT AROUND TO THE LEFT. AS THE INDUTION HEATER CONTINUES TO HEAT THE NUT, THE NUT GROWS, AND THE THREADS OPEN UP AROUND THE STUD. MOE CONTINUES TO

TRY TO PUSH THE CASTLE NUT AROUND TO THE LEFT THEN ALL THE SUDDEN THE NUT MOVES A LITTLE AROUND TO THE LEFT AS THE THREADS GROW DUE TO THE HEAT OF THE INDUCTION HEATER. MOE CONTINUES TO WORK THE NUT AROUND TO THE LEFT UNTIL IT FREES UP TO THE POINT OF ABOUT ONE INCH OFF THE TOP HALF OF THE HIGH-PRESSURE SHELL. MOE SIGNALS TO DOC TO CUT THE POWER TO THE INDUCTION HEATER AND JOHNNYOBOTT TAKES THE INDUCTION HEATER ROD AND GENTLY PUTS IT INTO THE TOP OF THE NEXT NUT. WITH THE INDUCTION HEATER OUT OF THE WAY THE NUT REMAINS HOT AS MOE CONTINUALLY TURNS THE NUT TO THE LEFT WITH THE BREAKER BAR UNTIL THE NUT REACHES THE TOP OF THE STUD. REMEMBER EACH NUT IS THE SIZE OF A SIXERS BASKETBALL AND WEIGHS ABOUT ONE HUNDRED POUNDS. ON THE LEFT SIDE OF THE HIGH-PRESSURE TURBINE THE TEAM WORKS THERE WAY AROUND THE HORIZONTAL JOINT.

NOSEALEO: Let's have the heat CAPPY.

CAPPY: Stick the rod in the hole of the nut first NOSEALEO, that way no one gets burned.

NOSEALEO STICKS THE ROD OF THE INDUCTION HEATER INTO THE NUT AND WAITS A FEW MINUTES.

JOWEEE: I think the navy taught me the nut is made of a little different type of US STEEL and heats up a little faster than the stud.

NOSEALEO: GOON told us we can't let the rod in there to long or the stud will also heat up and grow then we will have to let everything cool and start all over again.

JOWEE: That's why we must keep trying to turn the nut to the left with the bar as the nut heats up. So, you better get trying NOSEALEO!

AS THE HIGH-PRESSURE TEAM CONTINUES TO WORK THE WAY AROUND THE HORIZONTAL JOIN THE LOW PRESSURE TEAMS ARE MOVING TOGETHER TO THE "A" LOW PRESSURE TURBINE. ALL FOUR TORQUE MACHINES ARE NOW WORKING FROM THE CENTER OUT AND AROUND THE HORIZONTAL JOINT TILL THEY RELIEVE ALL THE TENSION ON THE STUDS OF THE "A" LP TURBINE. SUNNY, JAKE AND YUMYUM STAY BEHIND TO HELP THE RIGGERS REMOVE THE "C" LOW PRESSURE TURBINE BEARING CAPS AND TOP HALF OF THE BABBIT FACED BEARINGS. THE ELECTRICIANS ELANE AND ESKIN HAVE REMOVED THE VIBRATION PROBES ANDTHERMOCOUPLES FROM THE NUMBER EIGHT AND SEVEN BEARINGS AND VERY NEATLY SET THE CONTROL WIRE OUT OF THE WAY SO THET DON'T GET SKINNED WITCH COULD CAUSE A SHORT. LATER ON, DURING THE STEAM SIDE OUTAGE THE ELECTRICIANS WILL BE TESTING THE WIRES WITH DANDAMAN AND SJONG TO MAKE SURE EVERYTHING WORKS FROM THE BEARINGS TO THE CONTROL ROOM.

THE UNIT ONE CRANE IS CENTERED OVER THE NUMBER EIGHT BEARING CAP AS THE MACHINISTS ARE RECORDING AS FOUND MEASUREMENTS AND REPORTING THEM TO KRINE DOG AND BOWTIE.

KRINE DOG: Let's get the bearing to journal measurements before we remove the top half of the number eight bearing cap.

YUMYUM:	Feeler gage measurements along the horizontal joint of the top and bottom half of the bearing caps is zero.
KRINE DOG:	OK, how about the radial measurements between the rotor of the "c" low pressure turbine and the number eight babbitt faced bearing?
SUNNY:	I measure eight thousand inch around the journal and zero on the bottom, dead center.
YUMYUM:	Me to SUNNY eight thousand inch around the journal to the bearing. Make sure you wright that down JAKE.
JAKE:	I got it, but KRINE DOG and BOW TIE are standing right here.
SUNNY:	Remember double verification on all measurements.

THE UNIT ONE CRANE WITH SMARKEY AS OPPERATOR IS CENTERED DIRECTLY OVER THE NUMBER EIGHT BEARING CAP WITH THREE BOLTS ON EACH SIDE SECURING THE BEARING CAP TO THE INSIDE OF THE BEARING PEDESTOL. YUMYUM AND JAKE EACH PICK A SIDE AND USING A HAMMER AND PUNCH FLATTEN OUT THE METAL KEEPERS THAT ARE BENT OVER THE CORNER OF THE BEARING CAPS BOLTS TO MAKE SURE THEY DON'T VIBRATE LOOSE DURING OPERATION. THEN WITH A SMALL SLEDGE HAMMER AND THE PROPPER SIZED KNOCK WRENCH BANG THE BOLTS TO THE LEFT TO LOOSEN THEM. BLAZE AND BIG O ARE THE RIGGERS READY TO LIFT THE BEARING CAP OFF THE TOP HALF OF THE BEARING AND PUT IT DOWN ON THE LEFT SIDE OF THE UNIT.

BIG O TURNS A LIFTING EYE ALL THE WAY INTO THE BEARING CAP UNTIL IT SHOULDERS OUT THEN HOOKS A TWO TON CHAIN BLOCK TO DEAD CENTER ON THE TOP OF THE BEARING SADDLE THEN PULLS THE CHAIN TILL THE SLACK IS TAKEN OUT. BLAZE TAKES A CLOSE LOOK TO MAKE SURE EVERYTHING IS CENTER THEN GIVES BIG O THE GO AHEAD. BIG O PULLS HARD ON THE CHAIN BLOCK STRAIGHT DOWN. EVERYTHING TOTENS UP IN A HURRY AS BIG O TAKES ANOTHER BIG PULL ON THE BLOCK, BIG O TAKES A THIRD BIG PULL ON THE BLOCK AND THE TOP HALF BEARING CAP COMES UP OFF THE TOP HALF OF THE NUMBER EIGHT BEARING. AGAIN, BIG O TAKES ANOTHER BIG PULL ON THE BLOCKS TO MAKE SURE THE CAP IS CLEAR OF THE BEARING AS BLAZE SIGNALS SMARKEY IN THE UNIT ONE CRANE TO TROLLY TO THE LEFT SIDE AND PUT THE BEARING CAP DOWN. BLAZE DISCONNECTS THE HOOK FROM THE LIFTING EYE AND THE CRANE CENTERS UP ON THE TOP HALF OF THE NUMBER EIGHT BEARING.

SUNNY:	Wait a minute YUMYUM we must measure bearing deflection as we loosen the bearing bolts.
JAKE:	Yes, SUNNY that's why we set up the dial indicator. That way we can tell how much The upper half of the number eight bearing relaxes while we loosen the bolts.
YUMYUM:	Make sure were set to zero on the indicator.

JAKE AND YUMYUM BANG THE KEEPERS FLAT THEN SLOWLEY LOOSEN THE BEARING BOLTS.

SUNNY:	OK we have a reflection of six thousand (.006)
YUMYUM:	Make sure we wright that down.

THE MACHINISTS ARE QUICK TO REMOVE THE SIX UPPER HALF BEARING BOLTS THAT ATTACH THE UPPER HALF OF THE BEARING TO THE LOWER HALF AND MARK THEM APPROPRIATLY SO EACH BOLT GOES BACK TO THE SAME LOCATION DURING REASSEMBLY. THEN TOGETHER TAKE THE TOOLS AND MOVE TO THE NUMBER SEVEN BEARING CAP. BIG O TAKES THE LIFTING EYE AND TURNS IT INTO THE THREADED HOLE IN THE TOP OF THE BEARING UNTIL IT IS SHOULDERED OUT, ABOUT ONE INCH.

SMARKEY HAS THE UNIT ONE CRANE CENTERED UP DIRECTLY OVER THE NUMBER EIGHT BEARING TOP HALF AND BIG O HOOKS THE CHAIN BLOCK HOOK TO THE LIFTING EYE. USING EVERY OUNCE OF BODY WEIGHT BIG O TAKES A BIG PULL ON THE TWO TON CHAIN BLOCK AND EVERYTHING TOTENS UP. AGAIN, BIG O TAKES ANOTHER HUGE PULL ON THE CHAIN BLOCK AND NOTHING. THERE IS A SMALL COATING OF LUBE OIL THAT CREATES A SUCTION TYPE OF LOCK BETWEEN THE JOURNAL OF THE ROTOR AND THE BEARING. BIG O TAKES ANOTHER BIG PULL AS BLAZE MAKES SURE EVERYTHING IS DEAD CENTER. WITH BIG O'S FEET ALMOST OFF THE GROUND THE TOP HALF OF THE BEARING FINIALLY BREAKS FREE FROM THE JOURNAL OF THE 'C'LP ROTOR. AGAIN, BIG O TAKES ANOTHER COUPLE PULLS AND USING THE CHAIN BLOCK COMES UP OFF THE JOURNAL BY THREE INCHES OR SO.

BLAZE SIGNALS TO SMARKEY TO TROLLEY OVER TO THE LEFT SIDE AND LOWER THE TOP HALF OF THE NUMBER EIGHT BEARING DOWN WHERE HE UN HOOKS IT AND HEADS TO THE NUMBER SEVEN BEARING CAP. BOW TIE AND KRINE DOG ARE STANDING BY TO JOT DOWN ANY AS FOUND MEASUREMENTS THAT MIGHT BE CRUTCIAL COME TIME FOR REASSEMBLY.

JAKE:	The feeler measurements along the right and left sides of the number seven bearing cap is zero.
SUNNY:	OK how about the top bearing to journal JAKE?
JAKE:	I can get a ten thousand in the top. (.010)
SUNNY:	Right side?
JAKE:	Feels like a six thousand right side. (.006)
SUNNY:	Ok Jake now left side?
JAKE:	.007 seems right to me SUNNY.
YUMYUM:	I "m measuring the same SUNNY.

ON THE RIGHT AND LEFT SIDES OF THE BEARING CAPS ARE THREE BOLTS HELD TOTE BY STEEL KEEPERS WITH THE CORNER OF THE KEEPERS HAMMERED TOTE AGAINST THE CORNERS OF THE BOLTS TO KEEP THE BEARING CAPS TOTE TO THE BEARINGS DURING OPERATION. JAKE AND YUMYUM BANG THE KEEPERS STRAIGHT AND THEN TAKE A SMALL SLEDGE HAMMER WITH A SLUGGING WRENCH AND BANG THE BEARING CAP BOLTS TO THE LEFT TILL THEY ARE ABLE TO TURN THEM OUT WITH THERE HANDS AND REMOVE THE SIX BEARING CAP BOLTS THAT FASTEN THE CAP TO THE BEARING PEDESTOL.

BLAZE TURNS THE LIFTING EYE INTO THE TOP OF THE BEARING CAP THEN TAKES THE HOOK FROM THE CHAIN BLOCK AND ATTACHES IT TO THE LIFTING EYE. THIS TIME BIG O MAKES SURE THE HOOK IS DEAD CENTER OVER THE BEARING CAP AND GIVES BLAZE THE GO AHEAD. BLAZE TAKES A GOOD PULL ON THE BLOCK AND EVERYTHING TOTENS UP. BLAZE THEN TAKES A BIG PULL ON THE BEARING CAP AND STILL NO FLOAT. BLAZE, THIS TIME TAKES A BIG PULL WITH EVERYTHING HE HAS AND SLOWLY

THE BEARING CAP BEGINS TO COME UP OFF THE TOP HALF OF THE NUMBER SEVEN BEARING. BLAZE TAKES ANOTHER BIG PULL THEN THE BEARING CAP COMES CLEAR OF THE TOP HALF OF THE NUMBER SEVEN BEARING AND BIG O DIRECTS SMARKEY THE UNIT ONE CRANE OPPERATOR, TO LIFT THE NUMBER SEVEN BEARING CAP AND TROLLY TO THE LEFT SIDE AND GENTLY PUT IT DOWN AS BIG O QUICKLY DISCONNECTS THE HOOK AND TURNS OUT THE LIFTING EYE.

SUNNY: Ok JAKE set the indicator, so we can measure
                the deflection of the top half of the bearing.
YUMYUM: Let us straighten out the keepers first SUNNY.

YUMYUM AND JAKE STRAIGHTEN OUT THE KEEPERS AND SUNNY MAKES SURE THE INDICATOR IS SET TO ZERO. THEN JAKE AND YUMYUM WITH A SMALL SLEDGE HAMMER AND SLUGGING WRENCH BANG THE NUMBER SEVEN BEARING BOLTS TO THE LEFT AND LOOSEN THEM UP THE DIAL INDICATOR MOVES FOUR THOUSAND INCH (.004) AND SUNNY IS QUICK TO VERIFY THE MEASUREMENT, WRITE IT DOWN AND COMMUNICATE THE MEASUREMENT TO BOW TIE. BLAZE TURNS THE LIFTING EYE INTO THE TOP HALF OF THE NUMBER SEVEN BEARING AND BIG O MAKES SURE EVERYTHING IS DEAD CENTER OVER THE TOP HALF OF THE NUMBER SEVEN BEARING. BLAZE GRABS THE CHAIN TO THE BLOCKS AND GIVES A VERY STRONG PULL DOWN ON THE BLOCK, NOTHING.BLAZE TAKES HIS RIGHT OUTER WRIST AND WIPES HIS BROW AND AGAIN GIVES A STRONG PULL DOWN ON THE BLOCK. THE SMALL COATING OF LUBE OIL BETWEEN THE BABBIT FACED BEARING AND THE JOURNAL OF THE "C" LP ROTOR CREATES A LOCK THAT TAKES A LITTLE MORE TO BREAK THAT'S WHY IT'S IMPORTANT TO USE THE CHAIN BLOCK FOR THE

LIFT INSTEAD OF JUST USING THE CRAIN HOOK TO PULL IT OF SO YOU CAN FEEL THE HOIST OF THE UPPER HALF BEARING AND NOT CAUSE ANY DAMAGE.

IT'S IMPORTANT TO BE ABLE TO FEEL THE MACHINERY AS YOU ARE TAKING IT APART AND PUTTING IT BACK TOGETHER TO MINAMALIZE ANY POTENTIAL DAMAGE OR ISSUES WHEN START TIME HAPPENS. BLAZE GIVES A SUPER STRONG PULL ON THE CHAIN BLOCK AND FINIALLY BREAKS THE SEAL OF LUBE OIL BETWEEN THE BABBIT FACED BEARING AND THE JOURNAL OF THE ROTOR. BLAZE GIVES ANOTHER PULL ON THE BLOCK AND THE TOP HALF OF THE NUMBER SEVEN BEARING IS CLEAR AND BIG O SIGNALS TO TROLLY TO THE LEFT THEN GENTLY DOWN ON THE PROTECTED FLOOR WHERE HE CAN UN HOOK THE BEARING CAP AND MOVE ONTO THE NUMBER SIX BEARING CAP AND THE "B" LOW PRESURE TURBINE BEARING CAP. YUMYUM, SUNNY AND JAKE MOVE ALONG TO THE NUMBER SIX BEARING WITH BOW TIE AND KRINE DOG WAITING AND WATCHING THE REST OF THE CREW FINISH UP WITH RELIEVING THE TENSION ON THE "A" LP TURBINE, REMOVING THE NUTS AND STOREING THEM IN THE PROPPER BOLT BIN FOR CLEANING AND INSPECTION.

THE MEMBERS OF THE HIGH PRESURE TURBINE CREW MOE, JOHNNYOBOTT, JOWEE WITH HELP FROM DUDDLEY AND NOSEALEO ARE CAREFULLY TURNING THE BASKETBALL SIZE NUTS TO THE LEFT UNTIL THEY ARE READY TO BE REMOVED. TWO CREW MEMBERS OF A TIME GENTLY STAND THE NUTS UP ON THEIR SIDE AND SLIDE A SOFTENED LIFTING BAR THROUGH THE CENTER OF EACH NUT AND TOGETHER LIFT THE HUNDRED POUND NUTS AND SET THEM ON THE DECK IN A BOX FOR CLEANING AND INSPECTION. EACH NUT HAS BEEN NUMBERED AND THE

SIDE OF THE UPPER HALF SHELL ALSO NUMBERED IN SEQUENCE OF REMOVAL AND TO MAKE SURE THE NUTS STAY WITH THE CORRESPONDING STUD. RAYRAY CHONG OPPERATOR OF THE UNIT TWO CANE, WITH EEFFY, SKIN AND PAPALUCHI PAY CLOSE ATTENTION TO THE TOW OVERHEAD CRANES AND MAKE SURE THEY DON'T GET TO CLOSE AS THEY MOVE THE BOXES OF HIGH-PRESSURE TURBINE BOLTS OUT OF THE WAY FOR CLEANING AND INSPECTION. WHILE ALL THE ACTION IS TAKEING PLACE ON THE GOVONOR END SMARKEY AND THE UNIT ONE CRANE IS DIRECTLEY LINED UP OVER THE NUMBER SIX LP TURBINE BEARING CAP. SQUARE HEAD AND CORNOL HOGAN JOIN KRINE DOG AND BOW TIE NEAR THE NUMBER SIX BEARING PEDESTOL.

SQUARE HEAD:	GOON has CHARDY, LAZALOON, GONESKI, BOOGER, COOL EARL and OTTO ready to jack bolt the "C" low pressure inner cylinder half out of the fit and get it ready for removal.
KRINE DOG:	It takes a lot of hard work to get to the diaphragms and flow guides.
SUNNY:	Zero is the measurement along the horizontal joint of the bearing cap.
JAKE:	The feeler gage measurement for the bottom is also zero, right side measurement is left side measurement between the rotor journal and the babbitt faced bearing is six thousand .006. Top measurement is eight thousand .008 and left side is eight thousand.008.
YUMYUM:	I will confirm the measurements and I got the same measurements.

BOW TIE:	We like to add up the measurements then average them out to determine the oil wedge created by the lube oil lift pumps that protect the bearing face from the journal rotor turning at up to eighteen hundred rotations per minute.
KRINE DOG:	We also perform a thorough inspection on the journals of the rotors and the bearing faces to make sure there is no gouge in the bearing face or where the rotors turn inside the bearings, the journals.
JAKE:	The keepers are straight, and the bearing cap bolts are removed.
BIG O:	Let me in there JAKE.

BIG O TURNS THE LIFTING EYE INTO THE TOP OF THE BEARING CAP THEN WITH THE CRANE DIRECTLY CENTER OVER THE CAP HOOKS THE CHAIN BLOCK UP. BIG O GIVES A HARD PULL DOWN ON THE CHAIN BLOCK AND ALL THE SLACK IS QUICK TO DISIAPEER. BLAZE MAKES SURE EVERYTHING LOOKS CENTER AND GIVES BIG O THE OK. BIG O TAKES ANOTHER STRONG PULL DOWN ON THE BLOCK, THEN ANOTHER ONE AND THE NUMBER SIX BEARING CAP OF THE "B" LP TURBINE COMES UP OFF THE TOP OF THE BEARING. BIG O TAKES EVEN ANOTHER STRONG PULL AND THE BEARING CAP IS CLEAR AS BLAZE DIRECTS SMARKEY TO TROLLY OVER TO THE LEFT SIDE OF THE TRAIN AND GENTLY LOWER THE BEARING CAP TO THE FLOOR WHERE HE DISCONNECTS THE RIGGING AND ALLOWS THE CRANE TO RE CENTER OVER THE NUMBER SIX TOP HALF BEARING.

SUNNY:	The dial indicator is set to zero. Were ready to remove the six bolts JAKE and YUMYUM.

YUMYUM AND JAKE WITH A SMALL HAMMER AND PUNCH STRAIGHTEN OUT THE KEEPERS THEN TAKE SLEDGE HAMMER AND PROPPER SIZED SLUGGING WRENCH AND BANG THE BOLTS TO THE LEFT. IT REALLY DON'T TAKE MUCH TO KNOCK THE BEARING BOLTS LOOSE THEY ARE TORQUED TO A SPACIFIC FOOT POUNDS DURING REASSEMBLY.

YUMYUM: Ok SUNNY the bolts are loose

SUNNY: On the number six bearing we have a deflection of seven thousand.007.

BOW TIE: Deflection of the top half of the bearing is also taken into consideration. To much deflection could result in excessive clearance and to little deflection could lead to the bearing face getting wiped out.

KRINE DOG: So far, the numbers are looking pretty good, BOW TIE.

YUMYUM AND JAKE REMOVE THE BOLTS AND KEEPERS AND PUT THEM IN THE PROPPER BOLT BIN FOR CLEANING AND INSPECTION. BIG O AND BLAZE STEP IN AND HOOK THE RIGGING UP TO THE TOP HALF OF THE NUMBER SIX BEARING AND MAKE SURE THE HOOK OF THE CRANE IS CENTERED DIRECTLY OVER THE TOP OF THE BEARING. EACH BABBIT FACED BEARING HALF WEIGHS ABOUT ONE THOUSAND POUNDS. AGAIN, BIG O HAS TO USE ALL HIS STRENGTH TO PULL DOWN ON THE CHAIN BLOCK. AS SOON AS THE SLACK IS PICKED UP BLAZE MAKES SURE THE HOOK REMAINS DEAD CENTER OVER THE BEARING.

BIG O GIVES ANOTHER MAX PULL TO THE BLOCK THEN ANOTHER AND ANOTHER AND FINIALLY THE BEARING BREAKS FREE FROM THE JOURNAL AND COMES UP ABOUT TWO INCHES. BIG O PULLS HARD DOWN ON THE BLOCK AGAIN AND CLEARS THE PEDESTOL. BLAZE SIGNALS UP TO THE BOX WHERE SMARKEY IS OPPERATING THE CRANE TO TROLLY OVER TO THE LEFT SIDE AND DOWN GENTLY ONTO THE PROTECTED FLOOR. WHERE BLAZE DISCONNECTS THE RIGGING AND SENDS THE CRANE TO THE NUMBER FIVE BEARING WHERE THE CREW IS WAITING TO DO THE SAME THING OVER AGAIN ON THE AND THE NUMBER FOUR BEARING. ONCE THE CREW IS FINISHED WITH THE NUMBER FOUR BEARING THE UNIT ONE CRANE IS CUT LOOSE TO GO GET PREPARED TO LIFT THE UPPER HALF CYLINDER OF THE 'C' LOW PRESSURE TURBINE.

SUNNY, JAKE AND YUMYUM CONTINUE ON THE NUMBER THREE, TWO AND ONE BEARING CAP REMOVAL USING THE UNIT TWO CRANE WITH RAYRAY CHONG AS THE OPPERATOR. EEFFY, SKIN AND PAPALUCHI ARE WELL VERSED IN THE RIGGING ASPECTS OF THE TASK AND KRINE DOG ALONG WITH BOW TIE CONTINUE TO ACCOMPANY THE MACHINISTS TO MAKE SURE THE AS FOUND MEASUREMENTS GET RECORDED AND THE PROPPER CALCULATIONS CAN BE PERFORMED PRIOR TO REASSEMBLY. GOON HAS THE JACK BOLT TEAM FOLLOWING RIGHT ALONG PREPARING THE "C" LOW PRESSURE CYLINDER UPPER HALF FOR REMOVAL.

THE THREE UPPER HALF INNER CYLINDERS WEIGH ABOUT ONE HUNDRED TONS, HAVE SIX JACK BOLT FINE THREAD HOLES ONE IN EACH CORNER AND ONE IN THE MIDDLE OF EACH SIDE ALONG THE HORIZONTAL JOINT CONNECTING THE TOP HALF TO

THE BOTTOM HALF. THE JACK BOLTS ARE TWO INCH IN DIAMETER, TEN INCHES LONG AND FINE THREADS. CHARDY, LAZALOON AND GONESKI WILL MAN THE RIGHT SIDE WITH BOOGER, COOL EARL AND OTTO MANNING THE LEFT SIDE. EACH CREW MEMBER IS EQUIPED WITH INCH AND A HALF DRIVE AIR GUN AND A CARPENTERS RULE. THE AIR LINES HAVE BEEN RUN AND THE RIGHT SIZE SOCKET HAS BEEN INSTALLED BY LOPEZ, AIRYSUE AND MIC. GOON HAS POSITIONED HIMSELF SO EVERY ONE CAN SEE HIS DIRECTIONS. ALL THE PROPPER PPE IS REQUIRED ESPICIALLY HEARING PROTECTION.

FATTY JOE IS ALSO PRESENT TO MAKE SURE THE CYLINDER HALF COMES UP EQUALLY AND OUT OF THE INNER FIT TO THE FIRST STAGE FLOW GUIDE. GOON WAVES THE GO AHEAD AND THE CREW EACH ON A JACK BOLT START BANGING ON THE BOLTS TO THE RIGHT DRIVING THEM THROUGH THE FOUR INCHES THICK US STEEL CYLINDER HALF AND DOWN ONTO THE HORIZONTAL JOINT. THE CREW CONTINUES TO BANG ON THE JACK BOLTS AND STILL NO GAP APPEARS. GOON WAVES HIS HANDS AND THE CREW STOPS WITH THE BANGING. EVERYONE EVALUATES THE BOLTS AND MAKES SURE THEY ARE CLOSE IN REMANING LENGTH. THE JACK BOLTS ARE ABOUT FOUR INCHES THROUGH THE SHELL AND APPEAR READY TO START OPENING UP THE JOINT. GOON WAVES HIS HANDS AGAIN AND THE AIR GUNS START BANGING ON THE JACK BOLTS AGAIN. BANG. BANG, BANG, BANG, BANG THE NOISE IS DEFENING BANG, BANG, BANG, BANG, BANG THEN FINIALLY THE FINE THREADED JACK BOLTS BEGIN TO OPEN UP THE JOINT. FATTY JOE AND GOON ARE LOOKING VERY CLOSE AND ONCE THE UPPER HALF CYLINDER SHELL COMES UP OFF THE JOINT ABOUT ONE INCH GOON WAVES HIS HANDS.

THE CREW STOPS FOR A SECOND AND MEASURES THE DISTANCE BETWEEN THE TOP HALF AND THE BOTTOM HALF OF THE "C" LOW PRESSURE TURBINE CYLINDER. AGAIN, GOON WAVES HIS HANDS AND THE CREW PROCEEDS DRIVING THE JACK BOLTS HARD TO THE RIGHT LIFTING THE ONE HUNDRED TON CYLINDER WALL UP EVER SO SLIGHTLY. BANG, BANG, BANG, BANG THE CREW CONTINUES TO RUN THE JACK BOLTS UP. FATTY JOE AND GOON ARE MAKING SURE THE CYLINDER IS COMING UP EQUALLY AROUND THE JOINT UNTIL THE HORIZONTAL JOINT OF THE "C" LOW PRESSURE TURBINE UPPER HALF OPENS UP TO THREE INCHES. GOON WAVES HIS HANDS FOR A STOP AND THE CREW MEASURES TO MAKE SURE THE OPENING IN THE JOINT IS EQUAL ALL AROUND. FATTY JOE AND GOON ARE HAPPY WITH THE RESULTS. THE CREW STREATCHES THE AIR LINES OUT AND MOVE TO THE "B" LOW PRESURE UPPER CYLINDER HALF. LOPEZ AND THE TOOL CREW MAKE SURE THE PROPPER JACK BOLTS ARE IN THE HOLES SO THE CREW CAN MOVE RIGHT ALONG TO THE NEXT UPPER HALF SHELL. THE CREW ASSUMES THE SAME POSITIONS AND GOON DOSEN'T WASTE ANY TIME TO WAVE HIS HANDS. RIGHT SIDE AND LEFT SIDE WITH EACH CREW MEMBER HAVING THER OWN ONE INCH AND A HALF DRIVE AIR GUN WITH CARPENTERS RULE START BANGING ON THE JACK BOLTS TO THE RIGHT. BANG, BANG, BANG, BANG, BANG THE NOISE IS SO LOUD YOU CAN'T HEAR ANYTHING. GOON WAVES HIS HANDS AND WITH THE CREW UNDERSTANDING THE IMPORTANCE OF COMING UP TOGETHER STOPS FOR A SECOND.

THE BOTTOM OF THE JACK BOLTS HAVE BEEN RUN THRUOGH THE TOP HALF OF THE" B" LOW PRESURE CYLINDER AND APPEAR TO BE READY TO BREAK OPENED THE HORIZONTAL JOINT. GOON WAVES HIS HANDS AND THE CREW BANGS, BANGS, BANGS,

BANGS, BANGS ON THE JACK BOLTS TO THE RIGHT UNTIL THE JOINT OPENS UP ABOUT ONE INCH ALL AROUND. GOON WAVES HIS HANDS AND THE CREW STOPS FOR A MEASUREMENT. GOON AND FATTY JOE SEE IT'S UP ABOUT A HALF INCH ALL AROUND THEN GOON WAVES HIS HANDS THE CREW BEGINS BANGING ON THE JACK BOLTS AGAIN. THE FINE THREAD JACK BOLTS ARE RUNNING THROUGH THE FINE THREADED HOLES IN THE UPPER HALF OF THE CYLINDER AND JACK THE ONE HUNDRED TON UPPER HALF CYLINDER FROM THE LOWER HALF CYLINDER CREATING A GAP BETWEEN THE TWO HALVES AND OUT OF THE FIT OR KEY THAT IS GROVED INTO THE UPPER HALF TO HELP ALLIGN THE UPPER HALF WITH THE FIRST STAGE FLOW GUIDE. FATTY JOE AND GOON SEE THE CYLINDER GAP IS A LITTLE BETTER THEN THREE INCHES ALL AROUND AND ARE HAPPY TO MOVE THE CREW TO THE "A" LP. THE ONLY THING KEEPING THE ONE HUNDRED TON UPPER HALF CYLINDER SHELLS IN THE AIR AND OUT OF THE FIT IS THE SIX JACK BOLTS.

GOON, FATTY JOE AND THE CREW MOVE ALONG TO THE "A" LOW PRESURE TURBINE AND LOOK UP TO NOTICE RAYRAY CHONG AND THE CREW OF RIGGERS ARE ON THE WAY TO THE RIGGING CAGE TO RE DRESS THE UNIT TWO HOOK. JAKE, SUNNY, AND YUMYUM HAVE FINISHED UP WITH THE BEARING CAP AND BEARING AS FOUND MEASUREMENTS AND REMOVALS AND MAKE SURE BOW TIE AND KRINE DOG HAVE ALL THE NUMBERS REQUIRED TO MAKE THE CALCULATIONS FOR A SMOOTH REASSEMBLY.

BIG JIM AND SUAVE RICO HAVE BEEN BUSY MAKING SURE THE CRIBBING SET UP PRIOR TO THE STEAM SIDE OUTAGE ON UNIT TWO MAIN STEAM TURBINES ARE MEASURED OUT AND PERFECT

FOR THE RIGGERS TO SET THE UPPER HALF LOW PRESSURE AND HIGH-PRESSURE TURBINE CYLINDERS ON ONCE REMOVED. BIG JIM AND SUAVE RICO HAVE ALSO PERFORMED A THEROUGH SLING INSPECTION ON THE FOUR, TWENTY-FIVE FOOT KEVELAR SLINGS USED TO REMOVE ALL FOUR INNER SHELLS. (UPPER HALF CYLINDERS) THE UNIT ONE CRANE OPPERATED BY SMARKEY, BIG HOOK, SHAPED LIKE AN ANCHOR, IS DRESSED IN TWO, TWENTY-FIVE FOOT KEVLAR SLINGS WITH AN OPENED END AROUND EACH SIDE OF THE ANCHOR AND THE OTHER END OF THE SLING WILL GO AROUND THE OUTSIDE CORNER OF THE LIFTING HORNES, THAT ARE CAST INTO THE UPPER HALF CYLINDER'S. RAYRAY CHONG CENTERS UP OVER THE RIGGING CAKE DOOR AS THE BIG HOOK OF THE UNIT TWO CRANE IS BEING LOWERED DOWN.

THE RIGGING ON THE SMALL HOOK FROM THE BEARING WORK HAS BEEN REMOVED WITH THE SMALL HOOK ALL THE WAY IN THE UP POSITION OUT OF THE WAY. BIG JIM AND SUAVE RICO DRESS THE BIG HOOK SHAPED LIKE AN ANCHOR, WITH THE SAME SIZE, TWENTY-FIVE FOOT KEVLAR SLINGS AS THE UNIT ONE CRANE. WITH ALL THE SHELLS BEING UP ON THE JACK BOLTS AND OUT OF THE FIT, THE HEAVEY LOADS RIGGING CREW IS READY TO REMOVE ALL FOUR SHELLS SO THE MACHINISTS AND THE GOON SQUAD CAN START ROWING THE BOAT. RAYRAY CHONG SETS HIS UNIT TWO CRANE WITH THE BIG HOOK DIRECTLY OVER THE TOP OF THE "C" LP, "C" COUPLING END OF THE SHELL AND SMARKEY SETS THE UNIT ONE CRANES BIG HOOK DIRECTLY OVER TOP OF THE "C" LP "D" COUPLING END OF THE SHELL. THIS IS AN ALLHANDS EXCERSIZE FOR THE RIGGING TEAM WITH THE MORE EYES THE BETTER.

IT'S IMPORTANT AS THE SHELL IS BEING RAISED UP TO MAKE SURE IT DOSEN'T COME IN CONTACT WITH THE THREADS OF THE STUDS. EEFFY, SKIN, PAPPALUCHI MAN ONE SIDE OF THE INNER SHELL OF THE "C" LOW PRESSURE TURBINE AND BLAZE, BIG O, RAPPING RODNEY ON THE OTHER. BIG JIM WILL HANDLE THE SIGNALS AND THE CREW WILL WALK THE DECK WITH THE SHELL AND JOIN SUAVE RICO WHEN IT COMES TIME TO GUIDE THE UPPER HALVES DOWN ONTO THE CRIBBING, STAGED ON THE LEFT SIDE OF THE STILL OPPERATING UNIT ONE. ALL THE RIGGERS HAVE THE FLYER ORANGE VESTS ON AND HAVE DISSCUSSED THE PROPPER, MOST SAFE LOAD PATH FOR ALL THE SHELLS. EVERYONE KNOWS NOT TO BE UNDER A SUSPENDED LOAD EVER. THE PROPPER LOAD PATH IS STRAIGHT UP UNTIL EVERYTHING IS CLEARED, THEN BRIDGE THE CRANES IN UNISON DIRECTLY OVER THE OPPERATING UNIT THEN TROLLY LEFT, ADJACENT TO THE CORROLATING TURBINE WHERE THE CRIBBING HAS BENN PLACED WITH SUCH A HUGE SCOPE OF WORK FLOOR SPACE IS AT A PREMIUM. WITH EACH BIG HOOK IN PLACE AND THE SLINGS AROUND THE OUTSIDE CORNER LIFTING HORNS BIG JIM TAKES CONTROL OF THE LIFT.

SLOW UP, SLOW UP, SLOW UP AND THE SLACK OF THE TWENTY-FIVE FOOT KEVLAR SLINGS DISAPEARS. BIG JIM WAVES A STOP AND THE RIGGING TEAM CHECKS HOOK CENTERS AND POSITIONS OF THE SLINGS AROUND THE BIG HOOK AND THE LIFTING HORNS. THE SLINGS ARE SNUG BUT NOT TOTE. BIG JIM SIGNALS ANOTHER SLOW UP, SLOW UP AND REMEMBER HE IS SIGNALING BOTH CRANES AT THE SAME TIME. NOW THE SLING ARE VERY TOTE BUT STILL NO LIFT. BIG JIM NOW JUST SIGNALS TO RAYRAY CHONG, SCRATCHES HIS CHIN AND RUBS

HIS THUMBS AND FORE FINGERS TOGETHER AS TO SAY VERY SLOW, SMALL UP THEN WAVES A STOP.

THE RIGGERS ARE STATIONED AROUND THE SHELL PEERING DOWN THROUGH THE STUD HOLES MAKING SURE THE SHELL COMES UP DIRECTLY CENTER AND STRAIGHT UP. EVEN THOUGH THE SHELLS ARE UP ON THE JACK BOLTS THE THREADS OF THE STUDS ARE STILL ONLY ABOUT HALF WAY THROUGH THE SIX-INCH-THICK TOP HALF- INNER CYLINDER SHELLS. BIG JIM SIGNALS BOTH CRANES SLOW UP, SLOW UP AND EVERY EYE BALL IS ON THE LEVEL OF THE SHELL AND LOOKING FOR THE SHELL TO COME UP OF THE JACK BOLTS. BIG JIM WAVES A STOP AND LOOKS AROUND TO SEE IF ANY OF THE RIGGERS HAVE ANY CONCERNS. EVERYTHING IS LOOKS GOOD TO CONTINUE AND BIG JIM SENDS ANOTHER SLOW UP, SLOW UP THEN ALL THE SUDDENLY THE INNER CYLINDER, UPPER HALF SHELL OF THE"C" LP TURBINE IS UP OFF THE JACK BOLS AND THE HORIZONTAL JOINT.

THE UPPER HALF WEIGHS ABOUT ONE HUNDRED TON AND ONCE IN THE AIR BOUNCES AROUND A VERY LITTLE BIT. THE RIGGING CREW KEEPS IT STEADY AND MAKES SURE, THEIRE FINGERS AND FEET STAY AWAY FROM BEING BETWEEN THE TWO HALVES. BIG JIM SIGNALS THE CRANE OPPERATORS SLOW UP, SLOW UP SLOW UP AS THE INNER SHELL CLEARS THE STUDS THREDS AND LOOKS LEVEL. BIG JIM SIGNALS A STOP AND AGAIN THE RIGGERS TAKE A CLOSE LOOK TO TRIPLE CHECK THE LOAD FOR SLING POSITIONING BECAUSE IF SOMETHING IS NOT RIGHT THE INNER SHELL CAN BE PUT BACK DOWN ONTO THE JOINT WITHOUTT MUCH ALLIGNEMENT.

EVERYTHING IS IN ORDER AND BIG JIM SIGNALS ANOTHER SLOW UP, SLOW UP, SLOW UP AS THE CRANES ARE COMING UP TOGETHER KEEPING THE LOAD LEVEL. ONCE THE LOAD APPEARS TO BE CLEAR OF THE GENERATOR HOUSING AND DOG HOUSE BIG JIM WAVES A STOP. EVERYTHING LOOKS GOOD, EVEN TO FATTY JOE WHO IS AN OLD SCHOOL RIGGER WHEN ALL LIFTS WERE DONE WITH THICK WIRE ROPES BEFORE KEVLAR WAS AVAILIABLE. SMARKEY AND RAYRAY CHONG KNOW WHEN BIG JIM GIVES THE BRIDGE SIGNAL TO BRIDGE TOGETHER AT FULL THROTTLE, SO THEY BRIDGE TOGETHER ALONG THE CENTERLINE OF THE UNITS. BIG JIM SIGNALS THE CRANES TO BRIDGE AND THE INNER TOP HALF OF THE"C" LP TURBINE (SHELL) FLOATS ALONG THE TOP OF THE UNIT TWO GENERATOR HOUSING, OVER SOME OPEN FLOOR SPACE THEN OVER THE TOP OF THE OPPERATING UNIT ONE GENERATOR UNTIL IT IS RIGHT OVER THE TOP OF THE UNIT ONE"C" LP TURBINE. BIG JIM SIGNALS A STOP AND THE CRANES STOP. WITH THE CRANE OPPERATORS EXPERIENCE THEY KNOW WHERE THE SHELL IS GOING TO BE STAGED FOR CLEANING AND INSPECTION BUT STILL WAIT FOR BIG JIM TO SIGNAL.

BIG JIM SIGNALS TO TROLLY THE SHELL LEFT UNTIL DIRECTLY OVER THE TOP OF THE CRIBBING THEN SIGNALS THE CRANES A SLOW DOWN, SLOW DOWN, SLOW DOWN, SLOW DOWN, SLOW DOWN UNTIL JUST ABOUT SIX INCHES ABOVE THE CRIBBING. ALL THE RIGGERS ARE STATIONED AROUND THE SHELL AND MAKE SURE THE CRIBBING IS SET PERFECT TO SET THE SHELL ON TOP OF. THEY ALSO LET EACH OTHER KNOW TO KEEP FINGERS AND TOES OUT AWAY FROM THE FLANGE FACE AND THE CRIBBING WOOD. EVERYONE IS CLEAR AND BIG JIM SIGANALS SLOW DOWN, SLOW DOWN AND STOP THE CREW

THEN STEADYS THE SHELL AND BIG JIM SIGNALS A SLOW DOWN SLOW DOWN AS THE CREW GUIDES THE SHELL RIGHT ONTOP OF THE CRIBBING, PERFECTLY. BIG JIM SIGNALS A SLOW DOWN, SLOW DOWN AS THE "C" LOW PEASSURE, UPPER HALF, INNER CYLINDER SHELL COMES TO REST ON TOP OF THE CRIBBING. SUAVE RICO AND THE RIGGERS REMOVE THE SLINGS FROM THE OUTSIDE CORNERS OF THE LIFTING HORNS AND PROCCED TO REMOVE THE "B" LOW PRESSURE AND "A" LOW PRESSURE UPPER HALF, INNER CYLINDER SHELLS OF THE UNIT TWO MAIN STEAM TURBINES INSIDE THE GIANT ELECTRIC MACHINE.

THE LAST BUT NOTTHE LEAST UPPER HALF SHELL TO BE REMOVED IS THE ONE HUNDRED- AND TWENTY-TON HIGH PRESSURE TURBINE SHELL. WITH THE CREW OF RIGGERS STANDING BY. RAYRAY CHONG IN THE UNIT TWO CRANE LOWERS THE BIG HOOK IN FRONT OF THE RIGGING CAGE WHERE BIG JIM AND SUAVE RICO PERFORM A CLOSE INSPECTION ON THE KEVLAR SLINGS TO MAKE SURE THEY HAVEN'T BEEN STRETCHED EXCESSIVLEY.

THEY LOOK CLOSE AT THE TELL TALES THAT ARE BUILT INTO THE SLING, SO THE RIGGERS CAN TELL IF THE SLINGS HAVE BEEN OVER LOADED. USUALLY THE SLINGS ARE RATED WELL OVER THE ALLOWED LIFTING WEIGHT AS A BUILT IN SAFETY FEATURE BUT YOU CAN NEVER BE COMPLAICENT WHEN IT TO LIFTING ANY LOAD. ALSO, YOU WANT EACH LEG TO BE THE SAME LENGTH, SO THE SHELL COMES UP LEVEL FRONT TO BACK AND MOST IMPORTANTLY ON THE HIGH-PRESSURE TURBINE, SIDE TO SIDE BECAUSE OF THE LACK OF CLEARENCE DUE TO THE MAIN STEAM INLET PIPES CLEARENCES WITCH ARE ON THE RIGHT SIDE AND LEFT SIDE OF THE HP SHELL.

THE CLEARENCE WAS CREATED BY THE CREW PULLING THE MAIN STEAM INLET PIPES AWAY AROM THE FLANGE FACES WITH THE WIRE ROPE SLINGS AND COME ALONGS. BIG JIM AND SUAVE RICO ARE ASSURED OF THE KEVLAR SLINGS AND SEND RAYRAY CHONG ON HIS WAY TO SET HIS BIG HOOK UP OVER THE TOP HALF GOVONOR END HIGH PRESSURE SHELL. SMARKEY AND THE UNIT ONE CRANE THEN DOES THE SAME THING AS BIG JIM AND SUAVE RICO INSPECT THE SLINGS FOR EXCESSIVE STRETCH OR ANY TYPE OF INPERFECTION LIKE A TEAR OR FRAY. BOTH RIGGERS CHECK THE SLINGS AND THE TELL TALES AND SEND SMARKEY ON HIS WAY. THE REST OF THE RIGGING CREW IS WAITING AS THE HP SHELL IS UP ON JACK BOLTS. THE HIGH PRESSURE SHELL IS TEN INCHES THICK US STEEL AND WEIGHS A LITTLE MORE THEN ONE HUNDRED AND TWENTY TONS.

TO HAVE THE BIG HOOKS DEAD CENTER, PERFECTLY IN THE MIDDLE OF THE SHELL IS IMPORTANT. EACH LEG OF THE LIFT SHOULD GET TOTE TOGETHER AND EVERYONE WILL BE PAYING CLOSE ATTENTION. EVEN IF THE SHELL IS A LITTLE OFF TO THE RIGHT OR LEFT COULD CAUSE THE FLANGE FACES OF THE PIPES AND THE INLET FLANGES CAST INTO THE UPPER HALF OF THE HIGH PRESSURE SHELLS COULD GET DAMAGED BY SCORING OR GOUGEING. THE RIGGERS MAKE SURE THE METAL TALIC GASKETS ARE REMOVED FROM THE HIGH-PRESSURE SHELL, SO THEY DON'T FALL OFF DURING THE LIFT AND INJURE SOMEONE OR DAMAGE ANY EQUIPMENT. AGAIN, BIG JIM WILL BE THE SINGLE POINT OF DIRECTION FOR THE CRANE OPPERATORS.

THE BIG HOOKS ARE IN POSITION AND THE CREW OF RIGGERS SURROUND THE HIGH-PRESSURE SHELL. THE RIGGERS MAKE SURE THE SLINGS HAVE NO TWIST IN THEM COMING OFF THE BIG

HOOK AND STRAIGHT DOWN TO THE OUTSIDE CORNERS OF THE HIGH-PRESSURE SHELL AROUND THE LIFTING HORNS. BIG JIM GIVES THE SLOW UP, SLOW UP AND THE SLACK OF THE SLINGS EQUALLY IS REMOVED AND GET SNUG THEN BIG JIM WAVES A STOP. THE RIGGING CREW TAKE A CLOSE LOOK AND TRY THEIRE BEST TO MAKE SURE EVERYTHING LOOKS CENTER. YOU DON'T WANT TO COME UP OFF THE JOINT AND HAVE THE SHELL SLIDE INTO THE STUDS DAMAGEING THE STUDS. VERY IMPORTANT TO COME STREIGHT UP FRONT TO BACK, RIGHT TO LEFT.

THE CREW IS STANDING OVER THE TOP OF THE BOLT HOLES AND MAKING SURE THE STUDS STAY CENTER AS THE SHELL COMES UP OFF THE JOINT. BIG JIM SIGNALS SLOW UP, SLOW UP, SLOW UP AND ALL THE STREATCH COMES OUT OF THE SLINGS AND EVERYTHING IS REAL TOTE AND WAVES A STOP. THE RIGGERS TAKE ANOTHER LOOK AT THE WAY THE SLINGS ARE AROUND THE HOOK AND THE LIFTING HORNS ND ALSO FEEL THE TENSION OF EACH SLING TRYING THEIR BEST TO MAKE SURE THE TENSION ON THE SLINGS LOOKS AND FEELS EQUAL. BIG JIM SIGNALS THE CRANE OPPERATORS ANOTHER SLOW UP, SLOW UP AND UP JUMPS THE HIGH-PRESSURE SHELL. BIG JIM SIGNALS ANOTHER SLOW UP AS THE SHELL COMES CLEAR OF THE STUDS THEN SIGNALS A STOP. THE HIGH PRESSURE SHELL BOUNCES AROUND AS THE CRANES COME TO A STOP.

THE HIGH-PRESSURE SHELL IS THE SECOND HEAVIEST LIFT BESIDES THE FIELD OF THE MAIN GENERATOR WITCH WEIGHS ONE HUNDRED AND NINETY-EIGHT TONS. (VOLUME III MAIN GENERATOR) THE RIGGERS LOOK VERY CLOSE AT THE FLANGE FACES OF THE MAIN STEAM LINES AND STEADY THE SHELL. BIG JIM SIGNALS ANOTHER SLOW UP, SLOW UP, SLOW UP

AS EVERYONE HAS THEIRE EYES ON THE FLANGE FACES AND MAINTAINING THE TWO INCHES OR SO CLEARENCE ON EITHER SIDE. NOW THE UPPER HALF OF THE HIGH-PRESSURE SHELL IS ABOUT HALF WAY CLEAR OF THE MAIN STEAM INLET FLANGES. BIG JIM CONTINUES TO SIGNAL VERY SLOW UP, SLOW UP, SLOW UP AND THEN A STOP. THE SHELL BOUNCES AROUND IN THE SLINGS BRIEFLY AS THE RIGGERS WORK TO STEADY IT.

THE TEN INCHES THICK OF THE BOTTOM HALF OF THE UPPER HIGH PRESSURE SHELL IS ALMOST CLEAR OF THE FLANGE FACES AND BIG JIM GIVES ANOTHER SLOW UP, SLOW UP AS THE CRANES ARE COMING UP TOGETHER KEEPING THE LOAD LEVEL. THE HIGH PRESSURE SHELL BECOMES CLEAR OF THE MAIN STEAM SUPPLY PIPES AND LOOKS CLEAR TO THE GENERATOR AND BIG JIM SIGNALS THE STOP. AT THIS POINT THE HIGH-PRESSURE SHELL IS ABOUT THERTY FEET IN THE AIR AND LOOKS LIKE A KLINGON WAR SHIP. BIG JIM SIGNALS THE CRANE OPPERATORS TO BRIDGE ALL THE TO WAY THE OTHER END OF THE DECK AND WHEN THE HIGH-PRESSURE SHELL IS DIRECTLY OVER TOP OF THE UNIT ONE HIGH PRESSURE SHELL, BIG JIM SIGNALS A STOP THEN A TROLLY TO THE LEFT WHERE THE TEAM OF RIGGERS WAIT TO STEADY THE HIGH-PRESSURE UPPER HALF SHELL ONTO THE CRIBBING WHERE IT WILL BE CLEANED AND INSPECTED AND MADE READY FOR REASSEMBLY.

SQUARE HEAD, GOON AND FATTY JOE ARE WALKING THE CENTERLINE AS THE RIGGERS RE DRESS THE HOOK AND GET READY UNSTACK THE UNITS. THE SANDCRABS ARE PREPARING TO BECOME VERY BUSY AS SOON AS THE UPPER HALVES COME OFF THE UNIT, THEY KNOW IT'S TIME FOR THEM TO GET BUSY. SUNNY, JAKE AND YUMYUM ARE GETTING READY FOR FLOW GUIDE AND

DIAPHRAM REMOVAL BY HITTING THE ONE AND ONE EIGTH INCH CAP NUTS WITH RUST BUSTER.

GOON: You ready to row the boat?

SUNNY: As ready as we'll ever be GOON.

YUMYUM: Let's give the rust buster a chance to work first GOONY!

SQUARE HEAD: Remember as soon as we open the top halves we create a whole new FME zone.

JAKE: I don't understand why we can't use the air guns to remove the cap nuts.

GOON: We don't want to strip the heads, or run them off to quick and loose them in the main steam lines.

SQUARE HEAD: LOPEZ has the air bags ready to go once we have the "C" LP unstacked.

THERE ARE FIVE STAGES OF BLADES ON EACH TURBINE WITH THE FLOW GUIDES COVERING EACH STAGE AND FOUR DIAPHRAMS. EACH DIAPHRAM IS INBETWEEN THE STAGES OF BLADES AND ALLOWS THE STEAM TO MAINTAIN THE MOST EFFICIENT PRESSURE AND PATH AS IT PASSES THROUGH THE FLOW GUIDES ONTO THE BLADES. SAME AS THE HIGH PRESSURE AND LOW-PRESSURE CYLINDERS THERE ARE UPPER HALVES AND LOWER HALVES. THE UPPER HALF OF THE NUMBER ONE STAGE OF THE "C" LP TURBINE IS THE FIRST TO BE REMOVED. THE NUMBER ONE STAGE IS IN THE CENTER OF THE TURBINE SPINDLE AND THE LARGEST IN OVER ALL DIAMETER. FROM THE CENTER OUT YOU WILL FIND NUMBER ONE STAGE, SET OF DIAPHRAMS, NUMBER TWO STAGE, LESS IN DIAMETER, SET OF DIAPHRAMS, NUMBER THREE STAGE A LITTLE LESS IN DIAMETER, SET OF DIAPHRAMS,

NUMBER FOUR STAGE, LESS IN DIAMETER, SET OF DIAPHRAMS THEN WORKING YOUR WAY TO THE COUPLINGS IS THE NUMBER FIVE STAGE. EACH STAGE OF THE TURBINE BLADES IS COVERED BY THE FLOW GUIDES. THE DIAPHRAMS ARE SMALLER IN DIAMETER AND TAPER DOWN AS THE BLADE TIPS DIAMETER DECRESSES.

THE INSIDE OF THE DIAPHRAMS AND FLOW GUIDES ARE MANUFACTURED WITH BUILT IN CLEARENCE TO ALLOW THE SPINDLE OF THE FOUR TURBINES TO ROTATE UP TO EIGHTEEN HUNDRED ROTATIONS PER MINUTE. THE RUST BUSTER HOPEFULLY WORKED SOME MAGIC AND THE CREW IS GETTING READY TO REMOVE THE NINE CAP NUTS ON EACH SIDE OF THE "C" LP FOR A TOTAL OF EIGHTEEN ALLEN TYPE CAP NUTS.

JAKE:	SUNNY, YUMYUM come on let's get started. Looks like GOON is in drum beating mode.
YUMYUM:	I'm glad SUNNY is with us he has plenty of beef to put on the breaking bar.
SUNNY:	We have been hard at it and I'm getting tired but remember weebles wobble but they don't fall down.

JAKE TAKES THE INCH AND AN EIGTH ALLEN WRENCH, SHAPED LIKE A FLYERS HOCKEY STICK AND PUTS THE SHORT END INTO THE "C" LP, STAGE ONE, RIGHT SIDE CAP NUT. THE ALLEN WRENCH IS LANYARD TO JAKES WRIST SO IF THE WRENCH SLIPS OFF IT WON'T FALL INTO THE MAIN STEAM SUPPLY LINES. YUMYUM TAKES THE SIX-FOOT-LONG BREAKING BAR AND SLIDES IT OVER THE LONG END OF THE WRENCH. JAKE STANDS OVER THE CAP NUT WITH ONE HAND ON TOP OF THE ALLEN WRENCH AND CAP NUT AND THE OTHER HAND TOTE ON THE BREAKING

BAR. GOON IS STANDING ALONE, LICKING HIS LIPS EXPECTING THE CREW TO PERFORM QUICKLY AND PROFECIENTLY. SUNNY AND YUMYUM STAND BEHIND THE BREAKING BAR AND ON JAKES CALL BEGIN TO PULL THE BAR TO THE LEFT.

JAKE KEEPS HIS HAND OPENED AND ON TOP OF THE ALLEN AND CAP NUT. SUNNY, YUMYUM AND JAKE PULL ON THE BREAKING BAR HARD TO THE LEFT UNTIL THE BAR IS BENDING AND THEN ALL THE SUDDENLY THE CAP NUT BREAKS FREE AND GETS LOOSE. THE CREW REPOSITIONS THE WRENCH AND THEMSELVES AND USES THE BREAKING BAR A FEW MORE TIMES UNTIL THE CAP NUT CAN BE REMOVED BY HAND. THE CAP NUTS HAVE A SIX-INCH THREAD DEPTH AND ARE COUNTER SUNK INTO THE SIDES OF THE FLOW GUIDES AND DIAPHRAMS. EACH CAP NUT HOLDS DOWN THE UPPER AND LOWER HALVES TO THE HORIZONTAL JOINT WITCH HAS A POCKET TYPE FIT BUILT INTO IT FOR THE LOWER HALVES.

THE STUDS THREAD INTO THE BOTTOM OF THE HORIZONTAL JOINT POCKET OF THE LOWER HALF SHELL THEN PASS THROUGH THE BOTTOM HALVES OF THE FLOW GUIDES AND DIAPHRAMS ABOUT EIGHT INCHES ENOUGH TO CAPTURE THE UPPER HALVES AND TORQUE THEM DOWN WITH THE CAP NUTS. ONCE THE TEAM GETS THE UPPER HALF CYLINDER SHELLS OFF OF THE FOUR TURBINES, EVERYTHING ON THE INSIDE IS SUBJECT TO THE HARSH ENVIRORMENT OF THE MAIN STEAM PATH. FATTY JOE IS MAKING SURE THE WORK IS GETTING DONE ON THE "B" LP AS WELL. WITH ROPEY, PEACHES AND POOPDECK PAPPY.

POOPDECK PAP: Don't worry I got this, I don't need the lanyard. I'll keep my hands right where the wrench and breaking bar come together.

| ROPEY: | You sure POOPDECK? |
| PEACHES: | Ok ROPEY he says he's good. |

ROPEY AND PEACHES PULL THE BREAKING BAR HARD TO THE LEFT AND POOPDECK PAPPY HAS ONE HAND ON TOP OF THE ALLEN WRENCH AND CAP NUT AND THE OTHER WHERE THE BREAKING BAR SLIDES OVER THE ALLEN WRENCH. ROPEY AND PEACHES TOGETHER AREN'T AS BIG AS SUNNY AND REALLY HAVE TO GIVE IT ALL THEY HAVE, PAPPALI STYLE. TOGETHER THEY PULL WITH THEIRE FEET ALMOST SLIDING OUT FROM UNDER THEM, THE BAR IS BENDING THEN PEACHES COMES UP WITH A SUDDEN BURST OF POWER AND POP, THE CAP NUT GIVES SUDDENLY. SO SUDDENLY POOPDECK PAPPY IS TAKEN BY SURPRISE AS HIS HANDS JUMP UP OFF THE WRENCH AND HE LOOSES THE WRENCH DOWN INTO THE BOTTOM HALF OF THE "B" LP SHELL. BANG, BANG YOU CAN HEAR IT BOUNCE AROUND AND SLIDE DOWN THE SIDE OF THE SHELL AND DISSIAPEER UNDER THE LOWER HALVES.

POOPDECK PAP:	Oh no, you guys see that. The cap nut broke so quick it took me off guard.
ROPEY:	Hey POOPDECK PAPPY, that's why they want us to use a lanyard and break the nuts manually, instead of the air guns.
POOPDECK PAP:	I hope it didn't find its way into the pipe. I need a flashlight. Maybe I can see it.

FATTY JOE, SHAKING HIS HEAD, HANDS POOPDECK PAPPY A FLASHLIGHT AND POOPDECK PAPPY LOOKS VERY CLOSELY ALONG THE RIGHT SIDE OF THE "B" LP SHELL, UNDERNEATH THE LOWER HALF FLOW GUIDES AND DIAPHRAMS FOR ANY SIGN

OF THE ALLEN WRENCH. PEACHES HEADS TO LOPEZ LAND FOR ANOTHER ALLEN WRENCH SECRETLY TRYING NOT TO LET ANYONE KNOW ABOUT THE DROP.

POOPDECK PAP:	I can see the short end of the wrench under the bottom of the number three diaphragm.
FATTY JOE:	You sure POOPDECK?
POOPDECK PAP:	Yep!
FATTY JOE:	PEACHES you have confirm you see the wrench.
PEACHES:	Yep I can see the wrench FATTY. You're lucky POOPDECK.
FATTY JOE:	POOPDECK PAPPY, you should have had the lanyard on the wrench. If we lost it and couldn't see it we would have to fill out the drop log. Well if we see it we can grab it as we un stack the lower halves.
ROPEY:	Here you go POOPDECK PAPPY a lanyard and another inch and an eight allen wrench.

CORNAL HOGAN IS WATCHING AND COACHING THE CREWS ON THE "A" LP AND HP TURBINES STADING RIGHT BETWEEN THE TWO, NEAR THE A COUPLING. DELCO JOE, DUDDLEY AND K ARE READY TO MOVE TO THE LEFT SIDE OF THE "A" LP TURBINE. JOHNNYOBOTT, JOWEE AND MOE ARE WORKING TOGETHER ON THE CAP NUTS OF THE HIGH-PRESSURE TURBINE FLOW GUIDES AND DAIPHRAMS. THE HIGH PRESSURE TURBINE BLADES, FLOW GUIDES AND DIAPHRAMS ARE LESS IN TOTAL DIAMETER BUT THE CAP NUTS ARE THE SAME AND JUST AS TOTE.

MOE:	OK next nut, were ready.
COL HOGAN:	Come on OBOTT you got to give it your all!

CHARDY: Let me in there HOGAN I can help foot
                 the bar.

COL HOGAN: Go ahead CHARDY but make sure you have
                 nothing in your pockets. I don't want loose
                 Change or anything else falling into the steam
                 chest.

CHARDY MAKES HIS WAY TO THE RIGHT SIDE OF THE HIGH-
PRESSURE TURBINE TO HELP JOHNNYOBOTT AND JOWEE PULL
HARD ON THE BAR WHILE MOE WITH LANYARD ON WRENCH,
KEEPS THE BAR AND WRENCH SECURE ON THE TOP OF THE CAP
NUT. THE CREW IS PULLING HARD TO BREAK THE CAP NUTS
LOOSE. CHARDY STOPS FOR A SECOND THEN SITS DOWN ON
THE JOINT AND BRACES HIMSELF. CHARDY THEN TAKES BOTH FEET
AND PUTS THEM UP ON THE BAR AND USING HIS LEGS PUSHES
OUT HARD IN THE SAME DIRECTION AS OBOTT AND JOWEE ARE
PULLING, MOE HOLDS EVERYTHING STEADY. THE BREAKING BAR
HAS SO MUCH TENSION ON IT THAT ITS READY TO SNAP IN HALF.
IN A ROW BOAT TYPE OF ACTION AND CHARDY FOOTING THE
BAR THE AP NUT FINIALLY BREAKS FREE AND WORKS ITS WAY
LOSE. THE CREW, INCLUDING CHARDY REPOSITION THEMSELVES
IN THE SAME WAY AND WORK THE CAP NUT AROUND TO THE
LEFT.

A FEW MORE TIMES UNTIL THE NUT CAN BE REMOVED BY HAND
AND STORED IN THE PARTS BIN FOR CLEANING AND INSPECTION
MADE RAEDY FOR REASSEMBLY. BIG JIM AND SUAVE RICO RE
DRESS THE CRANE HOOKS FOR UPPER HALF FLOW GUIDE AND
DIAPHRAM REMOVAL. THE SMALL HOOK OF THE UNIT ONE AND
UNIT TWO CRANES EACH HAVE A SINGLE ONE INCH THICK,
BRADED, EYE AND EYE WIRE ROPE HANGING DIRECTLY OFF OF

IT AND ARE READY FOR UPPER HALF REMOVAL. SMARKEY IN THE UNIT ONE CRANE CENTERS THE HOOK DIRECTLY OVER THE TOP OF THE NUMBER ONE STAGE FLOW GUIDE WITH BLAZE AND BIG O TAKEING CARE OF THE RIGGING.

BIG O:	BLAZE, I can handle threading the inch and a half lifting eyes into the dead center, threaded holes and hook up the shackles if you want to handle the signals and landing the upper halves into the racks.

BLAZE:	That makes sense BIG O then we don't half to climbing up and down.

BLAZE SIGNALS SMARKEY OPPERATOR OF THE UNIT ONE CRANE TO LOWER THE HOOK AS BIG O LEANS OVER AND SCREWS THE LIFTING EYE INTO THE TOP OF THE FLOW GUIDE. BIG O HAS A SMALL PINCH BAR WITH A LANYARD TO HELP HIM TURN THE EYE INTO THE TOP HALF UNTIL IT SHOULDERS OUT ONTO THE TOP OF THE FLOW GUIDE, THEN USING A SHACKEL CONNECTS THE LIFTING EYE TO THE EYE AND EYE WIRE ROPE HANGING FROM THE HOOK. BLAZE AND BIG O LOOK CLOSELY TO MAKE SURE EVERYTHING LOOKS ALIGNED STRAIGHT UP AND DOWN PRIOR TO TOTENING EVERYTHING UP WITH A SLOW UP.

BLAZE:	Looks good from here BIG O.

BIG O:	Let me get out from between the flow guides and diaphragms and guide it center, over the studs so we don't booger up any threads. London's Calling GO BIRDS!

STANDING NEAR THE FLOW GUIDE RACK BLAZE SIGNALS SLOW UP, THEN A QUICK STOP AS ALL THE SLACK DISAPEERS. SLOW

UP, SLOW UP AND THE FLOW GUIDE GENTLY COMES UP OFF THE HORIZONTAL JOINT OF THE "C" LOW PRESSURE TURBINE. BIG O LEANS ON THE FLOW GUIDE JUST A LITTLE BIT AND WHILE IT'S SUSPENDED IN THE AIR GUIDES THE TWO TON FLOW GUIDE DEAD CENTER OVER THE STUDS AND MAKING SURE THE FLOW GUIDE DOESN'T COME INTO CONTACT WITH THE TIPS OF THE "C" LP TURBINE. RAPPING RODNEY JOINS BIG O FROM THE OTHER SIDE AND HELPS TO MAKE SURE THE UNIT WILL GET UNSTACKED WITHOUT ANY ISSUES. SLOW UP, SLOW UP AND BY NOW THE RIGGERS ARE FULLY EXTENDED WITH THERE ARMS IN THE AIR, STAYING OUT FROM UNDERNEATH AS THE FLOW GUIDE CLEARS THE TURBINES BLADE TIPS. BLAZE SIGNALS A STOP AND A TROLLY DIRECTLY OVER THE RACK BUILT FOR THE FLOW GUIDES AND SIGNALS A SLOW DOWN, SLOW DOWN, SLOW DOWN AND BRINGS THE NUMBER ONE STAGE "C" LP FLOW GUIDE TO REST IN THE POCKET OF THE RACK. BLAZE REMOVES THE SHACKLE FROM THE LIFTING EYE AND SENDS THE UNIT ONE CRANE BACK OVER TOP OF A DIAPHRAGM THAT SITS IN BETWEEN THE FLOW GUIDES.

RAYRAY CHONG AND THE UNIT TWO CRANE IS IN THE PROCESS OF UNSTACKING THE "B" LP TURBINES FLOW GUIDES AND DIAPHRAGMS. EEFY AND SKIN ARE GUIDING THE FLOW GUIDES AND DIAPHRAGMS AS PAPALUCHI IS SIGNALING THE CRANE AND REMOVING THE SHACKLE WHEN THE FLOW GUIDES AND DIAPHRAGMS ARE DOWN IN THERE SPACIFIC RACKS. ONE RACK IS BIG ENOUGH TO HOLD THE FIVE FLOW GUIDES TOP HALVES ANOTHER RACK WAS FABRICATED TO HOLD THE TOP HALF DIAPHRAGMS. FOR EACH LOW-PRESSURE TURBINE AND THE HIGH-PRESSURE TURBINE THERE ARE FOUR RACKS THAT HAVE BEEN FABRICATED BY BOOGER, OTTO, GONESKI, CARLY

AND LAURY PRIOR TO THE STEAM SIDE OUTTAGE. THE RACKS ARE REUSABLE FOR FUTURE OUTAGES AND ARE A VERY EFFECTIVE WAY TO DELIVER THE FLOW GUIDES AND DIAPHRAGS TO THE CRAB SHACK FOR SAND BLASTING, THEN TO THE WELDERS BOOTH FOR INSPECTION AND WASHOUT REPAIRS. SMARKEY AND THE UNIT ONE CRANE RIGGING TEAM ARE FINISHED REMOVING THE NINE UPPER HALF FLOW GUIDES AND THE EIGHT, SMALLER IN DIAMETER DIAPHRAGMS AND DELIVER THE RACKS TO THE CRAB SHACK.

FROM THIS MOMENT ON THE SAND CRABS WILL BE VERY BUSY. THE SAND CRABS HAVE A HOIST THAT RUNS ON THE EYE BEAM OF THE CRAB SHACK THAT ALLOWS THEM TO LIFT THE DIAPHRAGS OUT OF THE RACK THEN BRIDGE THE HOIST WITH THE DIAPHRAGM OR FLOW GUIDE INTO THE CRAB SHACK WHERE THEY SANDBLAST EACH FLOW GUIDE AND DIAPHRAGM THEN VACUME ALL THE SAND OUT OF THE PARTS AND BRIDGE THE HOIST OUT THE OTHER END OF THE SHACK WHERE THEY CAN LET IT HANG UNTIL A FULL RACK HAS BEEN COMPLETED. THEN THE UNIT CRANE MOVES THE RACK TO THE OTHER END OF THE CRAB SHACK, RE LOADS IT AND TAKES THE FULL RACK TO THE WELDER BOOTH WHERE THE FLOW GUIDES AND DIAPHRAGMS ARE REPAIRED OF ANY MAIN STEAM PATH WASHOUTS AND INSPECTED FOR ANY TYPE OF CRACK OR DAMAGE PRIOR TO REASSEMBLY. THE CENTERLINE TEAM IS CRITICAL PATH DUE TO THE EXTRAORDINARY AMOUNT OF WORK REQUIRED DURING A STEAM SIDE OUTAGE. THEY REMOVE ALL THE TOP HALF FLOW GUIDES AND DIAPHRAGS ALONG THE MAIN STEAM PATH AND LET THEM SIT IN THE RACKS NEXT TO THE UNIT. WHEN THE SAND CRABS ARE READY FOR MORE THE RIGGERS WILL FLY ONE RACK OUT TO THE WELDER BOOTH AND FLY ANOTHER RACK IN.

SUAVE RICO AND BIG JIM HAVE INSPECTED THE KEVLAR, ENDLESS SLINGS TO MAKE SURE THEY ARE UP TO THE NEXT TASK OF REMOVING THE THREE LOW PRESSURE TURBINES AND THE HIGH PRESSURE TURBINE AND SET IN THE ROLLERS FOR A CLEANING, BALANCING AND INSPECTIONS PRIOR TO REASSEMBLY.

BIG JIM: We must remove the "C" LP. turbine first then work our way to the HP. Turbine. That way the sand crabs can start cleaning the "C" LP because that's going to be going back into the machine first.

SUAVE RICO: The slings look good no signs of stress or abuse. Let's dress the hooks BIG JIM.

THE UNIT ONE CRANE LOWERS THE SMALL HOOK AND BIG JIM REMOVES THE EYE AND EYE WIRE ROPE THAT WAS USED TO HOIST THE UPPER HALF DIAPHRAGMS AND FLOW GUIDES. SUAVE RICO SIGNALS A FAST UP THEN TO LOWER THE BIG HOOK. SMARKEY THE CRANE OPPERATOR IS VERY FAMILIAR WITH THE TASK AT HAND AND KNOWS THE NEXT MOVE IS TO REMOVE THE FOUR TURBINES FROM INSIDE THE GIANT ELECTRIC MACHINE. THE BIG HOOK DOSEN'T MOVE AS FAST UP AND DOWN AS THE SMALL HOOK AND TAKES JUST A LITTLE LONGER FOR IT TO MAKE ALL THE WAY DOWN SO SUAVE RICO AND BIG JIM CAN DRESS THE HOOK. THE THREE LOW PRESSURE TURBINES WEIGH OVER SIXTY TONS EACH AND THE HIGH-PRESSURE TURBINE WEIGHS IN AT ABOUT TWENTY TONS. EACH TURBINE WILL REQUIRE BOTH CRANES AND IS A TWO POINT PICK.

ALL HANDS ARE ON DECK FOR THIS EVELOUTION BECAUSE MORE EYES THE BETTER WHEN THE MAIN STEAM TURBINES ARE HOISTED

OUT OF THE LOWER HALVES IT'S IMPERATIVE THE TIPS OF THE BLADES DON'T COME IN CONTACT WITH THE LOWER HALF FLOW GUIDES AND DIAPHRAGMS. BIG JIM AND SUAVE RICO DRESS THE UNIT ONE CRANE WTH A FIFTY FOOT KEVLAR, ENDLESS SLING WITH ONE SIDE OVER ONE SIDE OF THE ANCHOR STYLE HOOK AND WITHOUT A TWIST SO IT LAYS FLAT, THE OTHER SIDE AROUND THE OTHER SIDE OF THE ANCHOR STYLE HOOK.

BIG JIM SIGNALS A UP WITH THE BIG HOOK AND THE CRANE BRIDGES TOWARDS THE UNIT ONE END, OUT OF THE WAY OF THE RIGGING CAGE SO RAYRAY CHONG AND THE UNIT TWO CRANE CAN HAVE THE SAME THINGS DONE TO IT IN PREP FOR THE TWO POINT PICKS OF ALL FOUR MAIN STAEM TURBINES. THE UNIT TWO CRANE MOVES TO A LOCATION NEAR THE RIGGING CAGE AND LOWERS THE SMALL HOOK UNTIL SUAVE RICO CAN SAFELY REMOVE THE EYE AND EYE WIRE ROPE. QUICKLY ACCOMPLISHED BIG JIM SIGNALS THE UNIT TWO CRANE TO WINDE UP THE SMALL HOOK AND LOWER THE BIG HOOK.

THE BIG HOOK MAKES IT DOWN TO ABOUT KNEE HEIGHT AND BIG JIM SIGNALS A STOP. THE FIFTY FOOT KEVLAR SLINGS ARE NOT LIGHT BUT MUCH LIGHTER AND EASIER TO USE THEN THE OLD SCHOOL WIRE ROPES ARE LAID OUT ON THE FLOOR TO MAKE IT EASY FOE SUAVE RICO TO DRESS THE BIG HOOK IN THE SAME MANNER. THE UNIT TWO BIG HOOK IS DRESSED AND BIG JIM SIGNALS IT TO SET UP DIRECTLY OVER TOP OF THE "C "COUPLING. AS SOON AS RAYRAY CHONG AND THE UNIT TWO CRANE BEGINS TO MAKE ITS WAY TO THE "C" COUPLING SMARKEY IN THE UNIT ONE CRANE SETS UP ATOP OF "D" COUPLING.

WITH BOTH BIG HOOKS SET IN POSITION BIG JIM SIGNALS BOTH OPPERATORS TO LOWER THE BIG HOOKS. WITH THE BIG HOOKS CREEPING THEIRE WAY DOWN BIG O TAKES POSITION STANDING ON TOP OF THE LOWER HALF BEARING/ HORIZONTAL JOINT OF THE "D" COUPLING. SKIN ALSO TAKES A POSITION ON THE "C" COUPLING END STANDING ON TOP OF THE LOWER HALF BEARING/ HORIZONTAL JOINT OF THE "C" LOW PRESSURE TURBINE. AS THE BIG HOOKS CONTINUE TO CREEP THERE WAY DOWN THE RIGGERS GUIDE THE SLINGS TO THE OUTSIDE OF THE PEDESTOLS TO KEEP THEM FREE FROM POSSIBLE SNAGS OR OIL. THE BIG HOOKS MAKE THERE WAY TO ABOUT WAIST HIGH ON SKIN AND BIG O AND BIG JIM WAVES A STOP. SKIN AND BIG O EACH REMOVE THE RIGHT SIDE OF THE SLING FROM THE ANCHOR TYPE BIG HOOK, BEND DOWN WITH THE ONE SIDE OF THE SLING IN THERE HAND GO UNDER THE SPINDLE OF THE "C" LP. TURBINE AND HOOK THE SLING TO THE RIGHT SIDE OF THE ANCHOR STYLE BIG HOOK.

TRYING THERE BEST TO MAKE SURE THERE IS NO TWISTS IN THE BASKET STYLE LIFT. BIG JIM GETS A NOD FROM BOTH RIGGERS AND SIGNALS A SLOW UP, SLOW UP, SLOW UP AND THE RIGGERS MANAGE THE SLACK IN THE KEVLAR SLINGS UNTIL THE SLACK DISAPEERS. THEN BIG JIM WAVES A STOP. BOTH SLINGS LOOK GOOD NO TWISTS AND NOW NEED TO BE POSITIONED PERFECTLY IN BETWEEN THE NUMBER FIVE STAGE OF BLADES AND THE BEARING JOURNAL, ABOUT SIX INCHES ON THE INBOARD SIDES OF THE LOWER HALF BEARINGS. THIS IS A CRUCIAL LOCATION BECAUSE AT THESE SPACIFIC LIFTING POINTS, YOU ELIMINIATE THE POSSIBILITY OF CREATING RUN OUT ON THE SPINDLE AND ALSO WHEN YOU GO TO PUT THE TURBINE DOWN IT FITS PERFECT IN THE ROLLERS AND CLEANING STATION.

IF YOU LOWER THE SPINDLES INTO THE ROLLERS AND YOU CAN'T REMOVE THE SLINGS BECAUSE THE THE SLINGS ARE BETWEEN THE SPINDLE AND THE ROLLERS THE TEAM WILL HAVE TO PICK THE SPINDLE UP OFF THE ROLLERS AND PUT IT BACK INTO THE MACHINE READJUST THE SLINGS AND MAKE THE LIFT AGAIN. DURING THE PRE-JOB BRIEF THE CREW WAS REMINDED OF THINGS LIKE THIS PLUS FATTY JOE IS WATCHING. SKIN AND BIG O ADJUST THE SLINGS TO THE SWEET SPOT AND SIGNAL TO BIG JIM. SUNNY, JAKE, YUMYUM, ROPEY, PEACHES, POOPDECK PAPPY, RAPPING RODNEY ARE ALL POSITIONED AROUND THE "C" LP. TURBINE TO MAKE SURE THE TURBINE BLADES ARE GUIDED UP OUT OF THE LOWER HALF WITHOUT ANY DAMAGE. THE RIGGING CREWS ARE CLOSELY WATCHING TO MAKE SURE THE HOOKS ARE DIRECTLY OVER TOP AND CENTER FOR THE PICK. BIG JIM SIGNALS SLOW UP.

ITS IMPORTANT TO REMEMBER BOTH CRANES ARE WORKING TOGETHER AND AT THIS POINT OF THE PICK BIG JIM SIGNALS ARE FOR BOTH HOOKS. SLOW UP, SLOW UP AS THE SLINGS GET TOTE BIG JIM SIGNALS A STOP. SKIN AND BIG O CHECK POSITION OF THE SLINGS AROUND THE INBOARD ENDS OF THE JOURNALS THEN CHECK TOTNESS OF THE SLINGS. THE RIGGING CREW ARE LOOKING VERY CLOSELY AT THE CRANES CABLES COMING OFF THE DRUMS AND MAKE SURE THEY LOOK CENTER AND STRAIGHT TO THE HOOKS. BIG JIM GETS THE LOOK OF APPROVAL FROM THE CREW AND SIGNALS ANOTHER SLOW UP, SLOW UP AND A STOP. THE SLINGS AT THIS POINT ARE VERY TOTE AND LOOK LIKE THE NEXT UP AND THE CRANES WILL TAKE THE LOAD. BIG JIM SCRATCHES HIS CHIN AND SIGNALS ANOTHER SLOW UP, SLOW UP, SLOW UP AND THE "C" LP TURBINE "D" COUPLING END JUST BARELEY RISES UP OUT OF THE LOWER HALF

OF THE BEARING. BIG O WAVES A STOP. BIG JIM THEN SIGNALS RAYRAY CHONG ON THE "C" COUPLING END A VERY SLOW UP, SLOW UP THEN SKIN SIGNALS A STOP. NOW BOTH ENDS OF THE "C" LP TURBINE ARE UP OUT OF THE LOWER HALF OF THERE BEARINGS BY LESS THEN AN EIGTH OF AN INCH. AT THAT EXACT POINT OF THE PICK ITS IMPORTANT THAT THE CREW STATIONED AROUND TURBINE ARE PREPARED TO GUIDE THE SPINDEL BY GENTLY LEANING ON IT WITH THERE HANDS AND POSSIBLY GUIDING IT FROM FRONT TO BACK JUST TO MAKE SURE THERE IS NO CONTACT BETWEEN THE TURBINE BLADES AND THE LOWER HALVES OF THE FLOW GUIDES AND DIAPHRAGMS. THERE IS A VERY SLIGHT BOUNCE DUE TO LUBE OIL RESIDUE, IN THE SPINDLE AS IT BREAKS AWAY FROM THE LOWER HALF BEARINGS THAT ALSO REQUIRES THE ATTENTION OF THE CREW GUIDING THE TURBINE UP OUT OF THE FIT. ITS ALSO OF VITAL IMPORTANCE TO ONLY LIFT THE SPINDLE A VERY LITTLE BIT OUT OF THE LOWER HALF BEARINGS SO YOU DON'T ROLE THE BEARING FACES WITH THE WEIGHT OF THE TURBINE.

BIG JIM SIGNALS A SLOW UP, SLOW UP, SLOW UP AND THE CREW GENTLY GUIDES THE SPINDLE UP OUT OF THE LOWER HALF OF THE TURBINE SHELL. SLOW UP, SLOW UP, SLOW UP AS THE LOWER HALF OF THE TURBINE BLADES MAKE THERE WAY CLEAR OF THE FLOW GUIDES AND DIAPHRAGMS. THE CREW CONTINUES TO GUIDE THE SPINDLE UP OUT OF THE LOWER HALF AS IT WORKS ITS WAY CLEAR BY A FEW FEET OF THE LOWER HALF "C" LP SHELL. SLOW UP, SLOW UP SLOW UP THEN BIG JIM WAVES A STOP. THE "C" LP TURBINE SPINDLE IS NOW UP OUT OF THE MACHINE AND READY TO BE TAKEN TO THE ROLLERS SET UP NEAR THE SANDCRABS BOOTH.

WITH EVERYONE ON THE DECK FAMILIAR WITH THE PROPPER LOAD PATH AND THE CRANE OPPERATORS EXPERIENCE THEY WAIT FOR BIG JIM TO SIGNAL THE CRANES TO BRIDGE DIRECTLY OVER TOP OF CENTER LINE UNTIL THE TURBINE IS DIRECTLY PARALLEL WITH THE ROLLERS NEXT TO THE SANDCRABS BOOTH. BIG JIM THEN SIGNALS THE UNIT CRANES TO TROLLY OVER TOP OF THE ROLLERS. THE RIGGERS ARE WATCHING VERY CLOSELY AS THEY MAKE SURE THAT THE ROLLERS ARE SET PERFECTLY AND THE SLIGS WILL BE ABLE TO BE REMOVED AFTER THE SPINDLE FINDS REST ON THE ROLLERS. EVERYTHING LOOKS GOOD AS BIG JIM SIGNALS A SLOW DOWN, SLOW DOWN, SLOW DOWN AND A STOP. THE JOURNALS OF THE SPINDLE LINE UP PERFECTLY WITH THE POSITION OF THE ROLLERS AND BIG JIM SIGNALS ANOTHER SLOW DOWN, SLOW DOWN, SLOW DOWN UNTIL THE "C" LP TURBINE JOURNALS SET ON THE ROLLERS AND SLACK IN THE SLINGS BECOMES ENOUGH FOR MEMBERS OF THE RIGGING CREW TO CLIMB A LADDER AND REMOVE THE RIGHT-SIDE SLING FROM THE RIGHT SIDE OF THE BIG HOOK.

THE RIGGERS CLIMB DOWN THE LADDER WITH THE SLING IN THERE HAND AND BIG JIM SIGNALS THE CRANES TO TROLLY TOWARD CENTERLINE AND A STOP. THEN WITH THE HOOKS AWAY FROM THE RESTING SPINDLE SKIN TAKES HIS SLING AND PUTS IT BACK ONTO THE BIG HOOK. BIG O HOWEVER REMOVES THE SLING FROM THE LEFT SIDE OF THE UNIT ONE CRANE AND BIG JIM SIGNALS TO RUN THE BIG HOOK UP AND TO LOWER THE SMALL HOOK. THEN BIG JIM SIGNALS TO RAYRAY CHONG TO REPOSITION HIS BIG HOOK OUT OF THE WAY.

BLAZE:	We are going to set up CHARDY'S invention now, so the SANDCRABS can get started on Blasting the "C" low pressure spindle. BIG O I'll send the small hook over the hook goes directly into the center lifting eye of the steel frame of the five-sided curtain hanger.
BIG O:	That's the SIXERS blue thing that drapes over the turbines as the SANDCRABS sand blast them. The five-sided curtain hanger keeps all the sand in under the spindle and minimizes the sand from getting all over the place.
BLAZE:	Yes, BIG O that's it.

BIG O STANDS OVER BY THE CHARDY CURTAIN AND SMARKEY IS QUICK TO RESPOND LOWERING THE SMALL HOOK DOWN TO THE FLOOR SO BIG O CAN HOOK THE CHARDY CURTAIN. BIG O HOOKS THE CHARDY CURTAIN FRAME AND SIGNALS A UP, UP, UP, AND AS THE CRANE LIFTS THE CURTAIN FRAME THE CURTAIN UN FOLD UNTIL THEY ARE HANGING FROM THE FRAME. THE TOP OF THE CHARDY CURTAIN FRAME IS COVERED AND THE LIFTING HOOK IS ON THE OUTSIDE OF THE TOP CURTAIN WHILE THE OTHER FOUR SIDES DRAPE DOWN ABOUT TWENTY-FOOT-LONG. WHILE HANGING FROM THE HOOK THE CHARDY CURTAIN LOOKS LIKE A BIG BLUE BOX. WITH THE SMALL HOOK ABOUT ALL THE WAY UP BLAZE SIGNALS THE CRANE DIRECTLY CENTER OVER THE "C" LP TURBINE WITCH IS RESTING IN THE ROLLERS. THE CHARDY CURTAIN IS NOW DIRECTLY CENTER OVER THE SPINDLE AND SIGNALS A SLOW DOWN, SLOW DOWN, SLOW DOWN UNTIL THE CHARDY CURTAIN DRAPES OVER THE SPINDLE AND THE FRAME COMES TO REST ON TOP OF THE TURBINE. BIG O CLIMBES UP A LADDER AND WITH JUST A LITTLE SLACK REMOVES THE

SMALL HOOK FROM THE CHARDY CURTAIN FRAME AND SMARKEY COMES UP WITH THE SMALL HOOK.

BIG O CLIMBES DOWN THE LADDER AND TAKES THE LADDER TO THE NEXT SET OF ROLLERS. BLAZE IS WORKING WITH SMARKEY AND THE UNIT ONE CRANE TO DRESS THE BIG HOOK WITH THE SAME FIFTY FOOT ENDLESS SLING AND GET THE BIG HOOK POSITIONED OVER THE TOP OF THE "B" LP TURBINE "C" COUPLING. AND RAYRAY CHONG SETS UP OVER TOP OF THE "B" LP TURBINE "B" COUPLING. THE REST OF THE CREW IS IN POSITION AND AWAIT THE BIG HOOKS TO CREEP THERE WAY DOWN SO TOGETHER THEY CAN REMOVE THE "B" LP TURBINE FROM INSIDE THE GIANT ELECTRIC MACHINE'S UNIT TWO "B" LP LOWER HALF SHELL. EEFFY THIS TIME IS STANDING OVER TOP OF THE "B" TURBINE "B" COUPLING JOURNAL AND RAYRAY CHONG IS PARKED THE UNIT TWO CRANE RIGHT OVER TOP AND IS LOWERING THE BIG HOOK. SMARKEY IS QUICK TO POSITION THE UNIT ONE CRANE OVER TOP OF THE "C" COUPLING OF THE "C" LP TURBINE AND BIG O TAKES HIS POSITION STANDING ON TOP OF THE BOTTOM HALF BEARING WITH THE BIG HOOK WORKING ITS WAY DOWN SO THE RIGGER CAN SET THE SLING FOR A BASKET TYPE HOIST.

AS THE BIG HOOKS CREEP THERE WAY DOWN TO A WORKABLE HEIGHT THE TWO RIGGERS EACH REMOVE THE RIGHT SIDE OF THE SLINGS OFF THE ANCHOR STYLE HOOK. THE HOOKS CONTINUE DOWN AND THE RIGGERS GUIDE THE SLINGS TO THE OUTSIDE OF THE LUBE OIL PEDESTOLS. THE BIG HOOKS MAKE THERE WAY DOWN TO WAIST HEIGHT AND BIG JIM SIGNALS BOTH CRANES TO STOP. THE RIGGERS BEND DOWN AND FEED THE FREE END OF THE SLINGS DOWN AROUND THE INBOARD

ENDS OF THE SPINDLES JOURNALS SIX TO EIGHT INCHES FROM THE BEARINGS AND HOOK THE FREE ENDS OF THE SLINGS BACK ONTO THE RIGHT SIDE OF THE BIG HOOKS. BOTH RIGGERS MAKE SURE, THE BEST THEY CAN TO KEEP THE SLINGS FLAT WITH NO TWISTS THAT WAY THE BIG HOOK WON'T HAVE TO COME BACK DOWN FOR ANY ADJUSTEMENTS. BIG JIM SIGNALS THE CRANE OPPERATORS A SLOW UP, SLOW UP, SLOW UP UNTIL THE SLINGS GET ALMOST TOTE TO THE JOURNALS THEN A STOP. BIG O AND EEFFY POSITION THERE SLINGS IN THE PERFECT BASKET AND HOLD THE SMALL AMOUNT OF SLACK OUT OF THEM AS BIG JIM SIGNALS A SLOW UP, SLOW UP THE SLINGS GET TOTE ON THE BOTTOM OF THE "B" LP JOURNALS AND BIG JIM WAVES A STOP.

THE RIGGERS AND THE REST OF THE TEAM ARE SURROUNDING THE TURBINE AS IT SITS IN THE LOWER HALF OF THE "B" SHELLS FLOW GUIDES AND DIAPHRAGMS. THE RIGGERS ARE LOOKING VERY CLOSELY AT THE CRANES CABLES COMING OFF THE SPOOLS ALL THE WAY DOWN TO THE BIG HOOKS TO MAKE SURE THE CABLES ARE STREIGHT UP AND DOWN AND PERFECT RIGHT TO LEFT. AFTER A VERY CLOSE WATCH BY ALL HANDS BIG JIM SIGNALS SMARKEY TO COME DOWN WITH THE BIG HOOK AS BIG O HOLDS THE SLING UP ABOVE THE JOURNAL UNTIL THERE IS ENOUGH SLACK BETWEEN THE BIG HOOK AND WHERE BIG O IS HOLDING THE SLING. BIG JIM SCRATCHES HIS CHIN, WHICH MEANS VERY, VERY, VERY SLIGHT MOVEMENT OF THE HOOK TO TROLLY LIGHTLY TO THE LEFT SIDE AND A FAST WAVE STOP.

THEN BIG JIM THEN WAVES A SLOW UP, SLOW UP AS BIG O LETS THE SLING TOTEN UP UNDERNEATH THE JOURNAL AGAIN THEN WAVES ANOTHER QUICK STOP. EVERYONE ON THE CREW

AGAIN LOOK VERY CLOSELY AT THE CRANE CABLES COMING FROM THE SPOOL TO THE HOOK AND MAKE SURE EVERYTHING LOOKS STRAIGHT UP AND DOWN AND STRAIGHT RIGHT TO LEFT. ITS VERY IMPORTANT SO, WHEN THE SPINDLE COMES UP OUT OF ITS LOWER HALF BEARINGS IT COMES STRAIGHT UP OUT OF THE FLOW GUIDES AND DIAPHRAGMS LOWER HALVES THE BLADES DON'T COME IN CONTACT AND GET DAMAGED ALSO UP OUT OF THE BEARINGS TOGETHER AS TO MAKE SURE THE INBOARD AND OUTBOARD FACE OF THE BABBIT FACED BEARINGS DON'T GET ROLLED OVER.

BIG JIM SIGNALS A SLOW UP, SLOW UP AS THE KEVLAR SLINGS GET NICE AND TOTE UNDER THE INBOARD ENDS OF THE "B' LP JOURNALS THEN A QUICK STOP. AGAIN, EEFFY AND BIG O MAKE SURE THE THE SLINGS ARE SET PERFECT SO WHEN ITS TIME TO PUT THE SPINDLE DOWN ONTO THE SET OF ROLLERS THEY DON'T GET STUCK INBETWEEN THE ROLLER AND THE JOURNAL. THE MACHINISTS ARE STATIONED AROUND THE SPINDLE TO HELP GENTLY GUIDE IT UP OUT OF THE FIT WITHOUT CAUSING ANY DAMAGE. BIG JIM SCRATCHES HIS CHIN AND GIVES THE SLOW UP, SLOW UP, SLOW UP AS THE OVER SIXTY TON SPINDLE BOUNCES GENTLY UP OUT OF ITS LOWER HALF BEARINGS. AS THE SPINDLE COMES UP OUT OF THE BEARINGS THERE IS A SLIGHT OIL RESIDUE WITCH CREATES A SLIGHT BOUNCE WHEN IT BREAKS OFF THE BEARING FACES. THE CREW, HANDS ON, GUIDES THE BOUNCE AND MAKES SURE, THERE IS EQUAL CLEARENCES THEN BIG JIM WAVES A STOP. LOOKS AROUND TO CHECK WITH EVERYONE AND MAKES SURE EVERYTHING LOOKS PERFECT. BIG JIM SIGNALS A SLOW UP, SLOW UP, SLOW UP AND THE "B "LP TURBINE SLOWLY MAKES ITS WAY CLEAR OF THE LOWER HALF SHELL.

THE CREW STEADIES THE SPINDLE TILL THEY CAN'T REACH IT ANYMORE THEN BIG JIM WAVES A STOP. A SINGLE POINT OF CONTACT WHEN MAKING BIG LIFTS IS CRUCIAL FOR THE DIRECTION OF THE CRANES. SINCE THE SANDCRABS ARE STILL BLASTING THE "C" LP BIG JIM JUST HAS TO SIGNAL THE CRANES TO TROLLY LEFT TO THE SET OF ROLLERS SET UP. BOTH CRANES TOGETHER TROLLY LEFT SO THE SPINDLE IS DIRECTLY OVER TOP OF THE ROLLERS AND BIG JIM WAVES A STOP. THEN WAITING TILL THE SLIGHT SWING COMES OUT OF THE CABLES AND THE SPINDLE IS STILL BIG JIM SIGNALS A SLOW DOWN, SLOW DOWN, SLOW DOWN, SLOW DOWN UNTIL THE JOURNALS ARE JUST ABOUT READY TO COME DOWN ONTO THE ROLLERS THEN A STOP. THE RIGGERS TAKE A CLOSE LOOK TO MAKE SURE THE SLINGS WON'T GET STUCK BETWEEN THE TURBINE AND THE ROLLERS AND BIG JIM THEN SIGNALS A SLOW DOWN, SLOW DOWN, SLOW DOWN UNTIL THE "B" LP TURBINE COMES TO REST ON TOP OF THE ROLLERS WHERE IT WILL SIT UNTIL IT GETS SHUFFLED TO THE SANDCRABS CLEANING AREA. THE BIG HOOKS CONTINUE TO COME DOWN AS EEFFY AND BIG O GET CLIMB UP THE FOOTED LADDERS AND REMOVE THE SLINGS FROM THE RIGHT SIDE OF THE HOOKS. THEY REMOVE THE SLINGS FROM THE HOOKS AND BOTH CRANES TROLLY BACK TOWARD CENTERLINE STOP AND LOWER THE HOOKS SO EEFFY AND BIG O CAN PLACE THE LOOSE ENDS OF THE SLINGS BACK ONTO THE BIG HOOKS.

FATTY JOE: Two down, two to go. Next stop the high-pressure turbine because the high pressure spindle needs to get blasted next along with its flow guides and diaphragms. But "C" parts come first.

BIG JIM: Okay FATTY JOE to the high pressure we go.

THE TURBINE REMOVAL CREW MIGRATE TO THE HP. TURBINE WITH RAYRAY CHONG AND THE UNIT TWO CRANE LEADING THE WAY. THIS TIME PAPALUCHI SETS UP ON THE BEARING AND PROVIDES RAYRAY CHONG THE PERFECT TARGET FOR THE BIG HOOK. BIG O MOVES TO THE "A" COUPLING AND AGAIN, SETS UP STANDING ON THE LOWER HALF OF THE BEARING EXCEPT THIS TIME THE CREW WILL BE REMOVING THE HIGH-PRESSURE TURBINE FROM INSIDE THE GIANT ELECTRIC MACHINE.

THE HIGH-PRESSURE TURBINE SPINDLE IS AS LONG AS THE LOW-PRESSURE SPINDLES BUT THE DIAMETER OF THE STAGES IS MUCH SMALLER. REMEMBER THE HIGH-PRESSURE STEAM COMES IN FROM THE FOUR MAIN STEAM SUPPLY LINES THAT ARE FLANGED TO THE TOP RIGHT AND LEFT SIDES OF THE HIGH- PRESSURE SHELL. THE HIGH-PRESSURE STEAM BLASTS THE TURBINE BLADES DIRECTLY SO, THEY DON'T HAVE TO BE AS BIG IN DIAMETER. THERE IS STILL FIVE STAGES OF BLADES FROM THE CENTER OUT COVERED BY FLOW GUIDES WITH THE DIAPHRAGMS INBETWEEN EACH STAGE. THE HIGH-PRESSURE TURBINE DOSEN'T WEIGHT AS MUCH AS THE LP TURBINES SIXTY TONS, BUT STILL REQUIRES A TWO POINT PICK. THE HIGH- PRESSURE TURBINE WEIGHS ABOUT TWENTY TONS. THE CREW TAKES THERE POSITIONS AND UNDERSTANDING THE CRITICALLITY OF THE HOIST TAKE THER TIME AND UNDER BIG JIMS DIRECTION HOIST THE HIGH-PRESSURE TURBINE OUT OF ITS SHELL PAYING VERY CLOSE ATTENTION TO THE BLADE TIPS AND BEARING FACES. THE HIGH- PRESSURE TURBINE COMES UP OUT OF ITS SHELL AND IS TROLLIED OVER TO THE LEFT SIDE WHERE IT IS SET ON TOP OF THE ROLLERS AND WILL SIT UNTIL THE "C" LP IS FINISHED WITH THE SANDCRABS AND SENT TO THE TESTING AND INSPECTION SET OF ROLLERS. WITH THE "A" LOW -PRESSURE TURBINE STILL

AT REST IN ITS LOWER HALF SHELL SUAVE RICO DIRECTS THE
CRANES BACK TO THE RIGGING CAGE WHERE HE WILL UNDRESS
THE BIG HOOK AND DRESS THE SMALL HOOKS TO BE ABLE TO
MAKE TWO POINT PICKS FOR REMOVAL OF THE LOWER HALF
FLOW GUIDES AND DIAPHRAGMS. ONCE THE KEVLAR SLINGS
ARE SAFELY BACK ON THE BIG HOOKS BIG JIM SIGNALS BOTH
CRANES TO HEAD FOR THE RIGGING CAGE.

SMARKEY AND THE UNIT ONE CRANE BRIDGE PAST THE RIGGING
CAGE TO ALLOW RAYRAY CHONG AND THE UNIT TWO CRANE
THE ROOM TO HAVE HIS HOOK REDRESSED FIRST. THE BIG HOOK
MAKES ITS WAY DOWN TO WAIST HEIGHT AND SUAVE RICO
QUICKLY REMOVES THE FIFTY FOOT SLING OFF THE BIG HOOK.
RAYRAY CHONG WINDES UP THE BIG HOOK AND LOWERS THE
SMALL HOOK AT THE SAME TIME. THE SMALL HOOK MAKES ITS
WAY DOWN AND SUAVE RICO TAKES TWO, EIGHT FOOT, EYE
AND EYE WIRE ROPES AND SECURES ONE END OF THE ROPE TO
THE SMALL HOOK MAKING SURE THEY ARE SNAPPED IN BEHIND
THE MOUSE OF THE HOOK. RAYRAY CHONG SEE'S SUAVE RICO'S
HANDS OUT OF THE WAY, COMES UP WITH THE HOOK AND
PROCEEDS TO THE HIGH-PRESSURE TURBINE TO UNSTACK THE
LOWER HALF FLOW GUIDES AND DIAPHRAGMS. SKIN, EEFFY
AND PAPALUCHI ARE WAITING WITH THREADED LIFTING EYES. AS
SOON AS RAYRAY CHONG HEADS FOR THE LOWER HALF OF THE
HIGH-PRESSURE SHELL SMARKEY IN THE UNIT ONE CRANE MAKES
HIS WAY TO THE RIGGING CAGE AND LOWERS THE BIG HOOK.
SUAVE RICO TAKES SPECIAL CARE OF THE FIFTY FOOT SLINGS
AND AFTER REMOVING THEM FROM THE HOOK LAYS THEM OUT
FLAT KNOWING THEY ARE GOING TO BE USED FREQUENTLY
DURING THE MAIN STEAM OUTAGE OF UNIT TWO INSIDE THE
GIANT ELECTRIC MACHINE.

SUAVE RICO THEN DRESSES SMARKEYS UNIT ONE HOOK USING THE SAME EIGHT FOOT, EYE EYE, WIRE ROPES WITH ONE EYE HANGING FROM THE SMALL HOOK AND THE OTHER EYE IN POSITION FOR BEING SHACKLED TO THE LIFTING EYES WITCH ARE BEING SCREWED INTO THE LEFT AND RIGHT SIDES OF THE TOP HALVES OF THE LOWER FLOW GUIDES AND DIAPHRAGMS. JUST LIKE THE TOP HALVES THE LOWER HALVES WILL BE SET IN THE RACKS, IN ORDER FOR THE RIGGERS TO EASILY GET THE FLOW GUIDES AND DIAPHRAGMS TO THE SANDCRABS FOR CLEANING THEN TO THE WELDERS FOR REPAIRS AND INSPECTION. THE UPPER HALVES WERE REMOVED USING A SINGLE POINT PICK WITH ONE SHOULDERED, LIFTING EYE REQUIRED DEAD CENTER TOP FOR REMOVAL. THE LOWER HALVES REQUIRE TWO POINT PICK WITH A THREADED SHOULDERED LIFTING EYE ON THE RIGHT SIDE AND LEFT SIDE.

SO THE CREW AND THE SMALL HOOK CAN LIFT THE LOWER HALF FLOW GUIDES AND DIAPHRAGMS OUT OF THERE FITS IN THE LOWER HALVES OF THE LOW-PRESSURE AND HIGH-PRESSURE SHELLS. THE CREWS WORK DILIGENTLY REMOVING AND STACKING THE PARTS IN THE RACKS UNTIL THE ONLY THING LEFT IS THE LOW- PRESSURE TURBINES AND HIGH- PRESSURE TURBINE LOWER HALF CYLINDERS. WHEN THE SANDCRABS FINISH BLASTING THE "C" LP TURBINE THE RIGGING TEAM WILL BE READY TO MOVE THE "C" LP TURBINE TO THE BALANCING AND INSPECTION ROLLERS AND THEN MOVE THE HP TURBINE TO THE SANDCRABS BLASTING BOOTH THEN HAVE A SET OF ROLLERS FOR THE "A" LP TURBINE TO BE REMOVED AND LOWER HALVES BE UNSTACKED. AS THE FLOW GUIDES AND DIAPHRAGMS WERE BEING REMOVED FROM THE LOWER HALVES OF THE CYLINDERS THE MACHINISTS AND MILLWRIGHTS WITH HELP FROM HAIRYSUE

AND MIC INSTALLED AIR BAGS IN THE MAIN STEAM CROSS AROUND MAIN STAEAM SUPPLY LINES TO PREVENT ANY FOREIGN METERIAL FROM ENTERING THE SYSTEM. WITH THE SANDCRABS BEING VERY BUSY AND THERE WORK CUT OUT FOR THEM SQUARE HEAD BEGINS MAKING HIS ROUNDS. THE VALVE TEAM AND HIGH- PRESSURE CORE INJECTION PUMP TEAM BREAK OFF FROM THE REST OF THE CREW TO BEGIN DISSASEMBLY OF THE VALVES AND A MINOR INSPECTION OF THE PUMP.

THE REST OF THE CREW IS VERY BUSY CLEANING AND INSPECTING PARTS WHILE THE RIGGERS ARE SHUFFLING PARTS IN AND OUT OF THE SANDCRABS BLASTING AREA. THE RIGGERS WILL ALSO BE WORKING WITH THE VALVE TEAMS AS NEEDED IN THE DISSASSEMBLY OF THE NUMBER TWO MAIN STEAM CONTROL VALVE, NUMBER ONE STOP VALVE AND MINOR INSPECTION OF THE NUMBER THREE CROSS AROUND RELIEF VALVE. THE BTPASS VALVES WILL BE WORKED ON BY TWISTED STEELE, GEGGY AND A VERY OLD SPECIALIST NAMED CRANSTONIAN. FOR THE BYPASS VALVES A OVERHEAD CRANE IS NOT NECESSARY, AND THE CREW IS ABLE TO USE CHAINBLOCKS DUE TO THE VALVES BEING MUCH SMALLER AND LESS ACCESSABLE. HIGH- PRESSURE CORE INJECTION TEAM ARE IN THE BASEMENT INSIDE THE GIANT ELECTRIC MACHINE WITH THEIRE OWN OVERHEAD CRANE AND RAPPING RODNEY DOING THE RIGGING. SQUARE HEADS FIRST STOP WILL BE SCHAFFER CITY AND THE ELECTRICIANS WHO ARE REMOVING AND WORKING ON CLEANING THE BRUSHES FROM INSIDE THE DOG HOUSE.

SQUARE HEAD: We got our hands full this time SCHAFFER CITY I'm glad we aren't getting into the Main Generator. There are parts everywhere and we still have to remove the "A" LP turbine, flow guides and diaphragms.

SCHAFFER CITY: Tell me about it SQUARE HEAD parts are flying all over the place. HIGH VOLT, SISTER T, BRUCEY and CUPCAKE are under the belly of the generator working on the clam shells and links. SEESAW had to order all new beveled washers from CHICKEN SALAD KEITH for all the links where they bolt to the clam shells. Once the parts are all clean KRINE DOG and BOW TIE can inspect for wear and cleanliness before reassembly.

SQUARE HEAD: You guys are filthy.

DOC: We are pulling the brush assemblies out of the brush rigging, making sure they are labeled properly, get the dirt and heavy dust out of them, inspecting them and looking for wear.

CAPPY: The brushes barely meet the Main Generator's rotor and collect any phantom voltage and send it to ground. The brushes help protect personnel and equipment. We can only use denatured alcohol.

DOC: The brush assembly gets so filthy because the collector end is air cooled and as the Main Generator rotates and turns the alterex it sucks air in from the turbine deck through the filters in the water-cooled dog house where the brush assembly is located.

SQUARE HEAD:	CARLY and LAURY did the valve installation in the dog house during the last Unit Two MAIN GENERATOR outage so EAGLE ED and ICEMAN can isolate certain sections and replace any instrumentation that may be malfunctioning during the cycle.
SCHAFFER CITY:	CARLEY and LAURY already stopped over and made sure the UNIT I valves, witch have already been done functioned properly. They said they better check now before they get involved with flow guide and diaphragm repairs. Also, SQUARE HEAD I had to send RJ to the HIPCI team with WOBY. ESKIN and ELANE are checking the continuity of the control wires on the vibe probes and thermocouples along centerline with DANDAMAN and SJONG ringing the wires in the control room to make sure of proper locations of the annunciators.
SQUARE HEAD:	Sounds like the electricians also have your hands full. Don't forget DOC and CAPPY are going to be needed on the HIPCI and the valves.

SQUARE HEAD IS ALWAYS PAYING CLOSE ATTENTION TO WHATS HAPPENING ON THE DECK AND EVERYTHING THAT PRETAINS TO THE CREWS SCOPE OF WORK. THE SANDCRABS ARE FINISHED WITH BLASTING THE "C" LP TURBINE AND THE CHARDY CURTIAN HAS BEEN REMOVED. THE RIGGERS HAVE THE BIG HOOKS IN POSITION, LOWERED WITH EEFFY AND BLAZE ON THE FOOTED LADDERS POSITIONING THE THERTY FOOT LONG KEVLAR SLINGS

ABOUT EIGHT INCHES TO THE INBOARD ENDS OF THE TURBINES JOURNALS. BIG JIM IS READY TO SIGNAL THE CRANES SLOW UP, SLOW UP, SLOW UP UNTIL THE SLACK GETS TAKEN UP THEN A STOP. EEFFY AND BLAZE MAKE SURE THE SLINGS ARE POSITIONED PERFECTLY THEN NOD TO BIG JIM TO CONTINUE WITH THE PICK.

A CHOKE TYPE PICK IS NOT REQUIRED IT'S OK TO ALLOW THE SPINDLE TO ROLL IN THE BASKET EVER SO SLIGHTLY. BIG JIM SIGNALS SLOW UP, SLOW UP, SLOW UP AS THE TURBINE SPINDLE LIFTS UP OFF THE SANDCRABS CLEANING STATIONS ROLLERS. WITH THE CRANES WORKING IN UNISON THE TURBINE SPINDLE CLEARS THE ROLLERS AND BIG JIM SIGNALS A STOP. BIG JIM PAUSES AND MAKES EYE CONTACT WITH THE CRANE OPPERATORS TO MAKE SURE THEY KNOW THE TURBINE IS TO BE MOVED TO WHERE CHARDY IS STANDING AT THE TURBINE SPINDLE TESTING AREA. RAYRAY CHONG AND SMARKEY ASSURE BIG JIM OF THE LOAD PATH AND BIG JIM SIGNALS A TROLLY LEFT, TROLLY LEFT, TROLLY LEFT TILL THE TURBINE SPINDLE IS DIRECTLY OVER CENTERLINE THE A BRIDGE TOWARDS THE UNITS MAIN GENERATOR UNTIL IT'S DIRECTLY ON TOP OF THE EMPTY "C" LP SHELL THEN A STOP. BIG JIM THEN SIGNALS A TROLLY LEFT, TROLLY LEFT, TROLLY LEFT AND A STOP. THE RIGGERS ARE STANDING BY AND ALLOW THE SLIGHT SWING TO COME TO A REST. BIG JIM, EEFFY, BLAZE, BIG O AND PAPALUCHI LOOK VERY CLOSE AND MAKE SURE THE SIXTY TON "C" LP TURBINE IS LINEDED UP DIRECTLY OVER TOP OF THE TESTING ROLLERS AND BIG JIM SIGNALS A SLOW DOWN, SLOW DOWN, SLOW DOWN THEN JUST BEFORE THE JOURNALS COME IN CONTACT WITH THE ROLLERS BIG JIM WAVES A STOP.

PAPPALUCHI AND BIG O ARE ON EITHER END OF THE MASSIVE "C" LP TURBINE ATOP THE FOOTED LADDERS AND LOOK CLOSE AT THE LOCATION OF THE SLINGS SO THE SLINGS DON'T GET STUCK BETWEEN THE ROLLERS AND THE JOURNALS OF THE TURBINE SPINDLE. EVERYTHING LOOKS GOOD AND BIG JIM SIGNALS A SLOW DOWN, SLOW DOWN, SLOW DOWN AS THE TURBINE SPINDLE COMES TO REST ON TOP OF THE TESTING AREAS ROLLERS. PAPALUCHI AND BIG O ALLOW FOR THE BIG HOOKS TO COME DOWN ENOUGH SO THEY CAN COMFORTABLY REMOVE THE SLINGS FROM AROUND THE JOURNALS CLIMB DOWN THE LADDERS AND MOVE TO THE HIGH-PRESSURE TURBINES ROLLERS.

THE HIGH-PRESSURE TURBINE WILL BE THE NEXT ONE TO GO TO THE SANDCRABS BLASTING AREA BECAUSE IT TAKES MORE TIME DURING THE REASSEMBLY PROCESS TO PROPERLY STREATCH THE STUDS FOR THE CREW TO ACHIEVE THE TORQUE VALUES ON THE BASKETBALL SIZE NUTS. THE RIGGERS ARE SET UP AHEAD OF TIME AND SUCCESSFULLY RELOCATE THE TWENTY TON HIGH PRESSURE TURBINE TO THE SANDCRABS BLASTING AREA. BIG JIM SENDS RAYRAY CHONG OPPERATING THE UNIT TWO CRANE TO SET UP OVER THE "A" COUPLING END OF THE REMAINING LOW-PRESSURE TURBINE TO BE REMOVED FROM INSIDE THE GIANT ELECTRIC MACHINE. SMARKEY IN THE UNIT ONE CRANE POSITIONS IT OVER TOP OF THE RIGGING CAGE DOOR AND LOWERS THE BIG HOOK TILL SUAVE RICO CAN REMOVE THE THERTY FOOT KEVLAR SLING. SMARKEY RUNS THE BIG HOOK UP AND MAKES HIS WAY TOWARDS THE CHARDY CURTIAN WHERE HE LOWERS THE SMALL HOOK DOWN ALMOST TO THE FLOOR SO SUAVE RICO CAN HOOK THE CHARDY CURTIANS FRAME.

SUAVE RICO HOOKS THE CHARDY CURTIAN FRAME AND SMARKEY GENTLY ALLOWS THE CURTIAN TO UNFOLD AS THE HOOK MOVES UPWARD. WITH THE BOTTOM OF THE CURTIAN BEING CLEARED OF THE HIGH-PRESSURE TURBINE SMARKEY LOWERS THE CURTIAN SO IT DRAPES OVER IT AND COMES TO REST ON THE TOP OF THE SPINDLE. BLAZE THEN CLIMBES UP THE FOOTED LADDER AND WITH JUST ENOUGH SLACK IN THE HOOK DISCONNECTS THE CHARDY CURTIAN RACK THEN CLIMBES DOWN THE LADDER. SMARKEY OPPERATING THE UNIT ONE CRANE IS QUICK TO WINDE UP THE SMALL HOOK AND POSITION THE CRANE OVER TOP OF THE RIGGING CAGE AND AS THE BIG HOOK MAKES ITS WAY DOWN TO A COMFORTABLE HEIGHT SUAVE RICO RE POSITIONS THE THERTY FOOT KEVLAR SLING AND SENDS SMARKEY TO THE "B" COUPLING TO REMOVE THE "A" LP. FATTY JOE AND GOON HAVE POSITIONED THE TROOPS AROUND THE LOWER HALF OF THE "A" LP TURBINE IN PREPERATION OF THE PICK. BIG JIM WADDLES HIS WAY TO THE GOVONOR END OF THE MACHINE AND IS READY WITH THE SIGNALS. EEFFY AND SKIN HAVE MOVED DOWN BELOW THE DECK WHERE THE FLOOR PLUGS HAVE BEEN REMOVED WITH THE VALVE TEAM SO PAPALUCHI WILL TAKE CHARGE OF THE SLING PLACEMENT ON THE "A" COUPLING AND BIG O WILL HANDLE SLING PLACEMENT ON THE "B" COUPLING END OF THE "A" LP TURBINE. PLACEMENT IS CRITICAL DUE TO COMING UP EQUALLY AND WHEN ITS TIME TO PUT THE TURBINE DOWN ON THE ROLLERS THE SLINGS CAN BE REMOVED. SUNNY, YUMYUM, ROPEY, PEACHES, COOL DADDY, JOHNNY OBOTT, JOWEE, MOE AND K ARE ALL POSITIONED AROUND THE SHELL TO MAKE SURE THE SPINDLES BLADES COME UP OUT OF THE FITS WITHOUT MAKING ANY CONTACT WITH THE LOWER FLOW GUIDES AND DIAPHRAGMS.

WHILE MAKING THE LIFT THEY HAVE THE POWER TO STOP THE LIFT WITH A WAVE AT ANY TIME. WITH EVERYONE IN POSITION AND THE BIG HOOKS DEAD CENTER AND STRAIGHT UP AND DOWN BIG JIM SIGNALS A SLOW UP, SLOW UP, SLOW UP AND THE SLINGS TOTEN UP THEN A QUICK STOP. THE RIGGERS LOOK VERY CLOSE TO MAKE SURE THE CABLES COMING OFF THE DRUMS LOOK PERFECT STRAIGHT UP AND DOWN AND SIDE TO SIDE. BIG JIM THEN SIGNALS RAYRAY CHONG IN THE UNIT TWO CRANE OVER TOP OF THE "A" COUPLING TO COME DOWN, DOWN, DOWN TILL THERE IS JUST A SMALL AMOUNT OF SLACK. THEN BIG JIM SIGNALS RAYRAY CHONG TO BRIDGE LEFT, SCRATCHES HIS CHIN BRIDGE LEFT AND STOP PAPALUCHI SENDS BIG JIM A THUMBS UP THEN BIG JIM SIGNALS ONLY RAYRAY CHONG A SLOW UP, SLOW UP, SLOW UP AND A STOP. FATTY JOE, GOON AND SQUARE ARE ALL WATCHING CLOSELY AS REMOVING THE FINAL TURBINE FROM INSIDE THE GIANT ELECTRIC MACHINE IS A MAJOR EVELOUTION. BIG JIM MAKES SURE ALL HANDS-ON DECK ARE READY THEN SCRATHES HIS CHIN SLOW UP, SLOW UP, SLOW UP AND A STOP. PAPALUCHI AND BIG O CHECK THE SLING LOCATION AND THE TOTENESS AND NOD TO BIG JIM. BIG JIM SIGNALS TO THE JACK OF HEARTS SLOW UP, SLOW UP, SLOW UP AND THE "A" LP TURBINE COMES UP OUT OF ITS LOWER HALF BEARINGS PERFECTLY. AS IT BREAKS FROM THE LUBE OIL FILM THE TURBINE BOUNCES EVER SO SLIGHTLY WITHIN THE KEVLAR SLINGS THE CREW SURROUNDING THE SPINDLE CAUTIOUSLY GUIDE THE SPINDLE SO THE BLADES STAY CENTER IN THE FITS OF THE FLOW GUIDES AND DIAPHRAGMS. BIG JIM SIGNALS A STOP LOOKS AROUND FOR ANY CONCERNS THEN SIGNALS ANOTHER SLOW UP, SLOW UP, SLOW UP AND AS THE CREW GUIDES THE SPINDLE UP OUT OF THE LOWER HALF OF THE "A" SHELL IT SOON CLEARS.

BIG JIM CONTINUES WITH A SLOW UP, SLOW UP AND BEFORE YOU KNOW IT THE CREW CAN NO LONGER GET A HAND ON IT. BIG JIM SIGNALS THE CRANES TO TROLLY LEFT, TROLLY LEFT, TROLLY LEFT AND A STOP. BIG JIM ALLOWS THE SWING IN THE TURBINE TO SETTLE AND THEN SIGNALS THE CRANES TO BRIDGE TOWARDS THE GOVONOR END UNTIL THE SPINDLE LOOKS TO BE DIRECTLY OVER TOP OF WHERE THE HP TURBINE WAS RESTING. THE RIGGERS AGAIN LOOK VERY THEROUGHLY AND ALLOW BIG JIM TO CONTINUE. SLOW DOWN, SLOW DOWN, SLOW DOWN AND ANOTHER STOP.

PAPALUCHI AND BIG O CLIMB BACK UP THE LADDERS AS THE SPINDLE HANGS OVER TOP OF THE ROLLERS. MAKING SURE EVERYTHING LOOKS PERFECT BIG JIM SIGNALS A SLOW DOWN, SLOW DOWN, SLOW DOWN AND THE "A" LP TURBINE COMES TO REST ON THE ROLLERS. BIG JIM CONTINUES A SLOW DOWN, SLOW DOWN UNTIL THE BIG HOOKS CAN BE UNDRESSED. PAPALUCHI AND BIG O REMOVE THE RIGHT SIDES OF THE SLINGS AND SLIDE THEM UNDER THE JOURNALS THEN BACK UP ONTO THE HOOKS. SMARKEY AND RAYRAY CHONG MAKE ABSOLUTELY SURE THE SLINGS DON'T GET SNAGGED ANYWHERE AND RETURN BACK TO THE RIGGING CAGE WHERE RAYRAY CHONGS SMALL HOOK WILL BE DRESSED TO MAKE TWO POINT PICKS FOR REMOVAL OF THE "A "LP FLOW GUIDES AND DIAPHRAGMS. SMARKEY WILL HAVE THE UNIT ONE CRANES SMALL HOOK DRESSED TO MAKE FOUR POINT PICKS IN PREPERATION TO HELP THE SANDCRABS SHUFFLE THE RACKS OF FLOW GUIDES AND DIAPHRAGMS AROUND FROM THERE LOCATIONS TO THE SANDCRABS FOR BLASTING THEN TO THE WELDERS AND FITTER BOOTH FOR MAIN STEAM WASHOUT REPAIRS AND INSPECTIONS THEN BACK, NEXT TO THERE FINAL LOCATION IN ADVANCE

FOR REASSEMBLY. SQUARE HEAD, GOON AND FATTY JOE ARE PLEASED AND HAVE TO TIE IN WITH KISSY AND THE JOB PLANNERS TO MAKE SURE THE PAPPER WORK IS KEPT UP.

KISSY: I just got off the phone with the ADMIRAL and he suggested to fire up the grill so he and LOUIE can start cooking the old school Kielbasa.

SQUARE HEAD: We really don't have the man power to let the whole crew off the deck at the same time.

GOON: CORNAL HOGAN and the valve crew is just getting started.

FATTY JOE: WOBY with the HPCI crew just received the clearance to begin the minor work on the high pressure core injection pump.

PSU TOM: We spent time up front to make sure we have any parts on hold if needed. And all the parts are on the job already if we know we are using them according to procedures and history of the work being performed. Hopefully that will help us eliminate any part emergencies and allow the crew to focus on the work.

GENO: I can fire up the grill and bring the cooler full of Kielbasa to the ADMERAL and LOUIE So, everything is ready to go when the crew starts getting hungry.

SQUARE HEAD: Can you also let GEOR'GE the SANDWICH MAKER know the crew will be coming down to eat a little at a time. GEOR'GE also has extra rolls from CONSCHOCKEN and can help LOUIE and the ADMIRAL if required.

KISSY: I think we all know the goal is to keep the work being done on the deck in constant motion. Since we are critical path during the main steam maintenance outage INSIDE the GIANT ELECTRIC MACHINE.

SQUARE HEAD: The electricians are probably going to be the first group to eat they have a good jump on their work and are going to be very busy during reassembly. I have to get back to the deck and see if the crew has any concerns. I 'll let everyone know when they get a chance to stop in to see LOUIE and the ADMERIAL cooking the old school KIELBASA.

ON HIS WAY TO THE DECK SQUARE HEAD MADE HIS FIRST STOP TO CHECK IN WITH MITTS AND AMMO WHO ARE WORKING ON THE ELECTRO HYDRAULIC CONTROL PUMP. THE EHC PUMP MAINTAINS THE PROPPER HYDRAULIC PRESSURE IN THE SYSTEM THAT CONTROLS THE MAIN STEAM CONTROL, STOP AND CROSS AROUND INTERMEDIATE VALVES.

SQUARE HEAD: I'm on my way to make my rounds, we have all been very busy. Just making sure you re on schedule, to see if you need anything and to let you know to grab a bite when your hungry. The ADMERIAL and LOUIE are just getting started cooking the KIELBASA for the crew.

MITTS:	Just a minor inspection here SQUARE remove the head, inspect the lobes of the impeller replace the head gasket, coupling maintenance, mechanical seal inspection, make sure there is no soft foot or alignment issues and no vibration concerns.
AMMO:	We are also replacing the in-line filters of the hydraulic fluid.
SQUARE HEAD:	Ok, let me know if you need anything and when you get a chance grab a bite. WOBY and the HPCI team just got their clearance, that's going to be my next stop.

SQUARE HEAD MAKES HIS WAY TO THE BASEMENT OF INSIDE THE GIANT ELECTRIC MACHINE WHERE USUALLY YOU CAN HEAR A PIN DROP. WOBY AND HIS TEAM OF SPECIALISTS ARE JUST GETTING STARTED WITH THE MINOR INSPECTION. KRINE DOG AND BOW TIE ARE ALSO IN THE ROOM WITH ICEMAN. RAPPING RODNEY IS IN CONTROL OF A CHAIN OPPERATED VALVE THAT WILL ALLOW AUXILLARY STEAM TO FLOW INTO THE SYSTEM WHEN HE IS TOLD TO PULL DOWN ON THE LEFT SIDE OF THE CHAIN. DUDDLEY AND STRANGLEHOLD HAVE SET UP A SERIES OF DIAL INDICATORS TO CHECK FOR AXIAL MOVEMENT DURING START UP AND TO MAKE SURE THE UNIT TRIPS WHEN OVERSPEED IS REACHED. NOSEALEO IS ALSO ON HAND TO REPLACE THE LOCAL LUBE OIL FILTERS AND CHECK OIL PRESSURE GUAGES DURING THE RUN.

WOBY: Perfect timing SQUARE HEAD. NOSEALEO has just finished replacing the lube oil filters and ICEMAN is ready to give us the three count and let the Aux. steam into the steam chest of the turbine that drives the core injection pump.

KRINE DOG: The core injection pump is critical for the safety and well being of the public and plant workers. The pump floods the boiler with water continually to prevent any type of melt down inside the boiler in case of any emergency.

STRANGLEHOLD: We have a Kingsbury thrust bearing on the outboard end of the turbine and the coupling has been inspected, cleaned and greased.

RAPPING RODNEY: I'm on the job manning the valve chain open it slow or away it will go. Let the shell warm a little at a time the whistling steam is starting to scream

EVERYONE HAS HEARING PROTECTION, SAFETY GLASSES, HARD HATS AND GLOVES ON IT USED TO BE THE QUITEST PLACE INSIDE THE GIANT ELECTRIC MACHINE BUT NOT ANYMORE. WITH BOTH ARMS IN THE AIR ICEMAN SIGNALS TO RAPPING RODNEY FULL OPENED AND RAPPING RODNEY PULLS DOWN ON LEFT SIDE OF THE CHAIN ONE HAND AFTER THE OTHER UNTIL THE VALVE IS FULL OPENED. IT'S TO LOUD FOR DIALOUG RIGHT NOW AS THE AUX STEAM COMES FLOWING INTO THE STEAM CHEST OF THE TURBINE. NOSEALEO HAS A CLOSE EYE ON THE GAGES AND THE TURBINE CREEPS UP TO OPPERATING PRESSURE.

CHECKING A WATCH AND COMMUNICATING WITH EAGLE ED IN THE CONTROL ROOM ICEMAN AGAIN RAISES HIS HAND AND SIGNALS THREE, TWO, ONE AND AS BOTH HANDS FALL TO HIS SIDES THE MINI ROAR OF THE TURBINE KICKS IN. WITHIN TWO BLINKS OF AN EYE THE PUMP IS AT FULL CAPACITY AND YOU CAN HEAR THE WATER FLOWING THROUGH THE TWELVE INCH PIPES. EVERYONE IN THE ROOM HAS SOMETHING TO BE RESPONSIBLE FOR LEAKS, STEAM SUPPLY, PUMP SPEED, INTAKE AND DISCHARGE PRESSURE OF THE PUMP AND LUBE OIL PRESSURE FOR THE PUMP AND TURBINE BEARINGS. SQUARE HEAD IS ON THE MOVE AND HEADS FOR THE BACK STEPS, UP ABOUT 16 FLIGHTS OF STAIRS AND POPS OUT ON THE DECK OF UNIT I, THE OPPERATING UNIT INSIDE THE GIANT ELECTRIC MACHINE WHERE THE UPPER HALF CYLINDERS AND OUTTER SHELLS ARE BEING CLEANED AND INSPECTED. THE HPCI TESTING AND MINOR MAINTENANCE WORK CONTINUES, A RUN WHICH COULD LAST AN HOUR OR SO. SQUARE HEAD WALKS ALONG SIDE THE OPPERATING UNIT I UNTIL HE GETS TO THE "C" LOW PRESURE TURBINE INNER CYLINDER TOP HALF LOOKS AROUND AND SEES KUBBY, KOCHY AND MARTY. THE CREW HAS FULL HEARING PROTECTION, HARDHATS WITH SAFETY GLASSES AND FULL FACE SHIELDS. UNIT I IS AT FULL POWER AND IT'S VERY LOUD WORKING NEXT TO THE MACHINE.

SCHAFFER CITY IS ALSO CHECKING IN WITH THE CREW.

MARTY: Good to see you. We are removing the jack bolts, cleaning and chasing the threads.

SCHAFER CITY: Are you able to see inside the shell for a thorough inspection? How about if you have to use a wire wheel?

KOCHY:	YEA, YEA we're fine the electricians set us up for success. We are just going to have get the cylinder picked so we can re arrange the cribbing and make sure the upper half joint of the CLP turbine is ready for reassembly.
SQUARE HEAD:	Once we start going back together we are going to need the HP turbine cylinder right after the CLP upper half cylinder
MARTY:	Ok then the BLP and the ALP cylinders. GOT it.
SQUARE HEAD:	Most of your work is going to be on the high-pressure turbine shell so OTTO and BOOGER are going to help. Until then they are fixing flow guides and diaphragms. Let us know if you need anything. Work safe.

SQUARE HEAD AND SCHAFER CITY WALK ALONG SIDE THE OPPERATING UNIT I, PAST THE UNIT ONE MAIN GENERATOR, PAST THE LIFTING HATCH, PAST THE UNIT TWO MAIN GENERATOR TO THE "D" COUPLING, CENTERLINE. WORKING ON THE OIL SIDE IS YUMYUM AND ON THE STEAM SIDE IS SUNNY. SCHAFER CITY STOPPED TO TALK WITH ESKIN AND CLANE TO MAKE SURE THEY WERE OK WITH THE BEARINGS VIBRATION PROBES, THERMOCOUPLES AND CONTROL ROOM WIRING WITH DANDAMAN AND JONG. SQUARE HEAD IS STANDING AT" D" COUPLING STARING DOWN INTO THE LOWER HALF OF THE LOW-PRESURE TURBINE SHELL.

SQUARE HEAD:	How does the packing look SUNNY?

SUNNY:	As far as I can see it looks pretty good SQUARE HEAD. I have to check a few elevation pads, though and let KRINE DOG crunch the information.
SQUARE HEAD:	Seems like your off to a good start SUNNY, careful in there the packing is sharp and no Dropsies into the steam lines. Remember FME. Also, don't forget to grab a bite to eat.
YUMYUM:	We're getting pretty hungry, we all don't carry food around with us like BRUCEY.
SQUARE HEAD:	How does the oil side look YUMYUM? The bearing face and oil seals.
YUMYUM:	So far so good SQUARE HEAD we are going to use the laser to set the lower half bearings. I still need to get some measurements to. Like the journals of the turbine.
SQUARE HEAD:	Don't forget to grab a bite, before you know it the lower half diaphragms are going to be ready to get put back into the unit. Let me go see how the BLP is going.

SQUARE HEAD CONTINUES TO MAKE THE ROUNDS WITH THE NEXT STOP THE "B" LOW PRESSURE TURBINE SHELL AGAIN LOOKING DOWN INTO THE STEAM SIDE SHELL EXCEPT THIS TIME K IS WORKING THE ELEVATION PADS AND INSPECTION OF THE LOWER HALF STEAM SIDE PACKING. DELCO JOE IS WORKING ON THE OIL SIDE INSPECTION OF UPPER, LOWER HALF BEARING INSPECTIONS, OIL SEALS AND DEFLECTORS.

SQUARE HEAD:	How's things look K? Do you notice any signs of rubbing or wear of the packing?

K: I had to comb a few spots out but nothing serious. The packing looks good SQUARE HEAD. I have to make sure when the lower half flow guides and diaphragms start coming in they have a sound metal to metal fit.

SQUARE HEAD: Don't forget to grab a bite to eat the ADMIREAL, LOUIE, AND JIMMY O are on the grill with GOREGE the sandwich maker also opened for business.

DELCO JOE: My oil side inspection is going good GOON has been checking up on us.

SQUARE HEAD: As we begin to stack the unit SUAVE RICO is going to have the laser set to double check our lower half elevations. K keep up the good work.

SQUARE HEAD PUTS HIS HEAD DOWN AND HEADS FOR THE ALP LOWER HALF TURBINE SHELL. PEACHES IS WORKING THE STEAM SIDE AND ROPEY IS ON THE OIL SIDE INSPECTION. FATTY JOE IS ALSO STANDING BY.

SQUARE HEAD: We seem to be short handed on centerline FATTY JOE.

FATTY JOE: There's a lot going on SQUARE HEAD. The valve work, High pressure core injection pump, cleaning inspections of turbines, flow guides, diaphragms...

ROPEY: Ok already we get the point plus were all coming and going from break and a bite to eat.

PEACHES: The STEAM SIDE inspection is moving right along and the horizontal joint has been cleaned and stoned to remove any high spots around the bolt heads to help assure full and proper tightness.

SQUARE HEAD ONLY HAS TO TURN AROUND 180 DEGREES AND LOOK AT THE PROGRESS OF THE HIGH PRESURE TURBINE TEAM. JOHNNY OBOTT, JOWEE AND MOE ARE STONEING THE JOINT MAKING SURE THAT WHEN THE TOP HALF OF THE HIGH PRESURE TURBINE SHELL RETURNS FOR REASSEMBLY THERE IS NO RAISED FACE ANY WHERE ON THE JOINT.

MOE: Hey SQUARE HEAD, our oil side inspection is complete and we're ready for the laser to shoot the train's bearings.

SQUARE HEAD: Soon enough MOE, SUAVE RICO is the set-up guy.

FATTY JOE: SQUARE HEAD, I talked to the riggers and they have been able to sneak out for a bite and keep the job going. BIG JIM says they are very busy moving parts around for the SANDCRABS and the valve work.

SQUAREHEAD: Plus, RAPPING RODNEY is on the HPCI pump job. Like I said FATTY seems like we're a little shorthanded on centerline.

FATTY JOE: As jobs end more hands will become available for the reassembly process.

SQUARE HEAD: Let me go see how the valve gang is making out.

SQUARE HEAD IS MOVING RIGHT ALONG TO THE HOLE IN THE FLOOR WITH THE HANDRAIL AROUND IT LOCATED AT THE TOP OF CONTROL VALVE NUMBER TWO, CORNAL HOGAN IS THERE TO GREET HIM. JUST THEN THE UNIT TWO CRANE WITH RAYRAY CHONG OPPERATING WITH EEFFY AND SKIN GUIDING THE REBUILT CONTROL VALVE DOWN INTO THE OPENED VALVE BODY. JAKE, BIG MIKE AND MR URRIGHT ARE THERE TO GUIDE THE VALVE ASSEMBLY DOWN INTO THE VALVE BODY THEN HOOK UP THE LINKAGE. THE ELECTRICIANS DOC AND CAPPY WILL BE ALONG LATER TO TEST THE CONTROL AND SIGNAL WIRES THAT TERMINATE TO THE HYDRAULIC ACCTUATOR THAT CONTROLS THE STROKE OF THE VALVE. SKIN IS IN THE HOLE WITH THE VALVE GANG AND EEFFY IS STANDING ON DECK BY THE HANDRAIL. CONTROL VALVE NUMBER TWO ASSEMBLY IS HANGING FROM THE SMALL HOOK BEING LOWERED DOWN INTO THE HOLE.

CORNAL HOGAN: Don't forget the new gasket and make sure you measure it first, I got to remind you all the time. Use plenty of seize!

SQUARE HEAD: Ok CORNAL HOGAN I think they got it.

CORNAL HOGAN: No, no SQUARE HEAD I got to remind the gang all the time. We don't want to install a rebuilt valve and forget the gasket.

EEFFY SIGNALS RAYRAY CHONG AS HE LOOKS DOWN IN THE HOLE AT SKIN SLOW DOWN, SLOW DOWN SLOW DOWN THEN A STOP. THE BOLTS OF THE VALVE BONNET HAVE BEGUN TO PASS THROUGH THE HEAD AND ANOTHER SLOW DOWN, SLOW DOWN, SLOW DOWN AND THE UNIT TWO, NUMBER TWO CONTROL VALVE IS NOW IN PLACE. SKIN UNHOOKS THE RIGGING AND THE UNIT TWO CRANE GOES TO THE NEXT JOB.

SQUARE HEAD: How are the other valve jobs going CORNAL HOGAN?

CORNAL HOGAN: BUTCH and GOOGLY have completed the blue check on the number one MAIN STOP VALVE and are currently getting ready to torque up the valve bonnet. GEGGY and TWISTED STEELE are testing the two rebuilt bypass assembly and will soon be ready to rejoin the centerline crew.

SQUARE HEAD: Make sure you let your crew eat something COMANDER HOGAN and keep up the good work. Don't forget you gang still has a minor inspection on III CIV to work on.

CORNAL HOGAN: BUTCH, GEGGY, TWISTED STEELE and GOOGLY are going to be on that as soon as we can.

SQUARE HEAD: I have to check in on the fitters and repair techs next. Your valve gang needs to get the crane work done because it's almost time to start the full rebuild of the STEAM SIDE of the unit II main steam turbine INSIDE the GIANT ELECTRIC MACHINE.

SQUARE HEAD NOW IS HEADING TO THE WELD SHACK THAT WAS TEMPORALEY BUILT FOR A SAFE PLACE TO MAKE WASHOUT REPAIRES ON THE FLOW GUIDES AND DIAPHRAGMS. GOON IS STANDING BY WATCHING THE REPAIRES TAKE PLACE AND MAKING SURE THE SANDCRABS ARE BLASTING THE EQUIPMENT IN THE PROPER REBUILD ORDER. COOL EARL, CARLEY, LAUREY, BOOGER AND OTTO ARE VERY BUSY MAKING REPAIRES AND WORKING CLOSELY WITH THE UNIT ONE CRANE TEAM WITH

SMARKEY OPPERATING AND BLAZE, BIG O AND BIG JIM SHUFFLING PARTS BACK AND FORTH FROM THE SANDCRABS TO THE WELDERS AND SOON BACK INTO THE STEAM CHEST OF THE MAIN STEAM TURBINE. GOON SCRATCHES HIS CHIN THEN LICKS HIS LIPS.

GOON:	Looks like the SANDCRABS and the welders are finishing up with the lower half flow guides and diaphragm repairs for both the CLP and the HP.
SQUARE HEAD:	Oil side inspections and steam packing work is also finished up. Just waiting on TIE BOW and KRINE DOG to finish crunching the numbers on the bearing elevations. Du eat GOON?
GOON:	Yeah, we snuck down early before we got to busy. We might sneak back out for another quick bite while the riggers and machinists start to restack the unit.
SQUARE HEAD:	Hurry back then we need you to stay ahead. And FME.

THERE ARE PARTS BEING CLEANED AND INSPECTED EVERYWHERE. THERE ARE SO MANY PARTS IT'S HARD TO WALK AROUND. SQUARE HEAD, GOON AND SCHAFFER CITY BRIEFLY LEAVE THE DECK TO CATCH UP WITH KRINE DOG AND TIE BOW TO DISCUSS NUMBERS AND GRAB A BITE FROM GEOR'GE THE SANDWICH MAKER. FATTY JOE AND BIG JIM ARE STANDING BY WAITING TO START DELIVERING THE CLEANED AND INSPECTED RACKS OF LOWER HALF FLOW GUIDES AND DIAPHRAGMS BACK TO THERE FITS INSIDE THE STEAM CHESTS. THE SANDCRABS HAVE COMPLETE THE WORK ON THE HP TURBINE AND IS READY TO

SWAP OUT THE HP TURBINE FOR THE B LP. THE RIGGERS AND MACHINISTS ARE STILL ON STANDBY. KISSY, GENO AND PSU TOM ARE IN THE OFFICE TRYING THERE BEST TO KEEP UP WITH ALL THE PAPERWORK FROM ALL THE PARTS INSPECTIONS AND PARTS REPLACEMENTS. NOW THE VALVE WORK IS FINISHING UP BUTCH CAN ALSO HELP WITH THE PAPER WORK. SQUARE HEAD, GOON AND SCHAFFER CITY MAKE IT BACK TO THE OFFICE TO FIND OUT WHERE KRINE DOG AND TIE BOW ARE. THE CLOCK IS TICKING AND CENTERLINE, MAIN STEAM TURBINE UNIT TWO, INSIDE THE GIANT ELECTRIC MACHINE REMAINES CRITICAL PATH.

SQUARE HEAD: I don't think the boiler makers are going to help us this time.

PSU TOM: No not this time SQUARE HEAD. Looks like were critical path.

GENO: CHICKEN SALAD KEITH said to let him know if we need any emergency parts. The whole station wants to pitch in and help out. Anything they can do to help.

SQUARE HEAD: We really need to get the numbers and the clearances on the bearings. The bearings were all set precisely according to the laser.

KISSY: TIE BOW and KRINE DOG have already signed off on the bearing elevations and most of the parts inspections are ending. Oh, and WOBY just signed off on the second successful HPCI run. Minor adjustments and hopefully, another successful run and the HPCI crew can join centerline.

GOON: The sooner the SANDCRABS are finished blasting everything the better. They always do a good job cleaning up after themselves.

SQUARE HEAD: We are moving along but I still don't see the light at the end of the tunnel.

BUTCH: The valve work is starting to close up. Even the BYPASS valves with TWISTED STEELE and GEGGY are closed out. Just waiting on EAGLE ED and ICEMAN to test the stroke. JAKE just finished packing the stuffing box and torqueing the gland follower to the control valve number two.

JUST THEN CORNAL HOGAN SWINGS OPENED THE OFFICE PERSONEL DOOR DRESSED IN FULL SAFETY GEAR INCLUDING HARD HAT AND SAFTEY GLASSES, HEARING PROTECTION.

C O R N A L HOGAN: BIG MIKE, MR. URRIGHT and GOOGLY had to adjust the number three cross around relief valve. They had to de tension the pushrod and then start from scratch and make sure they finished with proper over travel. And coupling maintenance torque check.

BUTCH: That's great I can catch up on the paper work.

SQUARE HEAD: YO CORNAL HOGAN take out the ear plugs and please stop being so loud you're not on the deck; hey dja check in on MARTY, KOCHY and KUBBY lately?

KISSY:	They took a nice long break just to give them rest from all the noise. They are almost finished cleaning and inspecting the four upper half cylinders. KRINE DOG spent time with them inspecting the upper half of the high-pressure shell. Especially the horizontal joint. MITTS and AMMO are also finishing up on the electro hydraulic pump (EHC) and are ready to tie in with KULPURNICUS on the front standard.
PSU TOM:	How about HUMMER? Anyone see HUMMER?
KISSY:	HUMMER is in contact with EAGLE ED and is available to plan jobs incase something acts up with the operating unit. With SKIN helping the valve crew he is very busy.
SQUARE HEAD:	Speaking of the crew KISSY, I'm heading back to the deck to check in with BOOGER.
KISSY:	Dja eat something SQUARE?
SQUARE HEAD:	In my travels I've made it a point to eat and check up on LOUIE'S attention to detail. Make sure LOUIE'S grilling the kielbasa correctly.

THE STEAM SIDE OUTAGE OF THE MAIN STEAM TURBINE INSIDE THE GIANT ELECTRIC MACHINE REMAINS CRITICAL PATH. THE CREW REMAINS COMMITTED TO PRODUCEING HIGH QUALITY WORK, SAFELY. THE CREW HAS BEEN WELL TRAINED TO UNDERSTAND THE IMPORTANCE OF THE LONG TERM SUCCESS AND A BREAKER TO BREAKER RUN OF THE CYCLE. THE CREW KNOWS THE IMPORTANCE TO ATTENTION TO DETAIL AND UNDERSTAND THAT WHEN THE STEAM HITS THE TURBINES AND THE MACHINE STARTS TO WIND UP ANY ISSUES WILL STICK OUT LIKE A SORE THUMB AND EAGLE ED AND THE ADMIREAL WILL HAVE TO START ALL OVER AGAIN.

THE GIANT ELECTRIC MACHINE WILL BE OFF LINE AND UNABLE TO PROVIDE SAFE, RELIABLE, CLEAN ENERGY TO THE GRID. SQUARE HEAD QUICKLY MAKES HIS WAY BACK TO THE DECK. SQUARE HEADS FIRST STOP THIS TME AROUND IS THE WELDERS AND REPAIR TECHS WORKING ON THE DIAPHRAGMS AND FLOW GUIDES.

SQUARE HEAD: (Waiving his arms) BOOGER, BOOGER!

BEING INSIDE THE WELDERS BOOTH AND NOT WANTING TO GET IN THE WAY SQUARE HEAD TRIES TO GET BOOGERS ATTENTION. OTTO, CATCHES SQUARE HEAD OUT OF THE CORNER OF HIS EYE AND TAPS BOOGER ON HIS SHOULDER, TOGETHER THEY RAISE THEIR WELD SHIELDS AND WALK OVER TO TALK TO SQUARE HEAD.

SQUARE HEAD: Nice dew rags, how are you making out?
BOOGER: Were very busy, lucky to have the time to grab a bite.
OTTO: I'm glad we set the booth up under the box beam crane, it allows us to pick up the flow guides and diaphragms out of the rack for more thorough inspections and repairs.

BOOGER:	CARLEY and LAURY have been very attentive in fixing any areas the steam has washed out along the steam path's upper and lower half flow guides and diaphragms. OTTO and I are also helping with the wash outs then the high-speed grinding that brings the repairs to our satisfaction. COOL EARL and GONESKI are making sure to perform a sound foreign material check and making sure the flow guides and diaphragms are being put back into the proper rack for delivery and reassembly of the steam chest.
OTTO:	A lot of action SQUARE HEAD, but we are making progress all of the lower half flow guides and diaphragms have been delivered next to the steam chest and we are finished with the upper halves of the "HP". Turbine and the "C" LP. Turbine. And the SANDCRABS are non-stop getting the work done.
SQUARE HEAD:	A great example of quality to the line.

SQUARE HEAD TAKES A MOMENT TO LOOK AROUND AND ASSESSES THE JOB. THE LOWER HALF DIAPHRAGMES AND FLOW GUIDES HAVE BEEN REINSTALLEDAND TORQUEDTO THE PROPPER TORQUE VALUE ALSO THE "C" LP. TURBINE SPINDLE HAS ALSO BEEN REINSTALLED INTO THE STEAM CHEST. SQUARE HEAD SEES THE RIGGING CREW TAKING A PICK OF HIGH PRESURE TURBINE FROM INSPECTION AREA ROLLERS WHERE CHARDY HAS PERFORMED A VERY THEROUGH INSPECTION USING ULTRA SOUND AND OTHER MODERN TECHNOLOGY LOOKING FOR ANY SIGNS OF CRACKS IN THE BLADES OF THE ROTOR PRIOR TO RE ASSEMBLY AND AFTER IT HAS BEEN CLEANED BY THE SANDCRABS.

BIG JIM HAS THE RIGGING TEAMS ATTENTION AS THE PICK OF THE HIGH- PRESSURE TURBINE CONTINUES. SMARKEY IN THE UNIT ONE CRANE IS PARKED DIRECTLY OVER THE TOP OF THE INBOARD END OF THE HIGH PRESURE TURBINE AND RAYRAY CHONG AND THE UNIT TWO CRANE IS PARKED DIRECTLY OVER THE TOP OF OUTBOARD END OF THE HIGH PRESURE TURBINE. BOTH HOOKS ARE DRESSED WITH FIFTY FOOT ENDLESS, KEVLAR SLINGS AND THE SPINDLE HAS BEEN RETURNED TO A TWELVE O CLOCK POSITION SO, WHEN THE SPINDLE IS PUT BACK INTO THE STEAM CHEST THE COUPLING BOLT HOLES RETURN TO THE AS FOUND POSITION. BIG JIM SIGNALS SLOW DOWN, SLOW DOWN, SLOW DOWN AS THE HOOKS COME DOWN TOGETHER.

ON THE INBOARD END OF THE TURBINE BIG O IS ON THE LADDER MAKING SURE, OF THE PROPPER SLING LOCATION AROUND THE JOURNAL OF THE SPINDLE AND ON THE OUTBOARD END PAPALUCHI IS DOING THE SAME THING. SLING LOCATION PRIOR TO MAKING THE PICK IS CRITICAL DUE TO PLACEMENT OF THE SPINDLE INSIDE THE LOWER HALF BEARINGS. IF THE SLINGS ARE NOT IN THE RIGHT LOCATIONS YOU CAN'T PUT THE SPINDLE DOWN INSIDE THE BEARINGS BECAUSE THE SLINGS WILL BE IN THE WAY. A BASKET IS REQUIRED TO ALLOW THE SPINDLE TO ROLL A LITTLE WHILE IT'S BEING REINSTALLED. THE SLINGS ARE IN PLACE AS BIG JIM NOW SIGNALS A SLOW UP, SLOW UP, SLOW UP AS THE SLACK IN THE SLINGS DISAPPEARS. WITH THE SLINGS ALMOST TOTE BIG JIM WAVES HIS ARMS FOR A QUICK STOP THE REST OF THE RIGGING CREW LOOKS VERY CLOSELY AND MAKES SURE THE CRANES ARE LINED UP TO ASSURE A STRAIGHT PICK. BIG JIM AND THE CREW FEEL COMFORTABLE AND ARE READY TO PROCEED. SLOW UP, SLOW UP, SLOW UP AS THE SLACK IS GONE AND THE HIGH- PRESSURE TURBINE COMES UP OFF THE

TESTING, INSPECTION ROLLERS. WITH THE LOAD PATH CLEAR AND THE CREW WAITING AT THE STEAM CHEST. BIG JIM SIGNALS THE CRANE OPPERATORS ANOTHER SLOW UP, SLOW UP, SLOW UP UNTIL THE SPINDLE IS CLEAR OF THE ROLLERS THEN WITH A LONG ARM AND A POINTY FINGER BIG JIM POINTS TO THE HIGH PRESURE STEAM CHEST AS THE CRANES RESPOND WITH A STEADY, EQUAL SPEED TO THE LOCATION OF THE REST OF THE TEAM WAITING TO EASE THE SPINDLE BACK TO IT'S LOCATION. SQUARE HEAD MAKES HIS MOVE TO THE HIGH PRESURE TURBINE AREA WHERE FATTY JOE AND GOON ARE STANDING BY WATCHING THIS EVELOUTION.

THE HIGH PRESURE TURBINE IS IMPORTANT TO GET AHEAD OF BECAUSE IT TAKES AWHILE TO STREATCH THE UPPER HALF CYLINDER BOLTS, THEY ARE SO LARGE IN DIAMETER AND HAVE A HIGH TORQUE VALUE. MOE, K, JOEWEE AND JOHNNYOBOTT ARE STANDING BY TO GENTLY GUIDE THE HP SPINDLE BACK TO IT'S POSITION. THE RIGGING CREW FOLLOWS THE SPINDLE AND TAKES A POSITION AROUND THE STEAM CHEST. THE LOWER HALF DIAPHRAGMS AND FLOW GUIDES HAVE ALREADY BEEN PROPERLY LOCATED, LASER ALLIGNED FOR ELEVATION AND CLEARENCE MEASUREMENTS. BIG JIM SETS THE CRANES DIRECTLY OVER THE TOP OF THE STEAM CHEST AND SIGNALS A SLOW DOWN, SLOW DOWN, SLOW DOWN SLOW DOWN UNTIL THE NUMBER ONE STAGE OF THE HIGH PRESURE TURBINE BEGINS TO GET CLOSE TO THE FIT OF THE LWER HALF DIAPHRAGMS AND FLOW GUIDES THEN WAVES A STOP. THE HIGH PRESURE TURBINE IS SMALLEST OF THE FOUR SPINDLES. WITH THE CREW BEING STATIONED AROUND THE HP TURBINE BIG JIM SCRATCES HIS CHIN, AS TO SAY SLOWLY, SLOW DOWN, SLOW DOWN, SLOW DOWN THEN A STOP FOR A FINAL FME CHECK BY KRINE DOG

AND TIE BOW. FOUR THUMBS UP AND THE OK TO PROCEED. SLOW DOWN, SLOW DOWN AS THE CREW GENTLY GUIDES THE SPINDLE BACK DOWN INTO IT'S FIT AND BEFORE THE JOURNALS FIND REST IN THE LOWER HALF BEARINGS BIG JIM WAVES A STOP. EVERYONE AGAIN TAKES A CLOSE LOOK THEN FATTY JOE REMINDS EVERYONE TO NOT FORGET TO POUR SOME LUBE OIL INTO THE BOTTOM HALF OF THE BEARINGS BEFORE YOU ALLOW THE JOURNALS OF THE TURBINE TO COME TO REST ON THE BEARINGS.

SLOW DOWN, SLOW DOWN, SLOW DOWN AS THE HP SPINDLE COMES DOWN NICE AND LEVEL SO NO DAMAGE IS DONE TO THE BEARINGS OR TIPS OF THE TURBINE BLADES. STOP! WAVES BIG JIM FOR A FINAL LOOK AND THEN ANOTHER SLOW DOWN AS THE SPINDLE GENTLY COMES TO REST ON IT'S BEARINGS. SLOW DOWN, SLOW DOWN AS SLACK IN THE SLINGS INCREASE SLOW DOWN UNTIL THE SLINGS CAN BE REMOVED FROM AROUND THE JOURNALS OF THE HP SPINDLE. THE RIGGERS REMOVE THE SLINGS AND BIG JIM SIGNALS TO WIND UP THE HOOKS AND PROCEED TO THE NEXT PICK.

GOON:	After the riggers shuffle around the spindles, we can stack the HP turbine upper halves and set up for the upper half cylinder installation.
FATTY JOE:	BIG JIM is on board with the "B" low pressure turbine being finished with the SANDCRABS and going to CHARDY for testing. Then the "A" low pressure being moved to the SANDCRABS for being sandblasted and cleaned.

SQUARE HEAD:	Hopefully the spindles are balanced and crack free coming out of the CHARDY testing area it's crucial if we are to keep this tote schedule.
FATTY JOE:	If not we can fix them but it takes time.

WOBY ENTERS THE PICTURE FROM DOWN IN THE HPCI AREA.

WOBY:	I got some good news. The HIGH PRESURE CORE INJECTION pump is performing to within specs and we only have another run before we can sign off complete. If all goes well we can tie in with centerline for the reassembly.
SQUARE HEAD:	The more the merrier WOBY we welcome all the help we can get.
WOBY:	EAGLE ED and ICEMAN are working on the clearance right now it shouldn't be long.
GOON:	You really have to dot the I and cross the t when your working on that important piece of safety equipment.
WOBY:	We have always left the machine better then we found it and the room will be spotless.

SQUARE HEAD NODS AND HEADS FOR THE 'D' COUPLING AREA WHERE HE FINDS SUNNY AND YUMYUM CHARTING THE POSITION OF THE 'C' LP TURBINE AND GETTING READY TO STACK THE TOP HALF DIAPHRAGMS AND FLOW GUIDES.

YUMYUM: We're moving ahead SQUARE the riggers set the spindle almost perfect. Looks like we might have to bump the putt, putt gear just a bit to align the coupling bolt holes and we have room for the spacer when the time comes.

SUNNY: The steam packing all looks good and no foreign materials have entered the system. I have been focused on stoning the horizontal joint and making sure the studs are clean and threads look good. Sometimes when the upper half cylinder comes up off the joint it scrapes the studs and could roll the threads.

SQUARE HEAD: Another good reason to make sure we come straight up and down with our lifts. Either we spend time aligning the cranes or we fix the damage done because we hurried along. Keep up the good work.

SQUARE HEAD MAKES HIS WAY ALONG CENTERLINE TO THE 'B' LP STEAM CHEST WHERE HE FINDS COOL DADDY, PEACHES AND ROPEY PERFORMING AN FME CHECK IN PREPERATION OF SETTING THE LOWER HALF FLOW GUIDES AND DIAPHRAGMS.

ROPEY: We worked both lower half shells SQUARE HEAD so when the cranes are done with the spindle shuffle we will be ready to stack the lower halves in the "B" LP. and the "A" LP.

SQUARE HEAD: We want to set the upper half HP. Shell before we install your "B" and "C" spindles because it takes longer to stretch the bolts of the high-pressure shell.

COOL DADDY: Three passes and extentionometer measurements to reach the required stretch. Remember to remind them to work from the center out and around the joint to help flatten it out.

SQUARE HEAD: KRINE DOG and TIE BOW are already on it. They have made calculations to determine number of flats on the nut in relation to stretch of studs.

PEACHES: I'm glad engineering lets us dial up the torque machine for the low-pressure turbine shells even if we must acquire our bolt stretch in three passes.

ROPEY: And not have to use the extensionometer measurements. It seems to move a little faster when we can convert the gauge on the torque machine to pounds per square foot and know the studs are stretched accordingly anywhere between six and ten thousand of an inch, according to there location along the horizontal joint.

COOL DADDY: Once we set the lower halves SUAVE RICO can come behind us and double check on elevations and clearances with the laser alignment tools.

PEACHES: We set the elevation and clearance pads according to KRINE DOG and TIE BOW. Everything should be nice and tote.

SQUARE HEAD, GOON AND FATTY JOE ARE STANDING BY LOOKING LIKE THREE BIRDS ON A WIRE WHEN THE UNIT II OVERHEAD CRANE DRESSED IN A SINGLE LEG BRIDLE ROLLS PAST

AND SETS UP OVER TOP OF THE OF THE HIGH PRESURE TURBINE NOT FAR BEHIND ARE THE RIGGERS EEFFY, SKIN AND PAPALUCHI. THE RIGGERS HAVE ALREADY SET THE UPPER HALH RACKS OF FLOW GUIDES AND DIAPHRAGMS ON THE RIGHT SIDE OF THE TURBINE. THEY ARE READY TO PLAY PITCH AND CATCH. THE MACHINISTS HAVE THREE ON EACH SIDE DELCO JOE, DUDDLEY AND K ARE TOOLED UP AND READY TO GO. ON THE LEFT SIDE JOHNNYOBOTT, JOEWEE AND MOE WHO HAS A FLASHLIGHT IN HAND LOOKING CLOSELY, DOWN INTO THE STEAM CHEST OF THE HIGH PRESURE TURBINE. PAPALUCHI ESTABLISHES EYE CONTACT WITH RAYRAY CHONG THE CRAIN OPPERATOR, AND RASIES HIS RIGHT HAND. RAYRAY CHONG LOWERS THE ONE-LEGGED BRIDLE, MADE OF A BRAIDED WIRE ROPE RIGHT DOWN TO TOP, CENTER OF THE NUMBER ONE STAGE FLOW GUIDE. EEFFY HAS THREAD A ONE INCH LIFTING EYE INTO THE TOP OF THE FLOW GUIDE UNTIL IT SHOULDERS OUT. THEN EEFFY TAKES THE HOOK OF THE BRIDLE AND HOOKS IT TO THE STAGE ONE FLOW GUIDE OF THE HP TURBINE AND NODS TO PAPALUCHI. SLOW UP, SLOW UP, SLOW UP AS THE UPPER HALF FLOW GUIDE COMES UP OUT OF THE RACK THEN CLEARS IT.

EEFFY GENTLY ORRIENTS IT TO THE PROPPER DIRECTION AND WITHOUT STANDING UNDER GUIDES IT UP OUT OF HIS HANDS. RAYRAY CHONG HAVING DONE THIS TASK MANY TIMES BEFORE KNOWS WHER TO GO. SKIN IS ATTENTIVELY WATCHING THE LOAD PATH AND IS READY ON THE RECEIVING END. RAYRAY CHONG FROM THE BOX CENTERS UP THE FLOW GUIDE AND PAPALUCHI SIGNALS SLOW DOWN, SLOW DOWN AND AS THE FLOW GUIDE GETS CLOSE TO THE TIPS OF THE HIGH-PRESSURE TURBINE THE HOLE PROCESS SLOWS DOWN. SKIN REACHES OVER AND CENTERS UP THE FLOW GUIDE PERFECTLY. SKIN

LOOKS AT DELCO JOE ON THE RIGHT SIDE AND JOHNNYOBOTT ON THE LEFT, THERE TO GUIDE THE FLOW GUIDE AND FEEL FOR ANY HANG UPS. PAPALUCHI SCRATCHES HIS CHIN AND LOOKS UP AT RAYRAY CHONG AND WITH A QUICK SLOW DOWN, LOOK. QUICK SLOW DOWN, LOOK, SLOW DOWN THE FLOW GUIDE INCHES IT'S WAY DOWN TO COMPLETELY ENCOMPASS THE HIGH PRESURE TURBINE NUMBER ONE STAGE BLADES. THE FLOW GUIDES COMES RIGHT DOWN ONTO THE ALLIGNEMENT PINS AND SLACK APPEARS IN THE BRIDEL. SKIN REACHES OVER AND REMOVES THE HOOK FROM THE LIFTING EYE. PAPALUCHI SIGNALS UP AND RAYRAY CHONG IS ON HIS WAY BACK TO EEFFY WHO WILL BE PITCHING THE NUMBER ONE INBOARD UPPER HALF DIAPHRAGM.

RAYRAY CHONG POSITIONS THE HOOK DIRECTLY DEAD CENTER, TOP OF THE DIAPHRAGM. EEFFY IS WAITING AND HOOKS THE LIFTING EYE. PAPALUCHI SIGNALS SLOW UP, SLOW UP, SLOW UP AND GRADUALLY LIFTS THE DIAGHRAGM UP OUT OF THE RACK. EEFFY ORRIENTS THE DIAPHRAGM AND GENTLY PITCHES IT UP OUT OF HIS HANDS. THE MACHINIST AND SKIN STAY OUT FROM UNDERNEATH THE LOAD AS THE DIAPHRAGM IS NOW BEING LOWERED INTO AN ALMOST THERE POSITION. PAPALUCHI WAVES A STOP AS THE DIAPHRAGM GETS CLOSER TO THE TIPS OF THE TURBINE. SKIN AND THE MACHINIST KNOW THE DIAPHRAGM FITS IN BETWEEN THE NUMBER ONE AND NUMBER TWO STAGES OF THE TURBINE AND LOCATE IT DEAD CENTER OF ITS POSITION. PAPALUCHI ESTABLISHES EYE CONTACT AND POINTS TO HIS HEAD AS TO SAY STAY IN THE GAME CREW. PAPALUCHI SIGNALS VERY SLOW DOWN AND STOP TAKE A LOOK, VERY SLOW DOWN, STOP TAKE A LOOK VERY SLOW DOWN AND ALSO LISTENING

VERY CAREFULLY FOR ANY RUBS, VERY SLOW DOWN AND INCHING ITS WAY DOWN RIGHT INTO THE SIGNALS A STOP.

SKIN REACHES OVER AND DOWN IN ALONG THE SHAFT OF THE SPINDLE AND THIS TIME REMOVES THE HOOK FROM THE DIAPHRAGM AND THE TURNS OUT THE LIFTING EYE AND HANDS IT TO PAPALUCHI. NO FME IS CRUCIAL AT THIS TIME. NO SOONER SKIN SHOWS BOTH HANDS RAYRAY CHONG BEGINS TO WINDE UP THE HOOK AND HEAD BACK TO THE RACK WHERE EEFFY IS READY TO SEND HIM THE NUMBER ONE OUTBOARD UPPER HALF DIAPHRAGM OF THE HIGH PRESURE TURBINE.

HENCE THE PITCH AND CATCH METHOD. AFTER THE UPPER HALF OUTBOARD IS SET INTO PLACE THE NUMBER TWO STAGE INBOARD FLOWGUIDE IS SET, THEN THE NUMBER TWO STAGE OUTBOARD FLOW GUIDE. THEN NEXT WOULD BE THE NUMBER TWO INBOARD DIAPHRAGM AND THEN THE NUMBER TWO OUTBOARD DIAPHRAGM AND SO FORTH UNTIL THE HIGH PRESURE TURBINE IS FULLY STACKED WITH SIX STAGES STARTING FROM THE CENTER OF THE STEAM CHEST AND WORKING OUT ON THE INBOARD AND OUTBOARD ENDS. FOLLOWING UP BEHIND THE RIGGERS ARE JOWEE AND MOE ON THE LEFT SIDE AND JOHNNYOBOTT WITH DELCO JOE, DUDDLEY AND K ON THE RIGHT. THERE TASK IS TO TORQUE THE ONE INCH CAPBOLTS TO THE PROPPER SPEC. ONE HUNDRED- AND SEVENTY-FIVE-FOOT POUNDS THIS IS DONE MANUALLY USING A CALIBERATED TORQUE WRENCH FOUR FOOT TALL. IT TAKES ALL THREE MACHINISTS TO ACQUIRE THE TORQUE USING A STEADY PULL OR PUSH ACTION. NO AIR WRENCHES THE RIGGERS HAVE A VERY LITTLE BIT OF TIME TO DOUBLE CHECK THE TOTENESS ON THE COMEALONGS HOLDING THE MAIN STEAM PIPES OFF TO

THE SIDE SO WHEN THEY HAVE THE HIGH PRESURE SHELL IN THE AIR THEY HAVE COMPLETE CONFIDENCE THEY WILL BE ABLE TO INSTALL IT INTO PLACE WITHOUT ANY OBSTRUCTIONS.

WITH MOST OF THE JOBS STARTING TO GET CLOSED OUT A LOT OF THE CREW WHO HAVE BEEN WORKING ON THE VALVES, HIGH PRESURE CORE INJECTION PUMP AND THE ELECTRO HYDRAULIC CONTROL PUMP ARE RETURNING BACK TO THE DECK TO HELP OUT ON CENTERLINE. SCHAFFER CITY AND THE ELECTRICIANS ARE SPREAD OUT ON THE DECK WORKING ON THE BRUSH RIGGING ASSEMBLY LOCATED IN THE DOGHOUSE COLLECTOR END, THE VIBRATION PROBES AND THERMOCOUPLE CONTROL WIRING WORKING CLOSELY WITH DANDAMAN AND JONG WHO ARE LOCATED IN THE CONTROL ROOM RECEIVING CONTINUETY SIGNALS AT THE PROPPER ANNUNCIATOR. AND UNDER THE MAIN GENERATOR CLEANING THE LYNX WITH DENATURED ALCAHOL AND MAKING SURE, THE PARTS ARE CLEAN AND READY FOR REASSEMBLY. SQUARE HEAD TOOK A WALK WITH WOBBY DOWN TO THE BASEMENT OF THE PLANT FOR THE FINALE MINUTES OF THE HIPCI RUN. CORNAL HOGAN IS MAKING SURE THE AFTER-JOB HOUSE KEEPING IS COMPLETED ON THE VALVES PRIOR TO RETURNING THE FLOOR PLUGS BACK TO PLACE AND GOON WITH FATTY JOE ARE STANDING BY CENTERLINE READY FOR THE NEXT BIG MOVES. THE CHARDY CURTAIN COMES UP OFF OF THE "A" LP TURBINE AND PUT ASIDE. THE SANDCRABS HAVE FINISHED WITH THE SANDBLASTING OF THE STEAM SIDE OF THE TURBINE AND CHARDY IS FINISHED WITH THE ULTRA SOUND AND BALANCEING OF THE "B" LP TURBINE.

IMPORTANT TO REMEMBER THE STEAM SIDE OF THE TURBINES CONSIST OF ALL THE EQUIPMENT ALONG THE WAY OF THE

STEAM PATH. THE PARTS THAT NEED SANDBLASTING SUCH AS THE TURBINE BLADES, FLOW GUIDES AND DIAPHRAGMS. AND VALVE PARTS SUCH AS THE BALANCE CHAMBERS AND STRAINERS. THE OIL SIDE CONSISTS OF THE BEARING ENDS, THE ROTOR JOURNALS OF THE TURBINES, THE BEARINGS, LUBE OIL PUMPS, COUPLINGS, OIL DEFLECTORS AND COUPLING COVERS. THE SANDBLASTERS BLAST AND CLEAN THE STEAM SIDE OF THE MACHINE AS THE MACHINISTS USE SOAP STONES TO STONE THE JOURNALS OF THE TURBINE SPINDLES WITCH RIDE INSIDE THE BABBIT FACED BEARINGS THAT HAVE A CONSTANT SUPPLY OF LUBE OIL SUPPLYING THEM THEN RETURNING VIA THE OILPAN DRAIN DOWN TO THE LUBE OIL COOLERS BACK TO THE LUBE OIL RESERVIOR AND BACK UP THROUGH THE BEARINGS. WITH THE COUPLINGS OF THE TURBINES TURNING AT EIGHTEEN HUNDRED ROTATIONS PER MINUTE A LOT HAPPENING UNDER THE COUPLING COVERS ALL WITHIN FOUR TO EIGHT THOUSAND OF AN INCH CLEARENCE AND A THIN FILM OF LUBE OIL BETWEEN THE PARTS. FATTY JOE AND GOON ARE STANDING BY THE "B" LP TURBINE SHELL, STEAM SIDE, WATCHING THE CREW STACK THE UNITS LOWER DIAPHRAGHM AND FLOW GUIDE HALVES.

FATTY JOE: Looks like the valve gang is back to centerline GOON

GOON: The sooner the better FATTY JOE.

FATTY JOE: This is a lot of work.

GOON: COOL DADDY looks like BLP is stacked?

COOL DADDY: Were ready to row the boat and stake the tomb stones.

THE STACKING OF THE 'C' LP. TURBINE HAS ALSO BEGAN AND JUST LIKE STACKING THE LOWER HALVES OF THE "C" LP.

TURBINE AND THE HIGH-PRESSURE TURBINE THE RIGGERS ARE PERFORMING THEIRE WORK AND WILL SOON BE READY TO REINSTALL TO NEXT TWO LOW PRESSURE TURBINES. COOL DADDDY, GEGGY AND GOOGLY ARE ROWING THE BOAT ON THE RIGHT SIDE OF THE B LP TURBINE AND PEACHES, ROPEY, AND POOPDECK PAPPY ARE WORKING ON THE LEFT SIDE OF THE JOINT.

GOON: Come on COOL DADDY put some back into it!

THE TORQUE MUST BE ACHIEVED MANUALLY AS THE MACHINISTS ALONG WITH THE TORQUEWRENCH STRUGGLE TO REACH THE PROPPER TORQUE VALUE. THEY ALL MANAGE TO GET A DOUBLE CLICK ON EACH STAGE AND DIAPHRAMS CAP BOLTS AND TOGETHER THEY MOVE TOWARDS THE GOVONOR END TO THE "A" LP. WHERE THE RIGGERS ALONG WITH DELCO JOE, DUDDLEY AND K ARE STANDING BY TO HELP ROW THE BOAT. AS SOON AS THE LAST DIAPHRAGM AND FLOW GUIDE ARE SET THE RIGGERS HUSTLE AWAY TO GET THE BIG HOOKS DRESSED TO PICK THE FINALE TWO LOW PRESSURE SPINDLES BACK INSIDE THE GIANT ELECTRIC MACHINE. SUNNY, JAKE AND YUMYUM HAVE BEEN WORKING THE OILSIDE BEARING PEDESTOLS AND HELPED SUAVE RICO, ROPEY AND PEACHES WITH THE LASER ELEVATION AND CLEARENCE MEASUREMENTS.

FATTY JOE: I see we have staged lube oil at each bearing pedestal.
YUMYUM: SENIOR MANURE and the toolies.
JAKE: We will be able to pour plenty of lube oil onto and into the bearings during the reassembly.

FATTY JOE:	It's vital to lube oil the bottom half bearings before we set the spindles in, on the bearings. Don't forget FME practices and procedures. We don't want to loose anything down the steam supply pipes now.
SUNNY:	Looks like the riggers are ready to bring the "B" LP spindle?

WITH THE WHOLE CREW BEING DEDICATED AND COMMITTED TO THE SUCCESS OF STEAM SIDE OUTAGE INSIDE THE GIANT ELECTRIC MACHINE, THEY RELIZE IT'S TIME TO REFOCUS ON THE SAFETY AND QUALITY RESULTS THE ADMIREAL, LOUIE AND JIMMY O HAVE COME TO EXPECT. IT'S VERY IMPORTANT NOT TO BE COMPLAICENT AND IF SOMETHING DON'T LOOK OR FEEL RIGHT, STOP AND ASK QUESTIONS. KRINE DOG, TIE BOW AND STATION SUPPORT LIKE THE ANT HILL MOB ARE AVAILIABLE ESPICIALLY IF YOU ARE CRITICAL PATH. WITH THE WEATHER STARTING TO HEAT UP A LOT OF AIR CONDITIONERS ARE COMING ON LINE AND A STABLE ELECTRIC GRID IS ESSENTIAL TO PROVIDE CUSTOMERS WITH A SAFE, RELIABLE AND CONSTANT SUPPLY OF MECHANICALLY GENERATED ELECTRICITY. BIG JIM CONTINUES TO ORCASTRATE THE RIGGERS AND CLEAR TO ALL HAVE BEEN KEPT VERY BUSY. THE SCOPE OF WORK ISHUGE AND THE IMPORTANCE OF WORKING TOGETHER, SAFELY IS PARAMOUNT. THERE ARE SOME BIG PICKS AHEAD AND ATTENTION TO DETAIL IS AT THE FORFRONT OF EVERY CREW MEMBERS MIND.

WAY UP IN THE RAFTERS OF TURBINE HALL, SITTING IN THE UNIT TWO CRANE OPPERATORS BOX IS RAYRAY CHONG AND IN THE UNIT ONE CRANE BOX ALSO WAY UP HIGH IN THE RAFTERS OF THE BUILDING IS SMARKEY. BOTH CRANE OPPERATORS HAVE A

LOT OF EXPERIENCE AND HAVE WORKED CENTERLINE BEFORE. WORKING ALONG WITH RAYRAY CHONG AND THE UNIT TWO OVERHEAD CRANE IS EEFFY, SKIN AND PAPALUCHI. WITH THE UNIT TWO CRANE SMARKEY'S GROUND HANDS BLAZE, BIG O, BIG JIM, AND RAPPING RODNEY. SUAVE RICO IS PREPARING AND INSPECTING THE SLINGS BY THE RIGGING CAGE AND THE "B" LP TURBINE SPINDLE HAS AARRIVED DIRECTLY OVER TOP OF THE LOWER HALF CYLINDER. COOL DADDY, GEGGY AND GOOGLY ARE STANDING BY ON THE LEFT SIDE AND PEACHES, ROPEY AND POOPDECK PAPPY ARE THE GUIDES ON THE RIGHT SIDE. AT THIS POINT OF THE STEAM SIDE OUTAGE INSIDE THE GIANT ELECTRIC MACHINE EVERYONE IS ON THE SAME PAGE AND ONLY THOSE WHO ARE PART OF THE CREW ARE ON THE DECK. THERE IS TO BE NO DISTRACTIONS. BIG JIM AND THE RIGGERS ARE VERY CAREFUL TO TAKE THE APPROPRIATE TIME TO EYEBALL EVERY ANGLE TO MAKE SURE THE CRANES CAN COME STRAIGHT DOWN ON BIG JIM'S SIGNAL. SLOW DOWN, SLOW DOWN. SLOW DOWN AND A QUICK STOP. IF YOU LOOK CLOSELY YOU CAN SEE THE SPINDLE BOUNCE ALITTLE BIT IN THE SLINGS. THE TIPS OF THE LOW PRESURE TURBINS NUMBER ONE STAGE ARE JUST A FEW INCHES ABOVE THE LOWER HALF STEAM CHEST. EVERYONE SURROUNDING THE SPINDLE IS LOOKING TO IDENTIFY THE PROPPER STAGE OF THE TURBINE AND IT'S PROPPER FIT INTO THE FLOW GUIDES. SKIN AND RAPPING RODNEY ARE DOUBLE CHECKING THE SLING LOCATIONS IN REFERANCE TO THE LOWER HALF BEARINGS.

YUMYUM AND ROPEY MAKE SURE THE BEARINGS HAVE OIL POURED ON THEM. BIG JIM LOOKS AROUND AND THEN TOWARDS FATTY JOE THEN MAKES EYE CONTACT WITH THE CRANE OPPERATORS. SLOW DOWN, SLOW DOWN, STOP

AGAIN ALITTLE BOUNCE. THE TURBINE BLADES TIPS ARE NOW AT THE POINT OF JUST ENTERING THE FIT OF THE FLOW GUIDE. EVERYONE IS AWARE OF PINCH POINTS AND MAKE SURE THEIRE HANDS AND FEET ARE IN A SAFE PLACE. BIG JIM LOOKS UP TO THE CRANE OPPERATORS AND GIVES THEM THE SHOW ME THE MONEY SIGN THEN A QUICK SLOW DOWN, SLOW DOWN, SLOW DOWN AND A SOFT STOP. THE JOURNALS OF THE LOW-PRESSURE TURBINE SPINDLE ARE JUST ABOUT READY TO SQUASH THE OIL IN THE BEARING AND COMING TO REST. AGAIN, RAPPING RODNEY AND SKIN DOUBLE CHECK TO MAKE SURE THE SLINGS CAN BE REMOVED WHEN THE SPINDLE COMES TO REST ON IT'S BEARINGS. EYE CONTACT IS REESTABLISHED, AND BIG JIM AGAIN SENDS THE SHOW ME THE MONEY SIGN SLOW DOWN, SLOW DOWN VERY GENTLY BOTH ENDS TOGETHER NOT TO DAMAGE THE BEARINGS AND DOWN TO WHERE THE SLINGS DEVELOP ENOUGH SLACK FOR SKIN AND RAPPING RODNEY TO REMOVE THEM AND ATTACH THEM TO THE BIG HOOK. THE BIG HOOKS WINDE UP AND HEAD TO THE SANDCRABS AREA TO GET THE "A" LP SPINDLE AND DELIVER IT TO CHARDY FOR BALANCING AND CRACK CHECKS. RICO SUAVE IS STANDING BY THE RIGGING CAGE TO RE DRESS THE BIG HOOKS FOR THE HIGHPRESSURE TURBINE UPPER HALF SHELL, THE HEAVIEST PICK OF THE STEAM SIDE OUTAGE. GOON, FATTY JOE AND SQUARE HEAD ARE STANDING BY THE "A" LP WHEN KRINE DOG AND TIE BOW APPROACH THE STEAM CHEST.

SQUARE HEAD: So far so good. The crew has been doing an outstanding job.

GOON:	GORG'E the SANDWICH maker has a pot of fresh thorax ready to be applied to the high-pressure horizontal joint. Are we ready for the upper half high pressure shell KRINE DOG?
KRINE DOG:	Yeah, everything checks out, the lower half elevation pads the upper half clearance measurements, everything torqued our pinch checks on the bearings, were ready for the upper half high pressure shell.
GOON:	We can wait to thorax the joint until the riggers are bringing it.
KRINE DOG:	It's a very important milestone, and remember it takes three or sometimes four passes to stretch the bolts.
FATTY JOE:	Once CHARDY is finished with the inspections of the "A" LP turbine we can re install it and stack the units while the high-pressure team is acquiring the proper bolt stretch.

SUAVE RICO HAS FINISHED WITH BOTH CRANES BIG HOOKS AND THE RIGGERS MAKE THERE WAY ALL, THE WAY TO THE OTHER END OF TURBINE HALL, NEXT TO THE OPPERATING UNIT ONE HIGH PRESSURE TURBINE TO PICK UP AND TROLLY AND BRIDGE THE UNIT TWO HIGH PRESSURE UPPER HALF SHELL BACK TO IT'S LOCATION. EACH BIG HOOK HAS TWO THERTY FOOT KEVLAR SLING ON IT. THE ONE HUNDRED- AND TWENTY-TON LIFT REQUIRES A LOT OF ATTENTION. THE RIGGING TEAM SETS THE CRANES BIG HOOKS DIRECTLY CENTER OVER TOP OF THE TWO ENDS OF THE HIGH-PRESSURE TURBINE SHELL. AS THE BIG HOOKS WINDE THERE WAY DOWN THE KEVLAR SLINGS CAN GRADUALLY BE REACHED AND GENTLY PULLED DOWN ALONG THE SIDES OF

THE SHELL UNTIL YOU HAVE ENOUGH SLACK TO SET THE SLINGS AROUND THE LIFTING HORNS ON THE OUTSIDE CORNERS OF THE HP SHELL.

EVERYONE HAS THERE GAME FACE ON AND ALL THE RIGGERS ARE FAMILIAR WITH THE SAFEST LOAD PATH. DIRECTLY OVER TOP OF THE OPPERATING UNIT, OVER THE HATCH AND CONTINUE DIRECTLY OVER CENTERLINE UNTIL RESTING DIRECTLY OVER THE HIGH-PRESSURE TURBINE LOWER HALF. AS BIG JIM AND THE RIGGING TEAM PERFORM ANOTHER LIFT, THE MACHINISTS CONTINUE TO PREPARE THE LOWER HALF OF THE HORIZONTAL JOINT OF THE HIGH-PRESSURE TURBINE. THE CRANES WORKING IN UNISONE BRIDGE THE HIGH-PRESSURE SHELL DIRECTLY OVER TOP OF THE CENTERLINE AND EVERYONE WORKING BELOW KNOW NOT TO EVER BE UNDER THE LOAD. DELCO JOE, DUDDLEY AND K ARE STANDING BY ON THE LEFT SIDE HIGH PRESSURE TURBINE AND JOHNNYOBOTT, JOWEE AND MOE HAVE BEEN WORKING ON THE LEFT SIDE. RAPPING RODNEY, SKIN AND PAPALUCHI MAKE ABSOLUTLY SURE THE COME ALONGS ARE STILL TOTE AND KEEPING THE MAIN STEAM SUPPLY LINES OUT OF THE WAY SO THERE IS NO INTERFEARENCE WITH SETTING THE TOP HALF OF THE HIGH PRESSURE STEAM CHEST. WITH THE MEMBERS OF THE CREW FINISHED PAINTING THE THROAX ON THE JOINT, BIG JIM AND THE RIGGING TEAM POSITION THE TOP HALF SHELL DIRECTLY OVER THE BOTTOM HALF. BIG JIM MAKES EYE CONTACT WITH THE UNIT CRANE OPERATORS AND GIVES ANOTHER LOOK AROUND THE SHELL FOR ANY SIGNS OF A WAIT A SECOND OR HOLD ON BIG JIM BUT SEES NONE. THEN SENDS THE SLOW DOWN, SLOW DOWN, SLOW DOWN AND THEN A STOP THE BOTTOM HALF OF THE SHELL IS ABOUT READY TO BE LOWERED DOWN IN BETWEEN THE MAIN STAEM SUPPLY LINES FLANGE

FACES AND GENTLY OVER THE TOP OF THE FLOW GUIDES AND
DIAPHRAGMS AND DOWN AROUND THE SPINDLE OF THE HIGH
PRESSURE TURBINE TILL IT IS GUIDED DOWN BY THE RIGGERS
AND MACHINISTS WHO ARE LOOKING DOWN THROUGH THE
STUDS HOLES OF THE SHELL AND MAKEING SURE THE SHELL
DOSEN'T COME IN CONTACT WITH THE STUD AS TO CAUSE
DAMAGE TO THE THREADS. SLOW DOWN BIG JIM SIGNALS.

THEN SCRATCHES HIS CHIN SLOW DOWN, SLOW DOWN, SLOW
DOWN AS EVERYONE IS PAYING CLOSE ATTENTION TO THEIR
LOCATION MAKING SURE TO COME STRAIGHT DOWN UNTIL
THE TOP HALF, HIGH PRESSURE STEAM SHELL COMES TO REST
AND SQUEEZES ALL THE THROAX OUT ALONG THE JOINT. THE
SLINGS SLOWLY GAIN SLACK AND THE RIGGERS DISCONNECT
THE UPPER HALF STEAM CHEST AND BOTH CRANES HEAD FOR THE
RIGGING CAGE. SUAVE RICO IS AT THE CAGE READY TO DRESS
EACH HOOK FOR THE NEXT TASKS. SMARKEY OPERATING THE
UNIT ONE CRANE MOVES OVER THE UNIT ONE GENERATOR TO
GIVE RAYRAY CHONG PLENTY OF ROOM TO LOWER HIS HOOK
BY THE RIGGING CAGE WHERE SUAVE RICO IS PREPARED AND
WAITING. RAYRAY CHONG IS QUICK TO LOWER THE BIG HOOK
AS SUAVE RICO REMOVES THE TWO SLINGS USED TO LIFT THE
HP SHELL THEN CALLS FOR THE SMALL HOOK. RAYRAY CHONG
RESPONDSAND BEFORE YOU KNOW IT RAYRAY CHONG IS READY
TO DELIVER THE HUGE HIGH-PRESSURE NUTS INTO POSITION.
RAYRAY CHONG AND HIS RIGGING TEAM PROCEED TO THE
NEXT TASK AT HAND, DELIVERING THE CLEANED AND INSPECTED
HIGH PRESSURE NUTS TO THERE PROPPER STUDS LOCATION.
SMARKEY MOVES HIS CRANE AND LOWERS HIS BIG HOOK
DOWN FAR ENOUGH FOR SUAVE RICO TO REMOVE THE TWO
SLINGS FROM THE BIG HOOK AND AGAIN CALL FOR THE SMALL

HOOK. SMARKY ALREADY KNOWS WHAT'S NEXT BECAUSE OF HIS EXPERIENCE BUT A CRANE OPERATOR ALWAYS WAITS FOR AN APPROPRIATE SIGNAL BEFORE MAKING ANY MOVE. AN EYE AN EYE WIRE ROPE WITH A HOOK AND HIS GROUND HANDS HAVE THE THREADED LIFTING EYEYS REQUIRED TO STACK THE UPPER HALF FLOW GUIDE AND DIAPHRAGMS OVER TOP AND IN THE FITS OF THE "B" LOW PRESSURE TURBINE. SQUARE HEAD, FATTY JOE, GOON AND CORNAL HOGAN ARE STANDING BY THE TURBINE TESTING AREA WAITNG FOR CHARDY TO COMPLETE HIS TESTING.

COL. HOGAN: I can tell KOCHY, KUBBY and MARTY are doing a very thorough job cleaning and inspecting the upper half cylinders and really cleaning the upper half joint. When the upper half HP shell flew by I could see myself looking up at it.

SQUARE HEAD: I wouldn't let the ADMERIAL hear you say that. He'll think you were standing under the load.

GOON: Wonder how much longer CHARDY is going to be? Anyone seen GONESKI?

SQUARE HEAD: "A" LP is the last turbine we worked on two years ago, the engineers think it should be in pretty good shape.

ON THE HIGH-PRESSURE TURBINE RIGGERS EEFFY, SKIN, RAPPING RODNEY AND PAPALUCHI ARE PLAYING PITCH AND CATCH WITH THE BOLT BINS THE HP. NUTS ARE LOCATED IN MAKING SURE THEY GET THE NUTS AS CLOSE AS THEY CAN. MACHINISTS JOHNNYOBOTT, JOWEE, MOE AND SOME HELP FROM NOSEALEO ARE WORKING THE RIGHT SIDE AND DELCO JOE, DUDDLEY, AND K ARE WORKING THE LEFT SIDE. THE MACHINISTS ARE LOCATING

THE NUMBERED NUT WITH THE NUMBERED STUD AND USING A PADDED BAR TURN THE NUT ON IT'S SIDE SLIDE THE PADDED BREAKING BAR THROUGH THE NUT AND TWO MACHINISTS ONE ON EACH END OF THE BAR LIFT UP THE NUT AND CARRY IT OVER TO THE PROPER STUD. TOGETHER THEY STAND THE NUT UP RIGHT WITHOUT CRUSHING A FINGER THEN LIFT IT UP AND GENTLY PLACE IT ON TOP OF THE STUD NOT TO ROLL A THREAD.THEN USING THE SENSE OF TOUCH TURN THE NUT UNTIL THEY CAN FEEL IT PICK UP THE LEAD THREAD.

ONCE THEY PICK UP THE LEAD THREAD THE MACHINISTS TAKE THE BREAKING BAR AND CONTINUE TO TURN THE NUT ONTO THE STUD UNTIL THEY CAN NOT GET A FEELER GUAGE BETWEEN THE NUT AND THE SHELL. ONCE ALL THE NUTS ARE FEELER GUAGE TITE THE MACHINISTS TAKE A RELAXED READING OF THE STUD AND RECORD IT IN THE PROCEDURE. WORKING ON THE "B" LP BLAZE, BIG O AND BIG JIM, WHO IS DIRECTING THE PITCH AND CATCH OPERATION OF THE UPPER HALF FLOW GUIDES AND DIAPHRAGMS. COOL DADDY, GEGGY AND GOOGLY ARE HELPING GUIDE THE FLOW GUIDES AND DIAPHRAGMS GENTLY OVER THE TIPS OF THE TURBINS STAGES AND INTO THEIRE FITS. WHILE ROPEY, PEACHES AND POOPDECK PAPPY ARE STARTING THE CAP BOLTS ON THE PLACED FLOW GUIDES AND DIAPHRAGMS.

THE CREW IS READY TO ROW THE BOAT AND TORQUE THE FLOW GUIDES AND DIAPHRAGMS. JUST AS THE LAST STAGE HAS BEEN SET ON THE "B" LP THE LAST FEW NUTS HAVE BEEN LOCATED AND STARTED ON THE STUD OF THE HP TURBINES HORIZONTAL JOINT. THE OVERHEAD CRANES MAKE THERE WAY BACK TO THE RIGGING CAGE WHERE SUAVE RICO REMOVES THE RIGGING

REQUIRED FOR THE PAST TASKS AND HANGS A FOUR-LEGGED BRIDAL ON EACH SMALL HOOK AS THE RIGGERS LOOK TO CLEAR THE TURBINE DECK OF ANY EQUIPMENT THAT IS NO LONGER NEEDED. PLAINE BILL HAS LOCATED THE TRACTOR TRAILER AT THE BOTTOM OF THE HATCH AND IS READY TO HELP REMOVE THE EQUIPMENT FROM THE POWER BLOCK. FLOW GUIDE AND DIAPHRAGM RACKS, THE WELDERS SHACK AND THE CRABSHACK PLUS, THE ROLLERS THAT ARE NO LONGER BEING USED. OTTO, BOOGER, CARLY, LAURY AND COOL EARL HAVE BEEN WORKING HARD DISASSEMBLING AND STACKING SOME OF THE PANNELS FOR THE WELDERS BOOTH AND THE CRABSHACK. THE ELECTRICIANS SISTER T, HIGH VOLT, BRUCEY AND CUPCAKE HAVE ALSO BEEN BREAKING DOWN THE TEMPORARY ELECTRIC FEEDS USED TO SUPLY THE WELDERS BOOTH, CRABSHACK AND POWER ROLLER USED BY CHARDY TO INSPECT THE TURBINES FOR BALANCE AND CRACKS. CHARDY, KRINE DOG AND TIE BOW GIVE A FINAL BLESSING ON THE" A" LOW PRESSURE TURBINE.

THE RIGGING TEAM PREPARE TO HOIST THE TURBINE FROM THE ROLLERS AND TRANSPORT IT, TO ITS FINAL POSITION INSIDE THE LOWER HALF OF THE" A" LP STEAM CHEST, UNIT TWO, INSIDE THE GIANT ELECTRIC MACHINE. BIG JIM HAS THE UNIT TWO CRANE POSITIONED DIRECTLY OVER THE DEAD CENTER OF THE "A" COUPLING END OF THE TURBINE AND THE UNIT ONE CRANE IS SET DIRECTLY OVER THE CENTER OF THE JOURNAL OF THE "B" COUPLING END OF THE TURBINE. THE SLINGS HAVE BEEN POSITIONED PERFECTLY SO WHEN THE TURBINE COMES TO REST IN THE LOWER HALF BEARINGS THEY CAN EASILY BE REMOVED AND IN NO WAY CLOSE TO THE BABBIT FACED BEARINGS AND THE JOURNAL OF THE TURBINE. BIG JIM MAKES SURE THE LOAD PATH IS CLEAR AND EVERYONE IS READY FOR THE LIFT THEN

SIGNALS SLOW UO, SLOW UP, SLOW UP TILL THE SLACK IS ALMOST OUT THEN WAVES A STOP. LOOKS AROUND MAKES SURE EVERYONE IS PAYING ATTENTION AND SIGNALS A SLOW UP, SLOW UP, SLOW UP UNTIL THE SLACK DISSAPPEARS AND THE TURBINE IS HANGING FROM THE HOOKS OF THE OVERHEAD CRANES. BIG JIM THEN WAVES A STOP AND EVERYONE IS PAYING CLOSE ATTENTION ON THE PLACEMENT OF THE SLINGS SO THERE IS NO ISSUES WHEN THE TURBINE IS SET INTO THE OILED LOWER HALF OF THE BEARINGS. THE TEAM IS CONFIDENT WITH THE SLING PLACEMENT AND PROCEED WITH THE LIFT. BIG JIM SIGNALS SLOW UP, SLOW UP THEN A BRIDGE TO THE CENTERLINE AND A TROLLY TO THE UNIT TWO "A" LOW PRESURE STEAM CHEST.

CRANE OPERATORS RAYRAY CHONG IN THE UNIT TWO BOX AND SMARKEY IN THE UNIT ONE BOX KNOW EXACTLY WHERE TO GO WITH THE LOAD. THE CRANES ARE TMIED TO WORK TOGETHER SO ONE NOT TO GO FASTER THEN THE OTHER. THE CREW WORKING ON DIAPHRAGMS AND FLOW GUIDES AND THE CREW CHECKING ALLIGNEMENT AND BEARINGS ALL STEP OUT FROM UNDER THE LOAD UNTIL IT MOVES ALONG, ATOP OF CENTERLINE TILL IT IS CLOSE TO BEING DIRECTLY OVER THE TOP OF IT'S LOCATION. KRINE DOG, TIE BOW AND OTHERS PERFORM A FOREIGN METERIALS CHECK AND MAKE SURE, NOTHING IS LEFT IN THE MACHINE. BIG JIM AND THE RIGGING TEAM POSITION THEMSELVES AROUND THE STEAM CHEST WITH ROPEY, PEACHES AND POOPDECK PAPPY LENDING SOME EXTRA EYES MAKING SURE THE TURBINE IS GUIDED WITH PERCISION TO IT'S RESTING PLACE IN THE LOWER HALF BEARING AND STEAM CHEST. WITH THE TEAM PAYING CLOSE ATTENTION BIG JIM LOOKS

AROUND AND MAKES SOME VERY PRECISE MOVES ACCORDING TO THE DIRECTION OF THE OTHER RIGGING TEAM MEMBERS.

FATTY JOE, CORNAL HOGAN, GOON AND SQUARE HEAD LOOK LIKE BIRDS SITTING ON A WIRE AS THE JOB IS READY TO COMPLETE A MAJOR MILESTONE. IT'S IMPORTANT THE LOAD IS STILL PRIOR TO START COMING DOWN. BIG JIM MAKES EYE CONTACT WITH THE OPERATORS AND GIVES A SLOW DOWN SIGNAL, SLOW DOWN AND A STOP. THE TURBINE BOUNCES UP AND DOWN EVER SO SLIGHTLY AND COMES TO REST. THE TIPS OF THE TURBINE BLADES NUMBER ONE STAGE ARE JUST ABOUT READY TO PASS DOWN ALONG THE FIT OF THE FLOW GUIDES AND DIAPHRAGMS. EVERYONE IS ALWAYS LOOKING OUT FOR EACH OTHER MAKING SURE THERE HANDS AND FEET ARE NEVER IN A PINCH POINT OR UNDER THE LOAD. WITH THE LOAD HANGING FREE AND UN TOUCHED BIG JIM SIGNALS A SLOW DOWN, SLOW DOWN, SLOW DOWN AS THE TIPS OF THE TURBINE BLADES DISAPEER INTO THE BOTTOM TOF THE STEAM CHEST. BIG JIM WAVES A STOP AND DOUBLE CHECK EVERYTHING IS IN THE PROPPER FIT. THE RIGGERS ARE MAKING SURE THE SLINGS ARE IN THE RIGHT POSITION AND BIG JIM WAVES A SLOW DOWN, SLOW DOWN, SLOW DOWN AS THE TEAM GENTLY GUIDE THE TURBINE SPINDLE TO REST ON TOP OF THE LOWER HALF OILED BEARINGS. THE CREW MAKES SURE THEIRE FEET ARE CLEAR AND THEIRE HANDS ON TOP OF THE LOAD AS THEY GUIDE THE SPINDLE.

BIG JIM WAVES A QUICK STOP AND TAKES A FAST GLANCE THEN GENTLY HAS THE CRANES LOWER THE TURBINE SPINDLE TO REST IN IT'S LOWER HALF BEARINGS. BIG JIM GIVES A QUICK DOWN AND STOP AS THE RIGGERS REMOVE THE SLINGS AND

PREPARE TO STACK THE UNIT TWO "A" LOW PRESURE TURBINE WITH THE FLOW GUIDES AND DIAPHRAGMS. THE CRANES WILL TROLLY BACK TO THE RIGGING CAGE WHERE SUAVE RICO WILL SET THEM UP TO STACK THE "A" LP AND REMOVE UNUSED EQUIPMENT AND CONTINUE TO CLEAN UP THE FLOOR. ONCE RAYRAY CHONG AND THE UNIT TWO RIGGERS ARE FINISHED PLAYING PITCH AND CATCH WITH THE FLOW GUIDES AND DIAPHRAGMS THE TEAM WILL MOVE TOWARDS REINSTALLING THE UPPER CYLINDER HEADS, TOP HALF OF THE LOW PRESURE STEAM CHEST.

EEFFY, SKIN AND PAPPALUCHI ARE IN POSITION AND WAITING ON THE UNIT TWO CRANE AND RAYRAY CHONG TO BEGIN STACKING THE "A LP." UPPER HALF DIAPHRAGMS AND FLOW GUIDES. THE MACHINISTS AND MILWRIGHTS ARE ALSO WAITING TO ROW THE BOAT TO ACQUIRE THE PROPER TORQUE VALUE ON THE CAP BOLTS USED TO FASTEN THE UPPER TO THE LOWERS. NOSEALEO, TWISTED STEELE, PEACHES, ROPEY AND POOPDECK PAPPY ARE READY TO ROW THE BOAT. THE UNIT ONE RIGGING TEAM IS TRYING THEIRE BEST TO CLEAR THE DECK OF NO LONGER NEEDED EQUIPMENT AND TOOLING. THE TEAM HAS ALSO HELPED REPOSITION THE OUTTER LOW PRESSURE SHELLS FOR MARTY, KUBY AND KOCHY WHO ARE CLEANING THE UPPER HALF OF THE HORIZONTAL JOINTS. SUAVE RICO PERFORMS AN INSPECTION ON THE SLINGS THAT ARE GOING TO BE USED TO REINSTALL THE UPPER- HALF CYLINDERS OF THE A, B AND C LP.

TURBINES OF THE UNIT TWO MAIN STEAM CHEST INSIDE THE GIANT ELECTRIC MACHINE. IT'S EVERYONES RESPONSIBILTY TO KEEP FOREIGN METERIAL OUT OF THE UNIT AND AS THE TIME QUICKLY APPROACHES EVERYONE IS PERFORMING A FINAL

STEAM SIDE FOREIGN METERIAL EXCLUSION INSPECTION. ANY TOOL OR FOREIGN METERIAL LEFT BEHIND CAN POTENTIALLY GET INTRODUCED TO THE STEAM TURBINES AT EIGHTEEN HUNDRED ROTATIONS PER MINUTE AND CAUSE CATOSTROPHIC DAMAGE TO THE MACHINE. SOON AS THE FITH STAGE FLOW GUIDE, OUTBOARD END OF THE "A" LP. TURBINE IS SET DOWN INTO POSITION THE RIGGERS REMOVE THE RIGGING AND TOGETHER HEAD TO THE RIGGING CAGE. SAUVE RICO IS PREPARED TO DRESS THE BIG HOOK OF EACH UNIT CRANE WITH TWO THERTY FOOT LONG KEVLAR SLINGS. WHILE THE RIGGERS PREPARE TO MAKE THE FIRST OF THE THREE UPPER HALF CYLINDER LIFTS, THE MACHINISTS AND MILWRIGHTS CONTINUE TO WORK ON REACHING THE FINALE TORQUE VALUES ON THE FLOW GUIDE AND DIAPHRAGM CAP NUTS. SQUARE HEAD, FATTY JOE, GOON, CORNAL HOGAN AND NOW SCHAFER CITY ARE STANDING ALONG THE LEFT SIDE OF CENTERLINE LOOKING LIKE BIRDS ON A WIRE.

WOBY REMAINS IN THE BASEMENT WORKING WITH ICEMAN ON THE OVERSPEED HIGH PRESURE CORE INJECTION PUMP TESTING REQUIRED FOR START UP. BIG JIM HAS THE TEAM OF RIGGERS PARKED AND WAITING THE SIGNAL TO PROCEED WITH THE FIRST LIFT, UPPER HALF INNER CYLINDER OF THE "A" LOW PRESURE TURBINE. MOST OF THE TEAM HAS RETURNED TO CENTERLINE AND ARE READY TO CLOSE THIS BABY OUT. IT'S BEEN A LONG ARDJUST TASK WITH A BROAD SCOPE OF WORK. KRINE DOG AND TIE BOW COMPLETE A FINALE FME INSPECTION, SATISFIED WITH CLEARENCE/ELEVATION MEASUREMENTS OF THE FLOW GUIDES AND DIAPHRAGMS KRINE DOG GIVES FATTY JOE AND SQUARE HEAD THE GO AHEAD.

SQUARE HEAD:	Okay FATTY JOE we got the go ahead.
FATTY JOE:	SKIN, were ready to close the main steam chest A, B, C upper half, low presure turbines. Don't forget to grease the inside fit before we make the lift.
SKIN:	Got It. BIG JIM has us ready.
GOON:	Hey, POOPDECK PAPPY it's okay to apply the frax.

POOPDECK GIVES THE THUMBS UP AND LOOKS AT GOON WITH A WOBBLE. GOR'GE THE SANDWITCH MAKER IS PREPARING THE FRAX WITCH IS A MAPLE SYRUP LIKE SURFACE PROTECTOR THAT IS APPLIED THE HORIZONTAL JOINT JUST PRIOR TO THE REASSEMBLY. SOME OF THE MACHINISTS AND MILWRIGHTS ARE SURROUNDING THE STEAM CHEST WHILE OTHERS HAVE MOVED ALONG TO MAKE FINALE PREPERATIONS ON THE "B" AND "C" LOWER HALVES. SLOW UP, SLOW UP, SLOW UP BIG JIM SIGNALS THE CRANES IN UNISONE. THE SLINGS TOTEN AROUND THE OUTSIDE CORNER LIFTING HORNS AND BIG JIM WAVES A QUICK STOP. THE RIGGING TEAM EXAMINE THE SLINGS TO MAKE SURE THERE IS NO TWISTS AND ARE FULLY ENGAGED AROUND THE LIFTING HORNS AND NOD TOWARDS BIG JIM.

FROM THE SIDES BLAZE AND EEFFY MAKE SURE THE ANGLE OF THE CYLINDER LOOKS LEVEL AS BIG O IS STANDING BY TO REMOVE THE LEVEL THAT IS ATTACHED TO THE UPPER HALF CYLINDER. BIG JIM WAVES A SLOW UP, SLOW UP, SLOW UP AND THE TOP HALF CYLINDER COMES UP OFF THE CRIBBING. BIG O CHECKS THE LEVEL AND FINDS A SLIGHT ADJUSTEMENT IS REQUIRED. BIG JIM THEN MAKES SURE EVERYONE IS CLEAR AND GIVES A SLOW DOWN, SLOW DOWN, SLOW DOWN

UNTIL SLACK ENOUGH IN THE SLINGS IS MET. THE RIGGERS REPOSITION THE SLINGS AROUND THE LIFTING HORNS ON THE OUTBOARD END AND BIG JIM SIGNALS A SLOW UP, SLOW UP, SLOW UP AND THE SHELL IS BACK IN THE AIR. BIG O CHECKS LEVEL AND LOOKS TO BLAZE AND EEFY TO MAKE SURE THE ANGLE OF THE SHELL LOOKS PERFCT. THEY ALL LOOK TOWARDS BIG JIM WITH THE NOD OF APPROVAL. BIG JIM SIGNALS A SLOW UP, SLOW UP, SLOW UP UNTIL THE PROPER CLEARENCE IS ACHIEVED THEN SIGNALS THE CRANE OPPERATORS TO A STOP AND BRIDGE TOGETHER TO CENTERLINE OF THE OPPERATING UNIT ONE. BIG JIM THEN SIGNALS A STOP AND TROLLY TO OVER HEAD POSITION OF THE "A" LP STEAM CHEST. BIG O AND PAPALUCHI ACCOMPANY THE LOAD AND SOON POSITION THE TOP HALF OVER THE UNIT. BIG JIM ARRIVES AND SIGNALS A SLOW DOWN, SLOW DOWN, SLOW DOWN SLOW DOWN UNTIL THE TOP HALF GETS CLOSE THEN SIGNALS A STOP. THE TOP HALF BOUNCES EVER SO SLIGHTLY IN THE SLINGS AND COMES TO REST.

BIG JIM DOUBLE CHECKS TO MAKE SURE EVERYONES HEAD APPEARS TO BE IN THE GAME AND PROCCEDS WITH THE LIFT. SLOW DOWN, SLOW DOWN, SLOW DOWN AS THE CYLINDER NOW ENCOMPASSES THE FLOW GUIDES AND DIAPHRAGMS AND IS INCHING ITS WAY CLOSER TO CLOSING THE GAP OF THE HORIZONTAL JOINT. BIG JIM AND PAPALUCHI EACH SCRATCH THERE CHINS TO SLOW THE DOWNS A LITTLE BIT AS THE CYLINDER IS NOW APPROACHING THE INNER FITS OF THE FLOW GUIDES AND DIAPHRAGMS.LOOKING THROUGH THE TOP HALVES BOLT HOLES THE MACHINISTS AND MILWRIGHTS ARE NOW ABLE TO GUIDE THE TOP HALF DOWN AS THE CRANES LOWER IT OVER THE STUDS OF THE FIXED LOWER HALF. BIG JIM

SIGNALS A SLOW DOWN, SLOW DOWN, SLOW DOWN, AND A STOP AS NOW THE GAP BETWEEN THE LOWER AND UPPER HALVES IA ABOUT FOUR INCHES. THE MACHINISTS MAKE SURE TO HOLD THE CYLINDER STEADY TO MAKE SURE THE CYLINDER DON'T SWIPE THE STUDS AND ROLL THE THREADS. BIG JIM THEN LIFTS HIS HANDS IN THE AIR AS HIGH AS HE CAN STREATCH AND MAKES THE SHOW ME THE MONEY SIGN. DOWN, DOWN, DOWN INTO THE FIT AND FINIALLY AT REST. THE SLINGS GROW SLACK AND THE RIGGERS REMOVE THEM AND SEND THE OVERHEAD CRANES AWAY FOR THE "B" LP CYLINDER. THE TEAM PLAYS PITCH AND CATCH WITH THE REMAINING TWO LP CYLINDER UPPER HALVES AND THEN THE CRANES DISTRIBUTE THE NUTS TO THE MACHINISTS AND MILWRIGHTS. SENIOR'E MANURE, AIRYSUE AND MIC HAVE THE TORQUE MACHINES STAGED AND READY TO GO AS THE MACHINISTS REMIND EACH OTHER TO FLATTEN THE JOINT FROM THE INSIDE OUT AND IN THREE FULL PASSES. HOWEVER, THE HIGH PRSSURE TURBINE REQUIRES USING INDUCTION HEAT ON THE NUT TO ACQUIRE THE PROPPER STREATH OF THE STUD.

SQUARE HEAD, FATTY JOE, GOON, SCHAFER CITY HAVE FLOWN OFF THE WIRE AND UNDERSTAND A MAJOR MILESTONE HAS BEEN REACHED BY CLOSING UP THE MAIN STEAM CHEST AND ELIMINIATING FOREIGN METERIAL ZONES. NOW THEY NEED TO MAKE SURE THE PAPER WORK IS UP TO THE MOMENT. KISSY HAS BROUGHT IN SOME HELP, ELAINE, TO HELP WITH THE PAPERWORK. THE REST OF THE TEAM REMAINS ON CENTERLINE WORKING HARD TO ACQURIE THE PROPER TORQUE VALUES. KRINE DOG AND TIE BOW ARE STANDING BY THE HP. TURBINE WORKING WITH THE CREW. JOHNNY OBOTT, MOE, JOWEE AND NOSEALEO ARE WORKING ON THE RIGHT SIDE WITH DELCO

JOE, DUDDLEY, K AND CHARDY ON THE LEFT. BOTH SIDES HAVE MADE A SINGLE FULL PASS AROUND THE OUTSIDE OF THE HIGH-PRESSURE SHELL STARTING FROM THE MIDDLE NUTS AND WORKING OUT.

KRINE DOG: The nuts are back down to room temperature, so we can go for the second pass.

DELCO JOE: We laid everything out on both sides for the second pass, and all the studs' holes have vacuumed clean to make sue we have consistent measurements.

MOE: Looks like a flat and a half or so? KRINE DOG.

KRINE DOG: Our calculations are showing about eight to ten thousand an inch stretch per flat.

DELCO JOE: Let's get started.

ON BOTH SIDES OF THE HIGH-PRESSURE TURBINE THE CREWS BEGIN THE SECOND PASS OF TORQUE PROCEDURE. EACH SIDE HAS AN INDUCTION HEATER TO HEAT THE NUTS TO ALLOW THERMAL EXPANSION OF JUST THE NUT AND THEN USING A SMALL BAR TURNING THE NUT TO THE RIGHT BY ONE FLAT DOWN ONTO THE STUD. THEN ALLOWING TIME FOR THE TURBINE SHELL NUTS TO COOL AND TAKE ANOTHER MEASUREMENT. THE MACHINISTS AND MILWRIGHTS THEN TAKE A LENGTH OF THREE EIGHTS DRILL ROD CUT TO A SPECIFIC LENGTH, IN OUR CASE EIGHT INCHES AND SLIDE THE DRILL ROD DOWN INTO THE MACHINIED, SHOULDERED HOLE IN THE TOP OF THE STUD AND ALLOW THE DRILL ROD TO COME TO REST ON THE SHOULDER OF THE INSIDE OF THE STUD. ONE INCH OF THE DRILL ROD IS STICKING UP OUT OF THE STUD. THE MACHINIST THEN TAKES HIS TRAVEL INDICATOR AND SLIDES THE HOLDER OVER THE

DRILL ROD UNTIL THE INDICATOR HOLDER COMES TO REST IN THE TOP OF THE STUD. MAKE SURE EVERYTHING IS NICELY BOTTOMED OUT AND TAKE YOUR MEASUREMENT READING.

THE MEASUREMENT GIVES YOU A FIXED POSITIONED, OVERALL LENGTH OF STREATCHED STUD, LOCKED INTO PLACE BY THE SIZE OF A BASKETBALL NUT WITH FINE THREADS. THE TEAMS PAY CLOSE ATTENTION TO EACH MEASUREMENT AND MAKE SURE TO VERIFY AND DOUBLE VERIFY EACH MEASUREMENT. EVERY STUD HAS ITS OWN NUT TO MAKE SURE OF MATCHING THREADS. IT'S A TEDIOUS PROCESS BUT VERY IMPORTANT. YOU DON'T WANT TO OVER TOTEN OR THE NUTS COULD POP OFF LIKE A CANNON BALL. THE MACHINISTS AND MILWRIGHTS CONTINUE TO WORK TOWARDS ACQUIRING FINALE STREATCH AND UNDERSTAND THE THIRD PASS IS USUALLY A VERY MINOR ADJUSTMENT. OVERALL THE HIGH-PRESSURE TEAM LOOKS TO ACQUIRE ABOUT EIGHT TO TWELVE THOUSAND AN INCH STREATCH OF THE STUD. ALONG CENTERLINE THE TEAMS OF MILWRIGHTS AND MACHINISTS CONTINUE TO CLOSE THE JOINTS OF THE A, B, AND C LOW PRESSURE TURBINE STEAM CHESTS BY MAKING THREE PASSES WITH THE TORQUE MACHINE SET TO THE PROPER FOOT POUNDS PER SQUARE INCH. LIKE THE HIGH-PRESSURE TURBINE, YOU START WITH THE INSIDE NUTS AND WORK YOUR WAY OUT TO THE BEARINGS. SUNNY, YUMYUM AND JAKE ARE WORKING WITH COOL DADDY CHECKING BEARING CLEAREANCE AND PINCH CHECKS. THEY HAVE THIS OPPORTUNITY TO USE THE UNIT TWO CRANE RAYRAY CHONG OPPERATING. THE UNIT ONE CRANE CONTINUES TO MOVE THINGS DOWN THE HATCH AND CLEARING DECK SPACE. WITH HELP FROM ROPEY AND PEACHES THE BEARING TEAM HAS WORKED ITS WAY TO THE NUMBER FOUR BEARING.

EEFFY:	Watch out SUNNY the bottom half of the number four bearing is coming in.
SUNNY:	I can help you EEFFY.

THE SMALL HOOK OF THE UNIT TWO CRANE IS DRESSED IN A FOUR FOOT EYE AND EYE WIRE ROPE SLING AND A TWO TON CHAIN BLOCK. A SINGLE POINT PICK THE LOWER HALF BEARING NEEDS TO GENTLY GET STARTED IN THE RIGHT SIDE OF THE FIT THEN SLIDE DOWN AROUND THE BOTTOM OF THE JOURNAL OF THE TURBINE.

EEFFY:	Put the lifting eye in the bearing.

SUNNY REACHES DOWN INTO THE LEFT SIDE OF THE FIT OF THE LOWER HALF BEARING AND THREADS THE LIFTING EYE INTO THE HORIZONTAL JOINT OF THE BEARING THEN TAKES THE WIRE ROPE AND SHACKLE AND CONNECTS IT TO THE CHAIN BLOCK. EEFFY GENTLY PULLS THE SLACK OUT TILL THE LEFT SIDE IS TOTE. POURING SOME OIL DOWN INTO THE FIT, EEFFY PULLS UP ON THE CHAIN BLOCK THE LOWER HALF BEARING, AS EEFFY PULLS OP GRADUALLY WORKS ITS WAY AROUND THE FIT UNTIL THE LEFT SIDE OF THE BEARINGS HORIZONTAL JOINT MEETS WITH THE JOINT OF THE BEARING PEDESTOL.

EEFFY STOPS UP ON THE CHAIN BLOCK AND SUNNY IS QUICK TO DISCONNECT THE HOOK. EEFFY COMES UP ON THE CHAIN BLOCK UNTIL IT IS OUT OF THE WAY AND THE UNIT TWO CRAIN HEADS FOR THE UPPER HALF BEARING. STANDING IN THE BOTTOM HALF OF THE BEARING PEDESTOL PEACHES IS QUICK WITH THE FEELER GUAGES TO CHECK ON LOWER HALF BEARING CLEARENCE BETWEEN BEARING AND JOURNAL. DEAD CENTER

BOTTOM MEASUREMENT IS ZERO. THE JOURNAL OF THE TURBINE SPINDLE IS BOTTOM ON LOWER HALF BEARING. ALONG THE BOTTOM HALF RADIUS OF THE BEARING/ JOURNAL MEASURES THREE TO FOUR THOUSAND INCH AND AT THE TOP ALONG THE HORIZONTAL JOINT MEASURES AROUND FOUR THOUSAND INCHES. EEFY IS RETURNED WITH THE UPPER HALF BEARING AS RAYRAY CHONG CENTERS THE HOOK DIRECTLY OVER THE LOWER HALF, JAKE POURS LUBE OIL ONTO THE BEARING AND JOURNAL THEN EEFFY SIGNALS SLOW DOWN, SLOW DOWN, SLOW DOWN AND A STOP. THE UPPER HALF BEARING IS STILL A FEW INCHES AWAY. EEFFY PULLS ON THE BLOCK TO GENTLY LOWER THE UPPER HALF. PAPALUCHI AND SKIN MAKE SURE THE BEARING IS PROPPERLY ORRIENTED AND GUIDE THE UPPER HALF BEARING DOWN ONTO THE ALLIGNEMENT PINS OF THE LOWER HALF UNTIL THE SLACK IN THE CHAIN IS ENOUGH TO DISCONNECT THE HOOK.USEING FEELER GUAGES, PEACHES AND ROPEY MAKE SURE THE BEARINGS JOINT IS CLOSED AND EEFFY DISCONNECTS THE HOOK.

EEFFY DIRECTS THE CRANE TO THE BEARING CAP AS COOLDADDY, SUNNY AND JAKE TOTEN THE TOP BEARING BOLTS TO THE SPECIFIC TORQUE VALUE. EACH BEARING BOLT, TWO ON EACH SIDE HAVE AN INDICATOR ON THE TOP HALF OF THE BEARING NEXT TO THE BOLT HEAD. USING THE RIGHT SIZED SLUG WRENCH THE MACHINIST LOOSEN ONE BEARING BOLT AT A TIME THEN RE TOTEN IT. THE MACHINISTS AFTER LOOSENING ONE BOLT, MEASURE THE TOP OF THE BEARING FOR ANY TYPE OF DEFLECTION AND MAKE SURE THE BEARING WON'T ROCK BACK AND FORTH DURING THE OPPERATING CYCLE. THE MACHINIST FIND LESS THEN FOUR THOUSAND INCH DEFLECTION VERIFY IT THEN TOTEN THE BEARING NUTS USING A TORQUE WRENCH

SET TO THE PROPPER VALUE. THE MACHINISTS USE A THREE PASS X TYPE PATTERN TIL THE VALUE IS REACHED THEN BANG OVER THE KEEPERS. THE MACHINISTS MAKE SURE THE LUBE OIL BORES ARE PERFECTLY LINED UP AS THE CRANE SHOWS UP WITH THE BEARING CAP. ROPEY PEACHES AND YUMYUM ARE HANDELING THE LEAD CHECK TO MAKE SURE, THE BEARING CAP PUTS THE PERFECT AMOUNT OF SQUEEZE ON THE TOP HALF BEARING.

YUMYUM FOLDS A FOOT-LONG PIECE OF LEAD WIRE IN HALF, TWISTS IT TOGETHER LIGHTLY AND USING AN OUTSIDE MIC MEASURES IT TO .016. THEN SETS THE TWISTED WIRE DEAD CENTER ON THE TOP HALF OF THE BEARING. EEFFY, PAPALUCHI AND SKIN GENTLY GLIDE THE TOP HALF BEARING CAP DIRECTLY OVERTOP OF THE TOP HALF OF THE BEARING AND THEN SETTLE IT. EEFFY SIGNALS SLOW DOWN, SLOW DOWN, SLOW DOWN UNTIL THE BEARING CAP GETS CLOSE THEN A STOP. EEFFY SCRATCHES HIS CHIN AND LOOKS UP SLOW DOWN, SLOW DOWN, STOP. THE BEARING CAP FLOATS JUST ABOVE THE BEARING THEN EEFFY PULLS DOWN ON THE CHAIN BLOCK AND GENTLY LOWERS THE BEARING CAP INTO PLACE RIGHT ON TOP OF THE ALLIGNEMENT PINS AND SQUASHING THE LEAD WIRE. COOLDADDY, ROPEY SUNNY AND JAKE SPRING INTO ACTION AS SOON AS THE JOINT IS CLOSED AND THE SLING DEVELOPES SLACK. SINK A DOWEL FIRST ONE EACH SIDE THEN TOTEN THE BEARING CAP BOLTS TO THE PROPPER TORQUE VALUE. AS SOON AS THE TORQUE VALUE ON THE BOLTS ARE MET THE MACHINISTS DOUBLE VERIFY AND THEN LOOSEN THE NUTS. EEFFY THEN QUICKLY PULLS UP ON THE CHAIN BLOCK HARD UNTIL THE FILM OF OIL GIVES TO THE HOIST THEN CONTINUES TO PULL UP ON THE BLOCK.

GRADUALLY THE BEARING CAP GETS UP OUT OF THE WAY AND YUMYUM GRABS THE LEAD WIRE. USING A OUTSIDE MIC YUMYUM MEASURES THE SQUASHED PART OF THE WIRE AT .008 INCH. SUNNY AND ROPEY ARE THERE TO VERIFY THE MEASUREMENT AND ALL AGREE ABOUT AN EIGHT THOUSAND INCH PINCH ON THE BEARING. EEFFY AND THE RIGGERS GET THE APPROVAL TO SET THE TOP HALF BEARING CAP AND LOWER DOWN ONTO THE ALLIGNEMENT PINS OF THE BOTTOM HALF OF THE BEARING CAP. THE MACHINISTS ARE QUICK TO SET THE BEARING CAP AS THE RIGGERS REMOVE THE RIGGING AND AS SOON AS THE RIGGERS MOVE ON TO THE NEXT LIFT THE MACHINISTS WORK TOGETHER TO BRING THE TOP HALF BEARING CAP TO ITS FINIAL TORQUE VALUE. KRINE DOG AND TIE BOW WERE WITH THE CREW DURING THE ENTIRE EVELOUTION AND ARE PLEASED WITH THE RESULTS.

THE CREW POURS LUBE OIL DOWN INTO THE TOP HALF BEARING CAP AND PREPARE FOR "D" COUPLING. ESKIN AND CLANE ARE SETTING THE THERMOCOUPLES AND VIBRATION PROBES THEN TEST THE LOW VOLTAGE CONTROL WIRES WITH DANDAMAN AND JSONG WHO ARE STANDING BY IN THE CONTROL ROOM AND CONNECTING THE WIRE TO THE CORRECT ANNUNICATOR. THE EQUIPMENT IS USED FOR RECOGNIZING EXCESSIVE HEAT OR VIBRATION OF THE BEARINGS TO AVOID CATOSTROPHIC DAMAGE TO INSIDE THE GIANT ELECTRIC MACHINE. AS THE MACHINISTS, MILWRIGHTS CONTINUE TO STREATCH THE STUDS AROUND THE UPPER HALF CYLINDERS OF THE MAIN STEAM CHEST THE TOOLIES SENIORE MANURE, HAIRY SUE AND MIC ARE VERY BUSY KEEPING THE TOOL ROOM IN ORDER. THERES A LOT OF SPECIAL TOOLS REQUIRED TO BE CALIBRATED PRIOR TO USE. WHEN JOBS ARE COMPLETE THE TOOLIES RECEIVE THE TOOLS,

INSPECT THEM AND PUT THEM AWAY FOR A LATER USE. THEY ALSO STAGE TOOLS THAT ARE GOING TO BE USED IN ADVANCE AND MAKE SURE THEY ARE FUNCTIONING PROPERLY. THE TOOLIES HAVE STAGED THE COUPLING TOOLS AND HYDRAULIC JACK NEXT TO THE COUPLINGS AND ARE PREPAREING TO START THE COUPLING WORK. THE UNIT TWO CRANE WITH RAYRAY CHONG ARE DELIVERING THE NINETY POUND COUPLING BOLTS AS CLOSE TO THE COUPLINGS AS POSSIBLE AND THE UNIT ONE TEAM WITH SMARKY ARE LOWERING THE SANDCRABS SHACK DOWN THE HATCH TO PLAIN BILLS TRAILER. KOCHY, MARTY, CUBBY AND GONESKI ARE CLEANING THE BOTTOM HALF HORIZONTAL JOINT FLANGES OF THE OUTTER LOW PRESSURE SHELLS, PREPAREING THEM FOR REASSEMBLY.

EVERYONE HAS RETURNED TO THE DECK FOR A PREJOB BRIEF. THE COUPLING WORK REQUIRES QUALITY, CONCISE COMMUNICATION BETWEEN EACH COUPLING TEAM AS THEY WORK TOGETHER TO ACQUIRE A PERFECT ALLIGNEMENT. SUNNY, JAKE, YUMYUM AND TWISTED STEELE ARE STANDING BY THE "D" COUPLING. NAVY MIKE AND MR. URRIGHT ARE ALSO READY WITH THE CLEANED AND POLISHED SPACER THAT IS USED BETWEEN THE COUPLING FACES OF THE MAIN GENERATOR AND THE MAIN STEAM TURBINE INSIDE THE GIANT ELECTRIC MACHINE. AT "C" COUPLING COOLDADDY, GEGGY AND GOOGLY ARE TESTING THE HYDRAULIC PUMP AND MAKING SURE THE NUTS, BOLTS AND SLEEVES ALL MATCH PRIOR TO THE REASSEMBLY. REMEMBER EACH COUPLING BOLT IS SPECIFIC TO EACH COUPLING BOLT HOLES AND EACH SLEEVE IS TAPPERED TO THE SPECIFIC BORE. PEACHES, ROPEY AND POOPDECK PAPPY ARE WORKING ON THE "B" COUPLING AND DELCO JOE, K AND DUDDLEY ARE MONITORING THE "A" COUPLING AREA FOR NOW

AS THEY CONTINUE TO WORK ON THE FINALE STREATCH OF THE HIGH-PRESSURE STUDS. CAPP AND DOC TWO ELECTRICIANS ARE WORKING WITH EAGLE ED AND ICEMAN AS CULPURNICUS, AMMO, MITTS, OTTO AND BOOGER BRING THE ELECTRO HYDRAULIC SYSTEM BACK ON LINE EXCEPT FOR THE FRONT STANDARD, WHERE A DOUBLE BLOCK IS PLACED TEMPORALARY WHILE THE CREW CONTINUES WORK ON CENTERLINE.SQUARE HEAD GOON, FATTY JOE, SCHAFFER CITY AND WOBY RETURN TO THE DECK AND POSITION THEMSELVES ALONG CENTERLINE.

EACH BEARING ALONG CENTERLINE HAS A CREW MEMBER READY TO POUR LUBE OIL DOWN THROUGH THE BEARING CAP AND INTO THE BEARING PRIOR TO ANY MOVE WITH THE PUTT, PUTT. BIG JIM HAS RAYRAY CHONG LOWER THE SMALL HOOK TILL ITS EIGHT FEET FROM THE TOP OF THE "B" COUPLING AND PAPALUCHI SIGNALS A STOP. ROPEY INSERTS A PUTTER PIN IN THE OUTBOARD END, RIGHT SIDE OF THE "A" LOW PRESSURE TURBINE SPINDLE AS EEFFY IS QUICK TO USE A NYLON SLING IN A CHOKE AROUND THE PUTTER PIN JUST BELOW THE HORIZONTAL JONT. THEN PAPALUCHI SIGNALS SLOW DOWN, SLOW DOWN, SLOW DOWN, STOP AS EEFFY HOOKS THE SLING TO THE HOOK. MAKING SURE BOTH BEARINGS HAVE LUBE OIL POURED ON THEM PAPALUCHI GIVES THE SLOW UP AND A QUICK STOP AS THE SPINDLE IS GENTLY AND CAREFULLY ROTATED A HALF A COUPLING BOLT HOLE COUNTER CLOCKWISE TO ALLOW THE MACHINISTS AND MILWRIGHTS THE ABILITY TO LOAD THE COUPLING BOLTS TO THE PROPPER POSITION. THE HOOK IS QUICKLY DISCONNECTED AND THE PUTTERPIN REMOVED. THE MACHINISTS AND MILLWRIGHTS ARE CONFIDENT THE REST OF THE COUPLING BOLT HOLES WILL LINE UP AND ARE READY TO GET STARTED. RAYRAY CHONG AND THE RIGGING CREW SETS

UP OVER THE "D" COUPLING AND NAVY MIKE WITH MR URRIGHT STAND UP THE SPACER WITH THE LIFTING THREADS POINTING UP EEFFY IS THERE O THREAD THE EYE INTO THE TOP OF THE SPACER THEN PULLS THE SLACK OUT OF THE CHAIN BLOCK. WITH THE SPACER STANDING UP ON THE DECK LIKE A SILVER DOLLAR PAPALUCHI SIGNALS SLOW UP, SLOW UP AND GENTLY OVER TO THE "D" COUPLING SKIN IS THERE TO CATCH THE SPACER, ORRIENTS IT, TURNS IT AND STEADIES IT.

THE SPACER IS A FOOT ABOVE THE COUPLINGS. SUNNY, JAKE, YUMYUM, TWISTED STEELE USED OUTSIDE MICS TO MEASURE THE OUTSIDE DIAMETER IF THE SPACER AND A SET OF ADJUSTABLE PARRELLS TO MEASURE THE SPACE BETWEEN THE COUPLING FACES. SONNY ALSO TAKES THE "L" MEASUREMENT ALONG WITH JAKE AND FIND THE FACE OF THE "C" LOW PRESSURE TURBINE IS ABOUT FOUR THOUSAND INCHES FURTHER AWAY THEN THE AS FOUND PRIOR TO DISASSEMBLY. SONNY SEES THE INDICATOR ON THE GENERATOR COUPLING FACE PLUS ONE THOUSAND INCHES. DO NOT WANT TO GET THE SPACER WEDGED INBETWEEN THE COUPLING FACES. SKIN USINGTHUMB AND FORE FINGER LOOKING UP TO THE BOX OF THE CRANE SNAPS HIS FINGERS THEN POINTS DOWN WITH HIS THUMB REAL QUICK AND A STOP. THEN TAKES THE CHAIN BLOCK AND PULLS DOWN, PULLS DOWN, PULLS DOWN ON THE CHAIN BLOCK AS TWISTED STEELE AND SUNNY GUIDE THE SPACER DOWN INBETWEEN THE COUPLING SPACES AS YUMYUM AND JAKE ARE KEEPING A CLOSE EYE ON THE LINEING UP THE BOLT HOLES. SKIN SLOWS UP ON THE BLOCK AS THE SPACER NICELY, WITH NO INTERFEREANCE, MOVES BETWEEN THE COUPLING FACES UNTIL THE COUPLING BOLT HOLES MATCH UP, PERFECTLY.

ANOTHER REASON TO USE CHAIN BLOCK IS A MORE PRECISE TOUCH OF THE HOOK. RAYRAY CHONG WAITS AS THE MACHINISTS BEGIN TO LOAD THE COUPLING BOLTS FROM THE "C" LOW PRESSURE TURBINE COUPLING THROUGH THE SPACER THEN THROUGH THE COUPLING FACE OF THE MAIN GENERATOR INSIDE THE GIANT ELECTRIC MACHINE. TWISTED STEELE DELIVERS THE FIRST COUPLING BOLT WITH THE SLEEVE TO JAKE WHO IS STANDING AT THE RIGHTSIDE, "C" LP. END OF THE COUPLING AND YUMYUM IS STANDING ON THE GENERATOR END. SUNNY LINES UP "D" COUPLING BOLTS SO HE CAN PLAINLY SEE THE STAMPED NUMBERS ON THE BOLT AND SLEEVE. TWISTED STEELE TAKES EACH NINETY POUND COUPLING BOLT AND WALKS IT OVER THEN HANDS IT TO JAKE IN THE DIRECTION IT WILL BE SLID INTO THE COUPLING AND SPACER HOLES. JAKE TAKES THE COUPLING BOLT WITH THE FAT END OF THE TAPPERED SLEEVE LOOKING AT HIM AND SLIDES BOLT AND SLEEVE THROUGH THE COUPLING FACES AND SPACER. YUMYUM RECIEVES THE OTHER END OF THE BOLT AND STOPPING IT TO WHERE IT LOOKS CLOSE TO BEING HALFWAY. JAKE SLIDES THE SLEEVE ALONG THE INSIDE OF THE BORES TILL IT COMES TO A STOP. ALMOST TO THE EXACT MIDDLE OF THE COUPLING. TWISTED STEELE DELIVERS THE COUPLING NUTS AND YUMYUM AND JAKE THREAD THE NUTS ON HAND TOTE, AS FAR AS THEY CAN.

THE "D" COUPLING TEAM CONTINUES TO LOAD THE TOP HALF OF THE COUPLING BOLTS AND MAYBE ONE OR TWO BELOW THE HORIZONTAL JOINT. COOL DADDY, GEGGY, OTTO AND GOOGLY ARE WORKING THE "C" COUPLING. PEACHES, ROPEY, POOPDECK PAPPY AND BOOGER ARE WORKING THE "B" COUPLING AND DELCO JOE, DUDDLEY, K AND LAZALOON ARE WORKING THE "A" COUPLING. SQUARE HEAD, FATTY JOE, GOON AND WOBY ARE

SPREAD OUT CENTERLINE AND MAKE IT PERFECTLY CLEAR THE FAT PART OF THE TAPPERED SLEEVE SHOULD BE FACEING THE HIGH-PRESSURE TURBINE.

SISTER T IS STANDING BY WAITING TO GIVE CUPCAKE THE SIGNAL TO TURN ON THE PUTTER. EVERYONE ON DECK UNDERSTANDS THERE IS GOING TO BE A TURBINE ROLL. SQUARE HEAD IS WELL AWARE OF EACH COUPLING TEAMS PROGRESS AND MAKES SURE THE BEARINGS ARE WELL OILED THEN LOOKS TO FATTY JOE WHO TAPS SISTER T WHO SIGNALS TO CUPCAKE WHO CLOSED THE BREAKER TO THE PUTTER. WITH A BURST OF AIR, THE GEAR TO THE PUTTER IS DRIVEN UP INTO THE BULL GEAR OF THE TURBINE AND GRADUALLY BEGINS TO MOVE THE TRAIN IN THE COUNTERCLOCK WISE DIRECTION.

FATTY JOE KNOWS AS SOON AS THE TRAIN GETS UP ON THE OIL, TO TURN OFF THE PUTTER. PUTT, PUTT, PUTT, PUTT THE PUTTER GIVING IT ALL ITS GOT PUTT, PUTT THEN FATTY JOE WAVES A STOP. SISTER T SIGNALS CUPCAKE WHO WAS ANTICIPATING AND OPENS THE BREAKER TO THE PUTTER. THE ENTIRE THREE LOW PRESSURE TURBINES AND THE GENERATOR ARE ON A ROLL AND COAST INTO A PERFECT STOP WITH THE REMAINING BOLT HOLES ABLE TO BE ACCESSED TO INSTALL THE COUPLING BOLTS. THE COUPLING CREWS CONTINUE TO LOAD THE REMAINING BOLT HOLES MAKING SURE THE FAT END OF THE TAPPER IS FACEING THE HIGH-PRESSURE TURBINE. NEXT THE CREW WILL BE CLOSEING THE COUPLING FACES AND ALLIGNEING THE TRAIN. FROM THE MAIN GENERATOR TO THE HIGH- PRESSURE TURBINE. SQUARE HEAD IS READY TO BUMP THE TRAIN AND GET THE MACHINE BACK TO TOP CENTER. UP AND DOWN CENTERLINE EVERYONE IS CLEARLY COMMUNICATING AND UNDERSTANDING

THE PRIMARY TASK AT HAND. FATTY JOE AGAIN GIVES SISTER T THE GO AHEAD.

WITH LUBE OIL ON THE BEARINGS SISITER T SIGNALS CUPCAKE WHO CAUTIOUSLY LOOKS AROUND AND CLOSES THE BREAKER TO THE PUTTER. THE BURST OF COMPRESSED AIR PUSHES THE PUTTER GEAR UP INTO THE BULL GEAR OF THE TURBINE AND WITH ALL THE COUPLINGS JUST HAND TITE THE THREE LOW PRESSURE TURBINES, MAIN GENERATOR AND ALTEREX GRADUALLY GET UP ON THE OIL AND BEGIN TO TURN. AS SOON AS FATTY JOE SEES THE TIME IS RIGHT HE TAPS SISTER T WHO SIGNALS CUPCAKE WHO OPENS THE BREAKER AS THE MACHINSTS AND REST OF THE CREW WAIT AND SEE WHERE THE MACHINE COMES TO REST. THE PUTTER GEAR FALLS BACK OUT OF THE BULL GEAR AND THE TURBINE/GENERATOR COUPLING BOLTS AND COUPLINGS COME CREEPING AROUND LIKE THE MONEY WHEEL AND STOPS ABOUT AN INCH PAST TOP DEAD CENTER. ANYTHING OVER TWO OR THREE INCHES ITS PROBABLY BEST TO TRY AGAIN BUT FATTY JOE DID WELL, AND THE MACHINISTS CAN BEGIN TO CLOSE THE FACES OF THE COUPLINGS AND ALLIGN INSIDE THE GIANT ELETRIC MACHINE. IT ALL HAS TO START WITH THE "D" COUPLING. YUMYUM AND JAKE WILL BE WORKING THE COUPLING BOLTS SUNNY WILL OPPERATE THE HYDRAULIC PUMP AND TWISTED STEELE CAN TAKE FEELER GUAGE MEASUREMENTS, CHECK THE INDICATORS AND COMMINICATE WITH THE OTHER COUPLING TEAMS. JAKE'S BACK IS TO THE HIGH-PRESSURE TURBINE AND YUMYUM'S BACK IS TOWARDS THE GENERATOR.

WITH THE COUPLING STILL OPEN, JAKE REMOVES THE NUT FROM THE COUPLING BOLT, CENTERS THE SLEEVE, THEN SLIDES

THE HEAD OF THE HYDRAULIC JACK AROUND THE COUPLING BOLT TILL THE JACK IS TITE ON THE FAT END OF THE SLEEVE. JAKE HOLDS IT WITH ONE HAND AND THREADS THE BOLT ON WITH THE OTHER UNTIL EVERYTHING IS NICE AND TOTE. JAKE AND YUMYUM LOOK AROUND TO MAKE SURE EVERYTHING WAS RIGHT THEN SIGNALED SUNNY. SUNNY THUMBS THE ON SWITCH TO THE HYDRAULIC PUMP POP, POP, POP, POP, POP, POP, POP THE HEAD OF THE HYDRAULIC JACK IS TOTE AGAINST THE NUT OF THE COUPLING BOLT ON JAKES END AND ON THE OTHER END IS DRIVING THE TAPPERED SLEEVE TOWARDS YUMYUM EVERYONE ON THE JOB IS WATCHING AND LISTENING VERY CLOSE FOR ANY TYPE OF DRAG OR FRICTION AS ALL THE SUDDEN THE COUPLING CLOSES UP AND GETS VERY TOTE.

SUNNY VERIFYS THE GUAGE TWICE AND TURNS OFF THE PUMP AND RELEASES THE JACK HEAD. JAKE REMOVES THE NUT AND THE JACK HEAD FROM AROUND THE BOLT AND HAND IT TO TWISTED STEELE WHO SLIDES THE JACK HEAD AROUND THE NEXT COUPLING BOLT. THE FIRST COUPLING BOLT WAS AT THREE O'CLOCK AND THE NEXT ONE IS AT NINE O'CLOCK. JAKE MOVES OVER THE LEFT SIDE AND CENTERS THE SLEEVE, SLIDES THE JACK HEAD AROUND THE BOLT UNTIL IT SEATS ON THE TAPPERED SLEEVE THEN TOTENS THE NUT UP AS A STRONG BACK DOUBLE NUT. JAKE AND YUMYUM LOOK AROUND, ALONG WITH TWISTED STEELE AND SUNNY TO MAKE SURE EVERYTHING LOOKS GOOD THEN GIVES SUNNY THE GO AHEAD. SUNNY HITS ON THE THUMB SWITCH TO THE HYDRAULIC PUMP POP, POP, POP, POP, POP, POP, POP AS THE TAPPERED SLEEVE GETS PUSHED BY THE HYDRAULIC JACK HEAD INTO THE CENTER OF THE COUPLING FACES PULLING EVERYTHINHG TOWARDS THE MAIN GENERATOR AND CENTERING THE COUPLING BOLTS IN THE FACE AND ALSO

CENTERING THE COUPLINGS AND JOURNAL OF THE TURBINE IN THE BABBIT FACED BEARINGS. ON THE "C" COUPLING COOL DADDY IS READY TO GET STARTED.

NOW THE "D" COUPLING'S FACE HAS BEEN DRAWN IN TO THE SPACER AND THE MAIN GENERATOR ITS TIME TO SET THE "C" COUPLING. COOL DADDY WITH HIS BACK TO THE HIGH-PRESSURE TURBINE REMOVES THE NUT AT THE NINE O'CLOCK POSITION AND GEGGY IS WORKING THE INBOARD BOLT MAKING SURE IT'S CENTER IN THE COUPLING AND HIS NUT SNUG AGAINST THE FACE OF THE COUPLING. OTTO IS WORKING THE HYDRAULIC PUMP AND READING THE GUAGE AND GOOGLY IS DOUBLE VERIFYING THE GUAGE PRESSURE AND MAKING SURE TO COMMUNICATE WITH THE OTHER COUPLING TEAMS. COOL DADDY SLIDES THE HEAD OF THE HYDRAULIC JACK AROUND THE COUPLING BOLT AND SEATS IT ON THE FAT END OF THE TAPPERED SLEEVE THEN THREADS THE COUPLING BOLT NUT, DOUBLE NUT TOTE TO THE JACK HEAD HOLDING EVERYTHING SNUG. TAKES A LOOK AROUND, EVERYONE GIVES A THUMBS UP AND OTTO CLICKS THE THUMB SWITCH TO THE ON POSITION. POP, POP, POP, POP, THE JACK HEAD BEGINS TO PUSH ON THE TAPPERED SLEEVE AND BEGINS TO DRIVE THE COUPLING FACES TOGETHER TOWARDS THE GENERATOR END.THE THIN FILM OF LUBE OIL BETWEEN THE BABBIT FACED BEARINGS AND THE ROTOR JOURNALS IS IMPERATIVE. POP, POP, THEN THE COUPLING FACES GENTLY SLIDE TOGETHER AND THE PRE-SET PRESSURE ON THE GUAGE IS SATISIFIED. OTTO VERIFIYS THE PRESSURE AND GOOGLY DOUBLE VERIFYS AND THE PUMP IS OFF AND THE PRESSURE IN THE JACK HEAD RELEASED. COOL DADDY REMOVES THE COUPLING BOLTS ON HIS SIDE AND SLIDES THE JACK HEAD OFF THE SET, SLEEVED COUPLING BOLT.

GEGGY CHECKS THE FACE OF THE COUPLING TO MAKE SURE THE JOINT IS CLOSED. COOL DADDY THEN SETS THE JACK UP ON THE THREE O'CLOCK COUPLING BOLT OR AS CLOSE TO THE HORIZONTAL JOINT AS POSSIBLE. GEGGY DOUBLE CHECKS TO MAKE SURE THE BOLT IS CENTER IN THE COUPLING WITH THE SLEEVE SET PERFECTLY. COOL DADDY TAKES ANOTHER LOOK AND NODS TO OTTO, POP, POP, POP, POP, POP, THE PUMP DRIVES THE FAT END OF THE TAPPERED SLEEVE COUPLING BOLT TOWARDS THE MAIN GENERATOR AND CLOSES THE COUPLING FACE RIGHT UP. THE PRESSURE IS DOUBLE VERIFIED AND THE PRESSURE RELEASED. COOL DADDY REMOVES THE JACK ASSEMBLY AND MOVES TO THE NEXT COUPLING BOLT. THE" B" COUPLING TEAM OF ROPEY SETTING THE SLEEVES AND JACK, PEACHES CENTERING THE COUPLING BOLTS AND ADJUSTING THE NUTS, POOPDECK PAPPY ON THE HYDRAULIC JACK WITH BOOGER WORKING AND COMMUNICATING WITH THE OTHER COUPLING TEAMS. GOON IS ALSO STANDING BY.

GOON: Let's go were waiting on you.

JUST THEN EVERYONE LOOKS AT EACH OTHER AND THE PUMP TURNS ON POP, POP, POP, POP AS AGAIN THE THREE O'CLOCK POSITIONED, FAT END OF THE SLEEVE, COUPLING BOLT OF THE "B" COUPLING GETS DRIVEN BY THE JACK HEAD TOWARDS THE GENERATOR. EVERYONE IS CLEAR OF THE COUPLING FACE. POP, POP, POP, POP THEN ALL THE SUDDEN THE FACES OF THE COUPLING CLOSES UP AND GETS TOTE ALL THE WAY AROUND. POOPDECK DOUBLE CHECKS THE GUAGE PRESSURE ALONG WITH BOOGER THEN TURNS OFF THE HYDRAULIC PUMP AND RELIEVES THE JACK HEAD PRESSURE. ROPEY REMOVES THE COUPLING NUT AND REMOVES THE JACK HEAD FROM

AROUND THE COUPLING BOLT AND MOVES THE ASSEMBLY TO THE NINE O'CLOCK POSITION. PEACHES DOUBLE CHECKS THE CENER OF THE BOLT THROUGH THE COUPLING AND MAKES SURE THE SLEEVE IS SET AND HIS NUT TOTE. ROPEY SENDS POOPDECK PAPPY THE GO AHEAD AND THE PUMP KICKS ON AND DRIVES THE JACK HEAD INTO THE FAT END OD THE COUPLING BOLT TAPPERED SLEEVE AND DRIVES THE SLEEVE INTO THE COUPLING, CLOSES THE FACE OF THE "B" COUPLING INSIDE THE GIANT ELECTRIC MACHINE. AS THE COUPLING FACES ARE BEING CLOSED ALL THE MOVEMENT HAS BEEN TOWARDS THE GENERATOR END. THE "A" COUPLING TEAM FEATURES DELCO JOE SETTING THE SLEEVES AND JACK HEAD, DUDDLEY CENTERING THE COUPLING BOLTS AND K ON THE HYDRAULIC PUMP AND GUAGES ALSO LAZALOON TO VERIFY THE GUAGE READINGS AND COMMUNICATE WITH THE OTHER COUPLING TEAMS.

USING THE EXACT SAME METHOD PULL THE "A" COUPLING TOGETHER STARTING AT THE NINE O'CLOCK POSITION. POP, POP, POP, POP, THE JACK HEAD OF THE PUMP DRIVES THE TAPPERED SLEEVE TOWARDS THE GENERATOR WHICH CLOSES THE FACE OF THE COUPLING AND MAKES CLEAREANCE FOR THE STUB SHAFT. LAZALOON VERIFYS THE GUAGE READING AND K TURNS OFF THE PUMP AND RELIEVES THE PRESSURE IN THE JACK HEAD THEN DELCO JOE IS QUICK TO REPOSITION THE EQUIPMENT AND SIGNAL TO K. POP, POP, POP, THE JACK HEAD DRIVES THE TAPPERED SLEEVE ON THE RIGHT SIDE OF COUPLING "A" AND CLOSES THE FACE OF THE COUPLING. KRINE DOG AND TIE BOW ARE ALSO ALONG CENTERLINE FOR VERIFICATION AND FOLLOWING THE PROPPER PROTOCOL. K TURNS THE HYDRAULIC PUMP OFF AND RELIEVES THE PRESSURE OF THE JACK HEAD. DELCO JOE REMOVES THE JACK ASSEMBLY AND SLIDES IT ON

TO THE NEXT SLEEVED COUPLING BOLT. THE OTHER COUPLING TEAMS HAVE BEEN WORKING ON ALL THE COUPLING BOLTS THEY CAN GET, THEN WAITING FOR TURBINE ROLL. JOHNNY OBOTT, MOE AND JOWEE HAVE OBTAINED THE FINIALE BOLT STREATCH NUMBERS ON THE HIGH-PRESSURE TURBINE SHELL AND SINCE THEN HAVE BEEN WORKING ON REMOVEING ANY RAISED FACE AROUND THE COUPLING BOLT HOLES OF THE STUB SHAFT. RAYRAY CHONG AND THE UNIT TWO CRANE HAVE PICKED UP THE STUB SHAFT USING A TWO POINT, TWO-LEGGED PICK FROM TOP DEAD CENTER BOLT HOLES IN THE TOP OF THE HIGH SPEED, CARBON FIBER / KEVELAR TYPE OF METERIAL THEN PUT A LEVEL ON THE FOUR-FOOT-LONG, TWO FOOT COUPLING DIAMETERS, ORIENET IT PROPERLY AND BEGIN TO LOWER IT DOWN INBETWEEN THE TWO COUPLING FACES.SKIN WAVES HIS HANDS FOR A QUICK STOP ADJUS TS THE CHAIN BLOCK AND PAPALUCHI THEN SCRATCHES HIS CHIN AND SIGNALS DOWN, DOWN, DO, DOWN TILL THE BOLT HOLES MATCH UP. STOP! PAPALUCHI WAVES, AS THE MACHINISTS STEP IN.

WOBY STANDING BY MAKES SURE THE MACHINISTS TOTEN THE STUB SHAFT TO THE HIGH-PRESSURE TURBINE FIRST AND ACQUIRE FINALE TORQUE VALUE. JOHNNY OBOOTT AND MOE GET THE COUPLING BOLTS STARTED, AND SKIN COMES OFF THE RIGGING AND GETS OUT OF THE WAY. TOGETHER JOHNNY OBOOT, MOE AND JOWEE GET ALL THE COUPLING BOLTS STARTED AND USING THE PROPPER TORQUEING SEQUENCE AND THREE SEPARATE PASSES MEETS THE REQUIRED TORQUE OF THE HIGH- SPEED STUB SHAFT. AS THE MACHINISTS WERE ACQUIRING THE PROPPER TORQUE VALUE ON THE GOVONOR END THE COUPLING FACES WERE BEING CLOSED AS THE FRONT STANDARD ROTOR WAS PULLED TOWARDS THE GENERATOR. NOSEALEO, COOL EARL,

RAPPING RODNEY, LAUREY AND CARLY REPLACED THE OLD METALTALIC GASKETS IN THE FOUR MAIN STEAM INLET PIPEING OF THE HIGH PRESSURE.

RAPPING RODNEY:	I'm working STEAM SIDE send to the basement, working real hard. Off to centerline, just In time buckle this turbine up! Finish this pup! start up! Move on! RAPPING RODNEY is gone.

EEFFY, SKIN AND PAPALUCHI HAVE THE LADDER OUT AND RELEASING THE TENSION ON THE COMEALONG TO ALLOW THE BOLT HOLES TO LINE UP. THE FITTERS MAKE SURE TO CENTER EACH BOLT IN THE CENTER OF THE FACES AND CLOSE THE FLANGE FACE EQUALLY.

WHEN THE FLANGE FACES OF THE HIGH-PRESSURE TURBINES HAVE BEEN MADE WRENCH TOTE AND HAVE AN EQUAL GAP BETWEEN THE FACE THE FITTERS USE A FLEELER GUAGE AND TOTEN THE FLANGE FACES IN A STAR PATTERN IN THREE PASS AND ACQUIRE THE PROPPER TORQUE VALUE. THEN USING THE FEELER GUAGE TAKE ANOTHER MEASUREMENT SUBTRACT FROM FIRST MEASUREMENT AND DETERMINE THE PROPPER AMOUNT OF SQUASH ON THE METALTALIC GASKETS. DURING THE THIRD PASS THE FITTERS DOUBLE VERIFY THE TORQUE ON EACH FLANGE STUD. THE RIGGERS REMOVE THE RIGGING FROM THE INLET PIPES THEN FATTY JOE TELLS CHARDY TO REMOVE THE GAGS FROM THE SPRING CANS.WORKING SAFE, ATTENTION TO DETAIL, FOLLOWING PROCEDURES, QUALITY CRAFTSMANSHIP AMD TEAMWORK ALL COMING INTO PLAY ON CENTERLINE. WITH A MEMBER OF THE CREW STATIONED AT EACH BEARING POURING LUBE OIL DOWN THROUGH THE BEARING CAP AND

FLOODING THE TOP HALF SQUARE HEAD GIVES THE TURBINE ROLL AS FATTY JOE BUMPS SISTER T WHO SIGNALS CUPCAKE WHO KNOWS EXACTLY WHAT HE'S LOOKING FOR. WITH A QUICK BUMP THE PUTT PUTT GEAR GETS PUSHED INTO THE BULL GEAR OF THE "D" COUPLING AND SLOWLY AND STRUGGLING BRINGS CENTERLINE ON A FULL ROLL. PUT, PUT, PUT THE TURBINE/ GENERATOR GETS UP ON OIL AND CUPCAKE HESITATES FOR A SPLIT SECOND AND OPENS THE PUT PUTS BREAKER.

UNIT TWO TURBINE/GENERATOR UP ON LUBE OIL, RIDEING IN THE BABBIT FACED BEARINGS COASTS DOWN AND SLOWLY ENDS UP AT JUST ABOUT ONE HUNDRED AND EIGHTY DEGREES. ALL ALONG CENTERLINE THE MACHINISTS AND MILWRIGHTS WORK TO COMPLETE THE COUPLING BOLTS. THE CREW WORKING ON THE STUB SHAFT HAVE A CHANCE TO DOUBLE VERIFY AND SET SOME INDICATORS UP. OTHER TEAM MEMBERS ARE CLEANING AND PREPARING THE HORIZONTAL JOINTS OF THE TOP AND BOTTOM OF THE COUPLING COVERS AND BEARING PEDESTOLS. SOAPSTONEING THE JOINT REMOVING ANY RAISED FACE AROUND THE BOLT HOLES AND INSPECTING THE THREADS. AS SOON AS THE COUPLING BOLTS HAVE BEEN TORQUED AND DOUBLE VERIFIED THE CREW ALONG WITH THE TOOLIES PUT THE NO LONGER NEEDED EQUIPMENT OVER BY THE TOOL ROOM OUT OF THE WAY ANS DECREESING ANY LIKELYHOOD OF FOREIGN METERIAL ENTERING THE OIL SIDE INSIDE THE GIANT ELECTRIC MACHINE. SUNNY, JAKE, YUMYUM, COOL DADDY, GEGGY, ROPEY, PEACHES, JOHNNYOBOTT, JOWEE, K AND MOE SET INDICATORS FROM ONE END OF THE TURBINE TO THE OTHER END OF THE GENERATOR. TIE BOW AND KRINE DOG ARE STANDING BY WAITING FOR THE TURBINE ROLL. OTHER MEMBERS OF THE CREW ARE OILING THE BEARINGS AND

GREASING THE SKIDS. ESKIN AND CLANE ARE KEEPING A CLOSE EYE ON THE THERMOCOUPLES AND VIBRATION PROBES AND MAKE SURE NO ONE STEPS ON THEM OR PULLS THE CONTROL WIRE HARNESSES APART. SQURE HEAD GIVES THE GO AHEAD AS FATTY JOE IS QUICK TO TAP SISTER T WHO SIGNALS CUPCAKE TO CLOSE THE PUTT PUTT BREAKER AND LET IT GO FOR A LITTLE.

THE BURST OF COMPRESSED AIR PUSHES THE PUTT PUTT GEAR UP INTO THE BULL GEAR OF THE "D" COUPLING AND GRADUALLY BEGINS TO TURN THE TURBINE/ GENERATOR. GIVING IT EVERYTHING IT HAS THE SMAIN STEAM TURBINE / MAIN GENERATOR GETS UP ON LUBE OIL AS THE PUTT PUTT IS ALLOWED TO RUN AND BECOME FULLY ENGAGED, HAVING THE POWER TO ROTATE THE MAIN TURBINE/ GENERATOR JUST FAST ENOUGH TO TAKE DIAL INDICATOR MEASUREMENTS OF THE COUPLINGS. THE MACHINISTS, KRINE DOG, TIE BOW ARE STARTING AFROM "D" COUPLING AND VISITING EVERY COUPLING ALONG CENTERLINE. IN DAYS OF OLD TO ALLIGN THE TRAIN WOULD TAKE A PIANO WIRE, LEVEL, AND VERY IMPORTANT TO WALK THE COUPLING FACE TOGETHER A LITTLE AT A TIME. TODAY LASER ALLIGNEMENT, BEARING ELEVATIONS AND SLEEVED COUPLING BOLTS HELP BRING THE MACHINE IN LINE WITH LESS TIME FOR THE CREW. ALL ALONG CENTERLINE THE COUPLING MEASUREMENTS RANGE BETWEEN SIX THOUSAND OF AN INCHES TO ELEVEN THOUSAND OF AN INCHES SIDE TO SIDE. EXCESSIVE SIDE TO SIDE MEASUREMENTS WOULD RANGE OVER SIXTEEN THOUSAND TOTAL SIDE TO SIDE CLEAREANCE JOURNAL OF SPINDLE TO BABBIT FACED BEARINGS. KRINE DOG AND TIE BOW ARE SURE TO RECORD ALL MEASUREMENTS AND DOUBLE CHECK THE NUMBERS.

FATTY JOE TAPS SISTER T WHO SIGNALS CUPCAKE WHO OPENS THE PUTTER BREAKER AS THE MACHINE GLIDES ON THE LUBE OIL TO A STOP. FATTY JOE RECEIVED APPROVAL TO TAKE CARE OF THE THRUST CHECK AT THIS TIME, BEFORE THE START OF THE STEAM SIDE OUTAGE. SUNNY, YUMYUM, ROPEY, PEACHES AND DUDDLEY STANDING BY, BOOGER AND OTTO SET THE THRUST PLATES UP ON THE HORIZONTAL JOINT OF THE "B" COUPLING WITH THE JACKBOLTS SET TO MOVE THE TRAIN HARD TO THE GENERATOR END. GOON IS ALSO STANDING BY AND MAKES SURE THE JACKBOLTS ARE GREASED SO, THEY DON'T SCRATCH THE COUPLING FACE DURING THE MOVES. BOOGER AND OTTO BOLT THE ONE INCH THICK PLATES TO THE HORIZONTAL JOINT AND LINE UP THE JACKBOLTS. FATTY JOE IS HAPPY AND FAMILIAR WITH THE SETUP AND TAPS SISTER T WHO SIGNALS CUPCAKE WHO CLOSES THE PUTTER BREAKER. THE BURST OF AIR ENGAGES THE PUTTER GEAR INTO THE BULL GEAR AND BEGINS TO ROLL THE TURBINE. WITH PLENTY OF HANDS AVAILIABLE TO POUR LUBE OIL INTO THE TOP HALF BEARING SADDLES DUDDLEY AND BOOGER CRANK DOWN ON THE JACK BOLTS. GOON TAKES HIS FOREFINGER AND PUSHES HIS GLASSES UP, HIGHER ON HIS FACE, LICKS HIS LIPS, SHAKES HIS HEAD AND PUTS HIS HANDS BEHIND HIS BACK THEN ROCKS FRONT TO BACK AS DUDDLEY AND BOOGER PUT EVERYTHING THEY HAVE INTO TURNING THE JACKBOLTS. FINIALLY THE JACK BOLTS MOVE THE MACHINE SIX THOUSAND INCHES TOWARDS THE GENERATOR AS FATTY JOE TAPS SISTER T WHO SIGNALS CUPCAKE WHO OPENS THE BREAKER TO THE PUTTER. THE MAIN STEAM TURBINE/ GENERATOR INSIDE THE GIANT ELECTRIC MACHINE GLIDES TO A STOP. BOOGER, OTTO AND DUDDLEY QUICKLY RE POSITION THE JACKBOLTS AND GIVE FATTY JOE THE THUMBS UP. GOON MAKES SURE THERE IS PLENTY OF GREASE ON THE JACKBOLTS

THEN FATTY JOE TAPS SISTER T WHO SIGNALS CUPCAKE WHO CLOSES THE BREAKER TO THE PUTTER. TURBINE ROLL, FATTY JOE AND GOON PAYING CLOSE ATTENTION AS AND DUDDLEY WORK THE LARGE OPENED END WRENCHES ON THE JACKBOLTS ATTEMPTING TO MOVE THE MAIN GENERATOR/ TURBINE TOWARDS THE FRONT STANDARD. DUDDLEY AND BOOGER TURN THE

HEADS OF THE JACKBOLTS PUSHING THERE TIPS INTO THE FACE OF THE COUPLING TOWARDS THE HP. TURBINE. AGAINE PUTTING EVERYTHING THEY HAVE INTO IT, INSIDE THE GIANT ELECTRIC MACHINE THRUSTS TOWARDS THE HP TURBINE AND FATTY JOE TAPS SISTER T WHO SIGNALS CUPCAKE WHO OPENS THE BREAKER AS THE MACHINE GLIDES TO A REST. BOOGER AND DUDDLEY JUMP RIGHT BACK ON REPOSITIONING THE JACKBOLTS FOR ONE FINIAL PUSH TOWARDS THE MAIN GENERATOR. CORNOL HOGAN IS NOW STANDING BY AND REMINDS GOON TO GREASE THE JACBOLT HEADS. THE MACHINISTS AND MILLWRIGHTS HAVE A CLOSE EYE ON THE DIAL INDICATORS WAITING TO DOUBLE VERIFY THE FULL AXIAL MOVEMENT OF THE MAIN GENERATOR / STEAM TURBINE INSIDE THE GIANT ELECTRIC MACHINE.

FATTY JOE TAPS SISTER T WHO SIGNALS CUPCAKE WHO CLOSES THE BREAKER TO THE PUTTER. PUTT, PUTT, PUTT AS THE MACHINE GETS UP ON THE LUBE OIL WEDGE AND ROTATES. BOOGER AND DUDDLEY AGAIN MAN THE OPENED END WRENCHES AND TURN THE JACKBOLTS PUSHING THE MAIN TURBINE/ STEAM TURBINE TOWARDS THE GENERATOR END. EVERYONE ANXIOUSLY WAITING FOR THE MACHINE TO MOVE ARE STUDYING EVERY DIAL INDICATOR ALONG CENTERLINE. TO VERY STRONG CREW

MEMBERS DUDDLEY AND BOOGER GIVE IT EVERYTHING THEY GOT THEN POOPDECK PAPPY AND TWISTED STEELE, ONE ON EACH SIDE GET DOWN AND PUSH ON THE WRENCHES USING THE STRENGTH OF THERE RIGHT LEG AND ALL THE SUDDEN THE MACHINE THRUSTS EIGHTEEN THOUSAND HARD TO THE MAIN GENERATOR. KRINE DOG AND TIE BOW ARE HAPPY WITH THE RESULTS AND IT DOS'ENT TAKE LONG BEFORE SQUARE HEAD IS IN TOUCH WITH SUAVE RICO AND BIG JIM TO GET THE COUPLING COVERS AND BEARING PEDESTOLS READY FOR RE ASSEMBLY.

THE CREW HAS CLEANED AND STONED THE JOINT AND APPLIED A FRESH COAT OF FORM A GASKET ON THE BOTTOM HALVES. THE UNIT TWO CRANE WITH RAYRAY CHONG OPPERATING, EEFFY, SKIN AND PAPALUCHI WILL WORK THE "A" AND "B" COUPLING COVERS AND BEARING PEDESTOLS WHILE THE UNIT ONE CRANE WITH SMARKEY OPPERATING HAS BLAZE, BIG O AND RAPPING RODNEY WORKING ON SETTING THE "D" AND "C" COUPLING COVERS AND PEDESTOLS. SUAVE RICO AND BIG JIM ARE PREPARING THE RIGGING USED TO SET THE OUTTER HOODS OF THE LOW-PRESSURE TURBINES AND CLEANING UP THE RIGGING CAGE. AS SOON AS THE RIGGING TEAMS COMPLETE SETTING THE COVERS ON THE ALLIGNEMENT PINS THE MACHINISTS FOLLOWED BEHIND SETTING THE DOWELS FIRST THEN TORQUING THE BOLTS. BEING CRITICAL PATH AND HAVING ALL HANDS-ON DECK TOTETING THE COVERS DON'T TAKE LONG AND THE CRANES PREPARE TO LIFT THE FIRST HOOD. WITH THE OIL BORES LINEING UP AND THE COVERS ALL TORQUED TO THE PROPPER FOOT POUNDS EAGLE ED OKAYS THE RETURN OF THE MAIN LUBE OIL. ICEMAN OPENS THE VALVES ALONG CENTERLINE AND THE BEARING LUBE OIL LIFT PUMPS COME ONE AND BEGIN

FEEDING LUBE OIL TO THE MAIN GENERATOR/ STEAM TURBINE BABBIT FACED BEARINGS. COOL EAR, NOSEALEO, LAZALOON AND GONESKI ARE CHECKING OIL PRESSURE GUAGES ALONG CENTERLINE AND THUMBS UP TO FATTY JOE WHO TAPPS SISTER T WHO SIGNALS TO CUPCAKE WHO CLOSES THE BREAKER TO THE PUTTER. THE BURST OF COMPRESSED AIR BLOWS THE GEAR UP INTO THE BULL GEAR OF THE TURBINE AND WITH GREAT EFFORT THE PUTTER BEGINS TO ROTATE THE MAIN GENERATOR/ TURBINE. OTTO AND CHARDY CHECK THE RUN SCREENS AT THE LUBE OIL RESERVIOR. WITH THE MACHINE ON ROLL THE ELECTRICIANS FINISH UP THE BRUSH WORK IN THE DOG HOUSE AND ARE DOWN WORKING ON THE CLAMSHELS AND LYNX. THE PAPER WORK FROM SATCH AND THE CAPICATOR BANK IN THE SUBSTATION IS COMPLETE. KULPURNICUS, AMMO, MITTS WITH CARLY AND LAURY HAVE WORKED THE ELECTRO HYDRAULIC SKID AND CONTROLS. THE VALVES HAVE BEEN STROKED WITH OUTSTANDING RESULTS AND THE BLOCKS HAVE BEEN REMOVED TO THE FRONT STANDARD CONTROLS. ICEMAN HAS RESTORED THE EHC SYSTEM UNDER THE DIRECTION OF EAGLE ED. THE RIGGING TEAM IS READY TO SET THE FIRST HOOD OVER TOP THE "C" LOW PRESSURE TURBINE. BIG JIM HAS THE CRANES WORKING TOGETHER, CENTERED RIGHT OVER THE TOP OF THE "C" LOW PRESSURE TURBINE. SLOW DOWN, SLOW DOWN, SLOW DOWN THE OUTTER SHELL SOFTLY COMES DOWN OVER THE INNER CYLINDER OF THE "C" LOW PRESSURE TURBINE. SLOW DOWN, SLOW DOWN WITH RIGGERS AND MILLWRIGHTS GUIDING THE SHELL DOWN THE SHELL COMES DOWN PERFECTLY ON TO THE ALLIGNEMENT PINS AND THE SLACK GROWS IN THE SLINGS. THE RIGGERS REMOVE THE SLINGS FROM THE HOOD AND MOVE TOWARDS THE "B" HOOD THEN TO THE "A" HOOD. THE MACHINISTS AND MILLWRIGHTS ARE QUICK TO EMPTY THE

BOLT BINS AND GET ALL THE BOLTS STARTED AROUND THE BASE OF THE HOOD. RIGHT SIDE AND LEFT SIDE HAVE TWO ONE INCH DRIVE AIR GUNS TO TOTEN THE BOLT HEADS INTO THE OUTER HORIZONTAL JOINT. THE TEAM WORKS ITS WAY TO THE "A" LOW PRESSURE HOOD AS THE RIGGING TEAM GENTLY SET IT ON ITS MARK AND THE MACHINISTS TOTEN IT DOWN THEN GRADUALLY HELP CLEAN UP AND LEAVE THE DECK.

WOBY HAS AN EYE ON KOCHY, CUBBY AND MARTY WHO ARE FINISHING COVERING THE HIGH-PRESSURE TURBINE AND CLIMBING DOWN. YOU CAN HERE THE AUXILARY STEAM BEGIN TO FILL THE STEAM CHEST. SOUNDS LIKE A WHISTLE AT TIMES. THINGS GET WARM IN A HURRY AS THE TEAM OF ELECTRICIANS HIGH VOLT, BRUCEY, SISTER T, CUPCAKE, DOC, CAPPY, ESKIN, CLANE, SCHAFFER CITY AND SEESAW HAVE BEEN FOCUSED ON THE BRUSH WORK AND CLAMSHELL/ LINCKS THAT CONNECT THE MAIN GENERATOR TO THE GRID. AS THEY WRAP THINGS UP DANDAMAN AND SJONG FINISH IN THE CONTROLROOM WITH THE VIBRATION PROBES AND THE THERMOCOUPLES. BEING ON CRITICAL PATH THERE IS NO TIME TO MESS AROUND DURING RE START. THE AUXILARY STEAM CONTINUES TO FILL THE STEAM CHEST OF THE MAIN STEAM TURBINES. A VACUME IS CREATED FROM THE DRAW OF THE CONDENSERS AND THE AUX STEAM GRADUALLY HEATS THINGS UP. EAGLE ED IS THUMBS UP AS JIMMY O IS CROSSING HIS FINGERS HOPING FOR THE BEST. LOUIE AND THE ADMIREAL ARE STANDING BY IN THE CONTROL ROOM WAITING TO SINK TO THE GRID AND END THE MAIN STEAM OUTAGE. THE AUX STEAM COMES TO PRESSURE AND BEGINS TO DRIVE THE MAIN STEAM TURBINE THEN THE PUTTER GEAR DROPS OUT AND EAGLE ED GIVES THE THUMBS UP. ICEMAN OPENS THE MAIN STEAM, STOP AND CONTROL VALVES

AND NOW BEGINS TO FLOOD THE STEAM CHEST WITH MAIN STEAM. EVERYTHING LOOKS GOOD IN THE CONTROL ROOM AS THE VIBRATION AND THERMOCOUPLES PROVE TO BE USEFUL INFORMATION. EAGLE ED THUMBS UP TO ICEMAN AS HE OPENS THE VALVES TO TWENTY PERCENT.

YOU CAN HEAR THE STEAM WORKING ITS WAY ALONG THE PATH AS THE MACHINE ITSELF PINGS AND POPS DUE TO THERMAL EXPANSION. WITH THE RIGGING TEAM SETTING THE FLOOR PLUGS EAGLE ED TAKES THE CONTROL VALVES AND ICEMAN MOVES TO SINK THE MACHINE TO THE GRID. STANDING AT THE FRONT STANDARD OF UNIT TWO INSIDE THE GIANT ELECTRIC MACHINE ICEMAN WITH A HEADSET ON SQUARE HEAD, FATTY JOE AND THE MACHINISTS COOL DADDY, JOHNNY OBOTT AND JOWEE. INSPECTING THE OVERSPEED TRIP MECHANISIM. WITH ICEMAN IN PLACE EAGLE ED SETS THE CONTROL POWER TO FIFTY PERCENT AS THE TURBINE MAIN GENERATOR IS REALLY STARTING TO PICK IT UP IN ROTATIONS PER MINUTE. EAGLE ED OPENS IT UP AND DIRECTS ICEMAN TO SINK IT TO THE GRID AND WITHOUT HESITATION ICE PUSHES CLOSED THE DISCONNECT AT THE FRONT STANDARD TO SINK THE MAIN GENERATOR OF UNIT TWO INSIDE THE GIANT ELECTRIC MACHINE BACK TO THE GRID. THE SUBSTATION TEAM CLOSED THE YARD BREAKER AND ARE GRADUALLY ADDING THE CAPACITOR BANKS INTO THE OVERHEAD TRANSMISSION AND DISTRIBUTION CIRCUTS. AND THAT'S WHAT HAPPENS INSIDE THE GIANT ELECTRIC MACHINE DURING A STEAM SIDE OUTAGE.

THE END

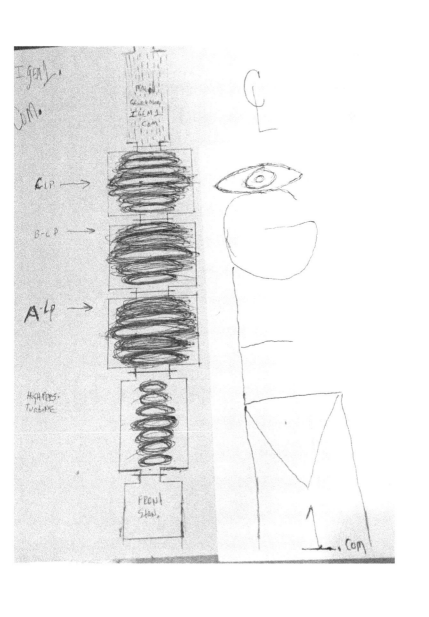

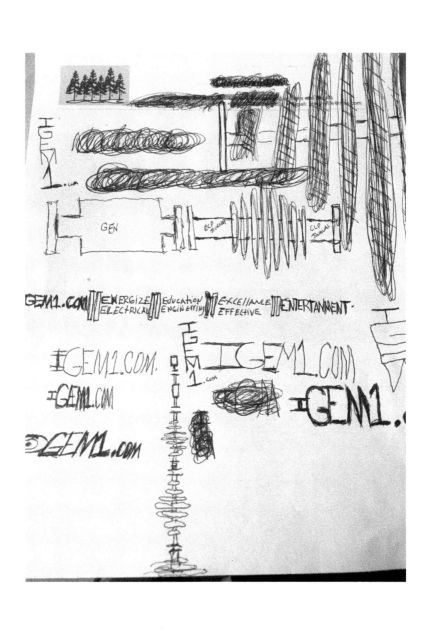